THE

STILL
SMALL
VOICE

THE
STILL
SMALL
VOICE

BRENDA STANLEY

LISTEN

Blue-green shimmer stretched and calling.
Stand with me here and listen.
There is no lie in tales never told.
Secrets in the fall forever kept and hidden.

—MILLIE JUAREZ

PROLOGUE

Blinding afternoon sun spread across the crisp grass at the base of the small valley as Dubby Woodruff approached the brush-covered secret trail that led to the overlook. The other campers were busily finishing up dinner and chattering madly about the dance to be held that night. It was their final day of the week-long camp.

It was called Aspen Veil, the oldest church camp in Utah. The large white wooden cabins hugged the edge of a lake surrounded by colorful jutting cliffs. It was God's country. The Mormon Church–owned property was a favorite destination for many youth groups looking for both recreation and spiritual retreats. Campers enjoyed a week filled with swimming, hiking, crafts, and fishing. Prayer preceded the activities and a message of appreciation for what the Lord had created followed.

Dubby had seen the girls steal away during dinner. He'd wondered why they had snuck off into the woods the previous nights—maybe skipping clean-up duty?—but the last five nights hadn't been anything special, with most of the campers huddled around campfires or listening to one of the leaders give a talk about the challenges and triumphs of living a Christ-centered life.

But this night would be different. It was the last of the trip and the most anticipated event of the week—the dance. It was a chance to be out under the stars, the dark mountain sky immense and inspiring, and dip your toe into the pool of possibilities regarding the opposite sex. It wasn't a free pass, but a limited ticket to connect, even touch that person that had piqued your interest in the days leading up to the event. They planned the dance and discussed it with giddy excitement even before they all arrived. What was it along that hidden path through the trees that rivaled the titillation of a dance?

The dry wind and high heat, even for August, had the ground so parched his sneakers crunched the straw-like grass with each step. With his new Canon camera around his neck, he cringed as he followed them farther into the woods. Hearing the chomp of his steps, he worried they would catch him and accuse him of lurking after them.

The trail began to climb, and soon he found rocks and pebbles tumbling around him as he had to find his grip and footing to stay on their path. At the top, he paused to catch his breath. He peered into the trees, wondering if he was still on the right route, but then heard distant voices, so he carefully followed.

He had been watching her all week. If she knew how he felt, she would probably just laugh. She belonged to someone else. He knew that, but it didn't stop him from longing for her. It was Sara, and even though he had known her since they were children, Dubby had always been so shy, so backward, it hadn't even occurred to him that she was aware he existed.

But that year seemed different. Twice she had smiled at him. It was so unexpected and elating that he wanted to catch it and keep it in a jar like a firefly. Just the bat of her eyes, even when she wasn't looking at him, made Dubby tingle inside. Her silky blonde hair bounced when she walked, and her lips were rosy even without the gloss the other girls were wearing. She hadn't led him on or encouraged him, so why he followed after them, he wasn't sure, but his fascination with her, as well as his curiosity, was strong. He kept going.

The large ponderosa pines with their deep crevassed bark towered above. Dubby was able to go from one to the next clandestinely because of their thick trunks and the mat of dropped pine needles. The louder and more distinct their voices became, the slower he went.

Soon the shadow of the trees was broken by silvery peeks of sunlight coming from the mesa. In the distance, he could see the vast canyon that spread out from the cliff's edge and the dark blue of Echo Lake below. He veered away from the trail, to where he could see the girls sitting on a bed of shaded grass in an alcove cut into the rocky hillside. It was a secluded nook to sit and enjoy the view.

For a moment, he just watched, but then his stomach dropped, and his heart began to pound. What he was witnessing was both shocking and improbable, so unbelievable he raised his camera and took frame after frame, sure that he would never be able to convince himself later of what he was witnessing.

The voice was there the moment he turned away and would speak to him often throughout his life. However, while he heard it whispering, he refused to listen.

CHAPTER 1

NOVEMBER 4, 2023
CENTRAL UTAH

adison Moore peered down from the plane's small oval window and saw the massive and familiar mountains of her childhood home.

Had they always been that immense? She felt her heart sink, realizing she had never appreciated their grandeur. They were simply part of her former life. A life that flooded back into her memories—some sweet but most sorrowful. Those mountains had watched her from above, but they felt more like a hovering, condemnatory presence rather than the majestic backdrop of her youth.

The overcast skies were a fitting return. Wisps of clouds clung to the tops of snow-covered peaks. Such a constant those crests and valleys had been in her life—as strong and constant as the shame her family had felt since she left their church.

Now, they reached up to her as if to say, see what you've been missing?

The diverse cultures and enticing nightlife of Las Vegas were exciting and certainly different, and her friends and co-workers were like a cozy blanket of comfort and support. And while she regularly traveled, mostly for fun, this was her only time coming home. She had left years ago, swearing she'd never return, but now she was back, and for the most unfortunate of reasons.

As tiny drops of condensation inched down the window, leaving weepy trails, she felt her throat tighten as she fought back the sting of tears. There was sadness laced with the fear, knowing her homecoming would be unwelcome, despite being requested—which was why she'd asked Taylor not to come. They'd only been married a few years. Taylor didn't deserve to be treated with disrespect because Madison had chosen to leave home rather than live the life her parents had planned for her.

It had been August of 2006 when she'd driven her over-packed, hand-me-down Toyota out of Orem, Utah, and eventually out of the state. The tears she cried then weren't just ones of leaving her home and family—she'd cried for the *loss* of home and family.

When she had made it to her dorm at the University of Nevada Las Vegas, she didn't call home to say she'd made it safely. They had made it clear that her choices went against all they believed. A full-ride scholarship in volleyball gave her a place to go; she found a job to cover basic needs. She had made it out, determined to show them that her decision was the right one.

The betrayal of her entire family remained fresh in her mind, how they had sent her away. She wondered if they, too, were thinking back to what happened and how it impacted their lives.

Madison could clearly envision the shock and disappointment on her mother's face when her brother Vincent, covering his own secrets, told the family that Madison was acting out against the church. Madison wanted to defend herself but knew they wouldn't listen to her. She'd tried to make them see she was still a daughter worth loving, tried to live up to their standards, but eventually she told them her true feelings: she no longer believed the way they did.

They kicked her out of the house.

And yet, now she was being asked to come back by those who had written her off.

When the plane landed, it was her Uncle Morey Woodruff who met her at the curb. He bounded out of the car, grabbing her suitcase with one hand while embracing her with the other. A completely opposite greeting from the one she expected from the rest of her family.

"It's so good to see you," he said, squeezing her tight. His bright red hair had almost completely turned gray, but his blue eyes were still as vibrant as she remembered. "We're the rare two percent," he always told her when she bemoaned her distinct red curls. "Shoulders back! We stand out in a crowd. Be glad you didn't get your dad's boring brown hair." And while it made her heart hurt to think it, she had secretly wished so many times that she not only looked like she was Morey's daughter but that she actually was.

It was such a comfort to have him there. They had monthly phone calls, but this was the first time she'd seen him in almost a decade. He was who Madison counted on. The one family member who hadn't abandoned her. While the others spoke of sin and shame, nothing she had done kept him from being there for her—even if it was long distance. The years had added some weight, and his smile, while still vibrant, was framed with the thin lines of time. His looks had changed, but he was the sweet and joyous Morey she had always loved.

They talked the entire forty-five-minute drive from the Salt Lake International Airport to the modest farmhouse where her ancestors had settled over a hundred years before. After Morey's second divorce, he moved there to help his parents manage the sprawling and fertile acres. At the time, they were into their eighties and in ill-health. It was convenient for them all, and being a contractor, Morey's ability to fix things and his access to equipment and resources made the arrangement work exceptionally well. When his parents died just months apart, he stayed. Madison remembered her grandparents fondly and loved that her Uncle Morey still lived at the old farm. He never had children, which could be why they were so close. Both appreciated the other for filling the hole in their lives.

As he drove slowly down the dirt laneway, he pointed to a small blue car. "It's not much, but it will get you around while you're here." He parked around back, and when they got to the porch, he opened the door and led her inside. "This door is never locked. I lost the key years ago, so if you ever want to rob me...."

She rolled her eyes, remembering her parents rarely locking their doors either.

"You sure you don't want to stay here?" he asked, setting her suitcase down.

She hugged him and nodded. "I promised Jenny I'd stay

with her, but thank you."

It was true, but also a bit of a lie. The farmhouse was so small, she knew he would insist on her taking the main bedroom, and he'd be sleeping on the foldout couch or a cot in one of the small upstairs rooms. It was the area of the farmhouse she knew well. Not only did she play in those rooms as a child, but she had also spent a few days living there while she waited for her room at her dorm to open—two days of officially being not just on her own but out.

Her parents had made it clear, there was only one way to stay a part of their world. After she finally told her parents she could no longer accept their beliefs, Morey had come to her aid. She often wondered if her parents knew of his role in her ability to leave or if they even cared.

"I don't leave until next Wednesday. We'll get together. I'm sure I'll need an escape from being with my parents. I'm still shocked they even asked me to come."

He started to refute her but instead shrugged, knowing what she said was true.

She looked around the farmhouse—same furniture, same photos on the walls, same warm, earthy smell she remembered. They went outside and walked the yard and the rows of trees that covered the old homestead. She smiled as she remembered some of the happier times from her past. Far in the distance, she noticed dust and some large pieces of equipment moving dirt.

"What's going on there?" she asked.

He hesitated and then sighed. "The beginning of the end."

She turned to him, confused.

"Long story, but the short version has to do with money.

Building computers is a more lucrative business than growing cherries." He contemplated the construction. "You can't expect everything to stay the way it was, but I hate the fact that it's changing when I'm still on this earth."

"You sold part of the farm?"

He smiled. "It wasn't mine to sell."

She looked out to rolling bulldozers and wafts of dust. "What do you mean? Isn't that Grandpa and Grandma's land?"

He nodded. "It was. But some things happened."

She felt her heart sink. She knew that farming was a feast or famine life, but the idea that he had to sell off part of the acreage that had been in their family for generations must have been devastating. And to have to watch and witness the resulting destruction of what he'd worked so hard to maintain. She sighed and put an arm around him.

"Why didn't you tell me?" she asked. It wasn't accusatory, but a mixture of surprise and sadness. They usually spoke at least every month on the phone, and now she wondered if she hadn't manipulated their time with her issues and events instead of being there for him. After all, she was no longer the estranged teenager forced to leave home.

She was now an educated, married, and resilient woman who should be there for the person who had always been there for her.

"It happened rather quickly, and there isn't anything you could have done." He took a deep breath. "I can't change it. But I sure wish I didn't have to sit here and watch."

They sat at the kitchen table, and he briefed her on what she'd find at her parents' house. Her father Saul was given just days to live and had started to refuse to see anyone, even Madison's brothers. Was it pride that had him slipping away both from illness and from others? Morey was unsure why his typically amenable and soft-spoken brother now stood his ground and wanted to die alone.

"And he wants to see me?" she asked, confused.

Morey nodded, but his face showed that he, too, was perplexed by his dying brother's request.

"He probably wants one more chance to tell me how disappointed he is," Madison quipped, but inside she wondered if that wasn't the truth. She hadn't relented and come back. She would not beg for forgiveness or wallow in shame. This could be her father's final chance to make sure she knew she wasn't the daughter he wanted.

As usual, Morey assured her it was her parents' loss. It didn't change her feelings, but she appreciated him trying to console her. Even ten years later, she needed that.

After another brief stroll through the row of cherry trees she had climbed as a child, he loaded her suitcase into the little blue car, hugged her again, and waved as she drove toward what would surely be a heartbreaking and angst-filled brush with her past.

What used to feel like a drive across the state took only fifteen minutes. She pulled up to the split-level brown-brick home of her youth. A large S.U.V. sat in the driveway behind her parents' 1976 blue wood-paneled station wagon, the same one she had driven in high school. Madison parked along the curb, as not to block anyone.

She hesitated, checked herself in the rearview mirror, and then took several deep breaths to calm her nerves.

"You're an adult, and they can't control how you feel or act. It's different now," she reassured herself against the niggling voice in her head. It was exceptionally loud today.

Wishing she had bought another mini-bottle of alcohol on the plane, Madison stepped onto the sidewalk. The light November breeze made her shiver, but it was a dry cold, she heard her mother's voice rationalizing. She smiled and rolled her eyes, and began the walk up to the door. She hated being cold, and today the air temperature wasn't the only thing giving her a chill.

The house was how she remembered it. Paint peeling on the wooden porch banister and the terra-cotta flower planters were the same ones her mother grew pink petunias in every spring. Now only the twisted and limp stems remained. The door was still a dark red, and she instinctively reached for the knob, only to catch herself and then step back. Before she could touch the doorbell, the door came open, and there stood a short but large woman holding a tiny boy with a mop of dark hair.

"Oh!" the woman exclaimed, obviously not expecting anyone. Her face went dour. "Madison," she said. "You came." It was her Aunt Katie. She was the wife of her Uncle Syd, her mother's older brother. Madison never could understand their pairing. Syd was arrogant and pious, nothing like their brother Morey, but he was charismatic and successful; while Madison wasn't particularly fond of Syd, she wondered what he ever saw in this pinched-faced and bitter woman.

Madison stood her ground, and Katie took a step back and adjusted the child onto her hip.

"Yes, I came," said Madison. "I'm here to see my dad."

Katie gave a suffered sigh. "He's in the back room. Your mother is with him now. Saul refuses to have anyone in there but her or Syd." She gave Madison a punctuated nod. "Syd just left but he's been here almost every day."

Madison cringed. She sighed, hoping that she wouldn't have Uncle Syd's constant presence.

Saul Woodruff, her father, was born in a small farming community in the northern part of Orem. He was a descendant of Wilford Woodruff, the fourth prophet of The Church of Jesus Christ of Latter-day Saints. The family was proud of their distinguished Mormon history. Of the six children born to Evelyn and Saul Woodruff, only two survived past the age of five. Saul Jr. was the younger of the two boys, and the chores on the farm kept them busy.

Both Saul and Morey graduated from Orem High School and then attended Brigham Young University. After so many years of hard labor on the farm, both boys chose different lines of work. Morey planned to be an architect but ended up leaving college early and working construction, eventually becoming a contractor. Saul studied religion and education, which led to a job as a seminary teacher at the same junior high he had attended as a boy.

The Mormon students walked across the street from the school to where the seminary building sat, and while it wasn't an official part of the school, they were allowed to take part of their school day to attend. For almost thirty years, Saul taught them the stories of *The Book of Mormon* and other scriptures aligned with their church. He had planned to retire at age sixty-five, but plans changed.

Madison stood outside the house she once called home. "Where's my mom?" she asked, annoyed that this woman felt in control.

Katie took an obvious "I'm going to be the bigger person" breath and hiked the child higher on her bulbous hip. "Come on in, and I'll get your mother." She backed up and gave Madison a sliver of space to slide through. Then she turned toward the hallway and announced, "Darlene, your daughter, Madison, is here."

Since Madison was the only daughter, it was annoying to have this pseudo-aunt act as though she was a stranger in the house.

The child began to squirm, and Katie bounced him. "This is Ephraim, Jed's youngest. I watch him on Tuesdays and Thursdays so his mother can work," she explained. "Jed just started his own carpet cleaning business. Lisa is cutting hair."

Madison nodded as though she was even aware of these people and their lives. She remembered her cousin Jed. He was several years older than her and was closer to her older brother Ben than he was to her. He was on a mission when things went awry with Madison and her family. She doubted she would even recognize him now.

"So, you're still working as a reporter?" Katie asked, half interested while trying to wrangle the fussy toddler.

"Yes." It wasn't entirely true. Madison was a reporter; however, she was a reporter without a job. It had been just over a month since the paper she had worked at for over five years went the way of so many other small newspapers and had to close. Madison was deciding what to do. She was lucky because Taylor's job as head chef at Café Nuevo brought in more than enough to pay their bills. However, Madison had never been dependent on anyone since she'd left the house she now stood in; the stress of having no paycheck was starting to wear on her. And being back home and in the most awful of situations didn't help.

She leaned back and looked toward the hallway, wishing her mother would come and relieve her from the awkward small talk, and yet she didn't know what to expect from her, either.

"She'll be out soon," Katie said, noticing Madison's glance. "He has good days and bad ones. But it seems like the bad ones are taking over. Last week we didn't expect him to still be here, but the Lord has other plans."

She paused, and when Madison didn't say anything, she pulled her keys from a large, quilted purse. "I need to get this one back home, so I'll leave you. I'm sure she heard me. Just wait here." She gave a curt smile and left Madison standing alone.

When the door closed, Madison stood for a moment more and then stepped into the small living room just off the foyer. The carpet was a pristine white, and the vacuum lines were straight and new. It was the "home teachers'" room—a place that many Mormon families designate in the home that is used to receive guests but is off-limits to anyone who actually lives there. The light blue sofa and matching love seat were spotless, just like when she lived there. Why wouldn't they be? They were only sat on once or twice a month.

A walnut upright piano was against the wall, with the hymnal open and a portrait of Jesus above it. Madison never remembered anyone playing that piano. The piano she practiced on when her mother forced her to take lessons was in the basement family room. On the wall behind the sofa was a large painting of the Salt Lake City temple in springtime and, like bookends, on one side was a portrait of the first prophet, Joseph Smith, and on the other, the current leader of the L.D.S. church, Russell M. Nelson.

Madison stepped lightly, trying not to disturb the carpet, and looked at the many framed photos of her brothers and their families arranged on the piano top. All were group portraits—father, mother, and children except the one of her—the one placed in the back. As Madison studied it, she realized it wasn't really her. Smiling up from the cheap gold frame was her sixteen-year-old self. The one, her parents, hoped she'd become again: sweet, obedient, and filled with faith. She picked it up and brushed the dust from the glass. When she heard footsteps padding down the hall, she quickly went to set it back but, in her scramble, knocked several of the other frames over, tumbling families and toothless grandkids in all directions.

"Hello, Madison." It was her mother.

Madison was righting the different photos, unsure where their original spots were. "Sorry," she said, and then she looked up. "Hi, Mom," she said, sadly. The woman she remembered hid under a thin skin of age and exhaustion.

Darlene had always been a slender and pretty woman. Her dark brown hair was shorter now and, along with her green eyes, had begun to fade.

Madison could feel her lips tremble as she tried to lick the dryness from them.

Her mother sighed and came to help arrange the photos. "You never could stay out of this room. The more I told you, the more intriguing you found it."

"I was a rebel," Madison said under her breath.

"Not always," her mother said. "You were strong-willed, but you had a sweet spirit."

"Had?" Madison chided her.

Her mother leaned into her and gave her an obligatory hug. "I'm glad you're here. Your father was so adamant that I call and ask you to come. Thank you for doing it."

"You didn't have to ask. When Morey told me Dad was sick I…"

Darlene rolled her eyes. "Morey," she groused. "I'm sure he has plenty to say about this."

Madison smiled inwardly. Her bond with Morey was both a comfort and another wedge with her family. Her uncle was the original black sheep of the Woodruff clan. He had stirred the pot since he was young, making the staunch and starchy bunch uncomfortable every time he was present. Brash and gregarious, he was an outspoken critic of the beliefs they held dear and the polar opposite of her father's quiet, humble nature. Madison loved him because he had no qualms about breaking rank with the others and helping her when her time to leave came to a head.

And from what she understood, he enjoyed telling them about her life while making sure they knew their shunning hadn't affected her in the least. It wasn't entirely true. Her rejection was painful then, and the wounds were still fresh.

Morey had always tried to make her feel like she wasn't missing out, but even he couldn't close that gaping hole of abandonment.

"He told me that Dad wasn't doing well. He knew I'd want to see him," Madison countered. And it was true. She did want to see him. Even with the heartache, the thought of never seeing her father again was as tragic as her reason for leaving. She didn't remember the cruel and condemnatory words as much as his sorrow-filled and disappointed eyes. She knew how he felt about the path of her life, but it was the others who made it clear she was no longer welcome because of that life choice.

It took over a year before Madison tried to make any contact. During a tipsy and especially lonely New Year's Eve, she called—a call met with cold and pointed undertones. She wondered if they were even happy to hear her voice and to know she was alive. The conversation turned predictable and probing, laced with comments about the blessings and gifts that being a faithful member had brought them, as if that would await her once she returned to the fold. Even with Madison's successes in life, nothing matched the life she could be living if she'd simply accepted that she had been misguided and was ready to repent and return.

That had been the last time she'd spoken to either of them, until her mother's awkward call to relay a request from her father to come home.

"He's sleeping right now. You can bring your things in, and he'll be awake soon," Darlene said.

Madison shifted and stumbled on her words. "I'm not staying here."

Her mother flinched.

It was hard enough to face them, knowing what they thought of her and her life. The last thing she imagined was that they would expect her to stay there at that house.

"I got a room." It wasn't entirely a lie, but if she told them where she was actually staying, it would have opened a whole new opportunity to degrade her.

"That seems like a silly waste of money," her mother said.

"I figured you'd need the space for others who were coming in." Others who were in their good graces.

Her mother gave her an annoyed smirk. "You know as well as anyone that there is no one coming in. They all live right here. You haven't been gone that long that you don't remember that. You're the only one who has left."

Madison wanted to snap back, but when she looked up, her father stood in the hallway, weak and disheveled in blue plaid pajamas. "Daddy," she whispered.

Her mother turned. "Saul William Woodruff, what on earth are you doing out of bed again?" She went to him, but he ignored his wife and stared with a weak, eager smile at Madison, who stood frozen.

His light brown hair was now completely gray, and his face was pale and tired. His sky-blue eyes were wet, and in them, she saw the man she remembered as if he were staring from inside a worn and weary suit.

"Hi, Maddie," he called to her. His voice was hoarse and brittle. He was the only one who called her that, except for Taylor, and to hear him say it with such fondness made her heart break. "You came. How are you?"

"She's fine, and she'll come and see you in your room," her mother urged, taking his arm and trying to direct him back to bed.

"I'm good, Dad," said Madison, ignoring her mother as much as he was.

He tried to take a step toward her but wobbled and caught the wall. Madison quickly went to him and, with her mother, helped him back to his room.

The room was dim, and the air smelled stale and somber. He moved slowly into the covers, and her mother fluffed two pillows behind his back and then touched his hand. He looked up at her.

Madison never could fault their bond. It was real, even if she saw little else in their life that was.

"You're supposed to be sleeping," Darlene scolded him.

He shook his head. "I'll have plenty of time to rest. I only have a few days with my little girl."

"That doesn't mean you have to wear yourself out." She turned to Madison and, seeing her eyes shimmer with tears, talked to her quietly but pointedly. "This isn't the time for resolutions."

Madison knew what she meant, and it made her heartsick. Why else would he have summoned her home if he didn't want to make amends? She reluctantly gave her a nod of compliance.

Darlene spoke to Saul. "I'll give you an hour, and then you have to rest."

He sat up as straight as he could. "Fine," he agreed. He shooed her with his hand, wanting to be alone with his daughter.

Her mother gave a huff and went to the door. "I'll be in the kitchen if you need anything."

Taking a seat on the bed, Madison grappled with what to say to him. He was dying. The doctors at the hospital gave him just days to live and then sent him home; nothing more they could do. Her Uncle Morey had warned her that he was fragile, but to see it for herself was heart-wrenching.

It was over a year ago that Morey had told her the grave news. Initially, she was shocked and refused to believe the diagnosis. Lung cancer. Such an improbable and ironic thing for a man who had never smoked. He had no vices. He had never touched a drop of alcohol in his life. He had been faithfully married to Darlene for almost thirty-six years. And the one time Madison remembered him swearing—the word "damn," hardly a worthwhile curse—he apologized almost immediately after uttering it.

In the months that followed Morey's grave call, she stewed about what to do. Should she visit? Should she try to make amends for the conflict that had pushed them apart? She'd wondered if it was finally the time to dismiss her fears and bring Taylor out to see the place that had been her home. Except for Jenny, no one from her past life had ever met Taylor. Most weren't even aware that Madison had gotten married. But why would she tell them, knowing they would never look upon her marriage outside of the church with anything but scorn?

When she'd first heard the news about her father from her uncle, she'd felt there was a chance things could be different if she saw him now. But then her trepidations stopped her, made her waste days and weeks with inaction, believing she'd have more time to come to grips. Instead, her good intentions had evaporated with the ring of her cell phone. It was a call from her mother telling her that her father's time was coming to an end and that he was pleading specifically for her.

It surprised her, saddened her, and had her wondering if he had finally realized he was wrong and wanted to make it right. Did it take facing death to have him choose his daughter over his church?

"Thank you for being here," he said softly.

She smiled. "Of course, and I wanted to come sooner, but I . . ."

He hushed her.

They just sat and let it sink in for several moments that she was there, and he soon wouldn't be. Tears rose in her eyes, and seeing this, his filled as well.

"This isn't why I asked you to come," he said. "I've been the reason for so many tears, and I don't want to spend my last days causing even more."

She couldn't disagree with him. His turning against her when she needed him most was the most painful time in her life.

They had cast her out. No calls, no visits, no support. And yet, she felt the urge to be here. Was it for him or for her?

He took a labored breath, and his face grimaced. He was so ill and in so much pain.

"There is something I need to do. It's something I should have done a very long time ago. I need to apologize, and I need your help to make things right."

Madison wiped her eyes, her brow scrunched in question. Was this what she longed to hear for so long? Was he finally going to accept her and apologize for the way he shut her out of his life just because her beliefs weren't his?

"Yes?" she asked in anticipation.

He glanced at the closed door and back at her. "There's something in my wall safe, behind that large photo," he said, motioning to a large landscape of the red rocks of southern Utah hanging on the bedroom wall. "Can you get it for me?"

She stood a moment and admired the photo. It was one her father had taken. He had always loved photography. The framed landscapes and numerous examples of his work hung throughout the house. Growing up, she'd loved to watch him get himself and the camera in position and focus on a subject. But this hobby also brought sadness: she wished her father could share this passion with Taylor, who was also an amateur photographer. It was actually an obsession, and they had filled their home with images from their life. Wouldn't it be nice to be able to share that with her father?

She lifted the photo off the hook and set it against the wall on the floor. There she saw the small door of the safe and combination dial. She looked over to him. "What's the combination?"

He hesitated a moment, making Madison wonder why he asked for her help if he didn't trust her, but then he glanced toward the door before quietly giving her the numbers.

"Eight, seven, eighty-one." It was almost a whisper.

Madison spun the dial, stopping at each number, then turned the small crank. Inside was a blue photo album sitting atop a brown and bulky paper bag. She lifted the album and showed it to him.

He nodded. "Yes, that's it. Bring it here, but close the door and put the picture back first."

She lifted the paper bag to ask if he wanted that as well. It was heavy, and as soon as he saw it, his face turned to horror. "Not that," he said. "Leave it."

The urgency in his voice was surprising, and Madison was overwhelmed with curiosity about what the brown bag held, but she did as he said, closing the safe and replacing the picture.

The album was dark blue with a yellowed plastic cover. A white sticker and the words "Youth Camp 1981" were written in black marker along the spine. It was filled with a small number of faded photos, held in separate plastic sleeves. She brought the album to him and wondered what it had to do with his apology to her. He reached out, and she placed it in his frail and shaking hands. As he opened it, he tried to clear his throat.

"Do you need some water, Dad?"

He shook his head, obviously determined to continue with what he'd planned to show her. His eyebrows creased as he studied the images, and he closed his eyes for a moment after turning the thick plastic-covered pages and stopping on the photo he wanted. When he opened his eyes, they were filled with regret. He pointed to a girl in the picture and turned the book toward Madison.

"This is a girl named Sara. She was in my ward when I was young. Her family lived just down the road from us," he explained. The ward, each neighborhood's congregation boundary in the Mormon Church, was the same one they were in today. Her childhood home had been in the family for generations and was part of the large farm that once spread for acres at the mountain's base. Acres that were now almost entirely filled with homes.

"I took these photos during a Mutual camping trip," he said. "It was at Camp Aspen Veil."
Madison thought back to her days in Mutual, the church's youth organization. But she was perplexed by what this had to do with anything now. "Okay?"

He looked up at her, and his entire face was so wrecked with sorrow, it startled her. "Dad, what is it?"

"Something terrible happened on that camping trip. It was so awful."

"What happened?" she asked.

Now he sat hunched over, with tears falling onto the pages. He sniffed and reached for his white handkerchief on the nightstand. He pinched his nose with it and wiped his cheeks. "Sara fell off a cliff and died."

"Oh my God, that's terrible," Madison said.

Her father flinched back at her using the Lord's name in vain. Then he turned several pages and pointed out another girl. "This is Amelia Johnson. She was also a girl in my ward." He swallowed, struggling to continue. He laid back against the pillows. "She was blamed for pushing Sara that day, and she went to prison." He paused. With red, wet eyes, he looked up at Madison. "But she didn't do it."

Madison reeled back, stunned. "She didn't do it? What do you mean?"

"Amelia didn't push Sara."

"How do you know this?"

"I have the proof." He took a deep and thoughtful breath. "I've kept it a secret all these years."

"You didn't tell anyone?" Madison exclaimed loudly.

His face turned to horror, and he looked to the door. He waited, but when nothing happened, he hushed her and continued. "I felt guilty. I was scared and didn't know what to do. I told my father right after it happened. He told me to stay quiet, so I did. She took the blame."

"Why?" Madison asked, dismayed.

He didn't answer, but his eyes drifted back to the photo. "I need you to help me. I don't want anyone else to..."

"What's going on in here?" It was her mother. She looked at the photo album and huffed. "What's that?"

Madison was startled and then felt like a child trying to hide candy she wasn't supposed to have. She felt the compulsion to steer her mother away from the matter. Her instincts were confirmed when her father began to cough. While Darlene was distracted looking for something to help him, Madison felt her father gingerly close the book and try to hide it away in the bedsheets.

When Darlene came to the bed with the pitcher and a glass of water, she saw the half-hidden album. "Youth Camp 1981," she read, seeing the label on the album.

Madison felt the need to help him keep his secret. "We were just looking at some old pictures."

"You think 1981 is old?" she remarked with a lilt.

While it sounded like good-natured goading, Madison knew that coming from her mother, it was more of a rebuke.

"It *was* over forty years ago," Madison countered.

Her mother tightened—another huff.

Darlene had grown up just a few houses from Saul, and while they never dated while in high school, they knew each other from the church, and after Saul returned from his Mormon mission in upstate New York, a four-month courtship led to marriage.

"What was he telling you?" She spoke as though her husband wasn't lying right there.

Madison straightened at her mother's accusatory tone. "He was just remembering old times." She emphasized the word old and then smirked.

Darlene reached for the bed covers and smoothed them around her husband.

Madison saw that her father had already dozed off.

Darlene picked up one of the medicine bottles by the bedside. "I think these are making him..." she mouthed the word "delusional" and raised her eyebrows. "He tries to leave the house, and I've found him wandering outside. And he seems to do nothing but cry anymore."

Madison peered down at her father. His face was slack, and his breathing was rhythmic and loud.

"He needs his rest. He sleeps almost all the time now." Her mother motioned her toward the door. "You can talk to him more later."

Madison reached for the album and slid it carefully from her father's limp hands. "Can I take this?"

Her mother sighed but gave her a relenting shrug.

"It will give me something to look at."

Darlene nodded, staring at the album in Madison's hand.

Madison realized her gaze wasn't on the album—her

mother was staring at her wedding ring. "It will be three years in June," Madison said. It wasn't to make a point or remind her mother that she was married. She was simply talking about her life. However, as long as Taylor wasn't the active L.D.S. young man and returned missionary that her parents had hoped for, her parents would never accept their love or their union.

When her mother gave her a disaffected raise of her eyebrow, it cut worse than if she had flat-out admitted that she didn't approve or even care. The older woman turned toward the door. "Do you want a sandwich or some water?"

Madison stood for a moment, trying to process her mother's blatant disinterest in her life. They hadn't spoken in over ten years, and she had nothing to ask her except if she was hungry? Her entire body roiled with sadness. "No," she finally blurted. "I need to leave."

"Leave?" her mother asked. "You just got here."

"I mean, I need to check in at the hotel."

It was an escape. She had come to find closure with her dying father, not to be in an awkward and uncomfortable position with her mother. She needed to leave to keep from lashing out and turning the first few moments back home into the same scene that played out so many times years ago.

She had talked herself through it before she even stepped on that plane and made a vow to herself that she wouldn't let them bring her to the red-faced fury and sharp-tongued defensiveness like before. That would just prove they were right—what they had been saying all along was true—that she was only doing these things to hurt them. That her decisions to go her own way, leave the church, and rebel against the gospel's teachings weren't what she really believed; it was just her continued immature rebellion.

Madison walked out of the room as her mother turned back to Saul and carefully tucked the covers around her dying husband.

Down the hall was the door to her old room. She hesitated in front of it. Every day for almost eighteen years, she'd found solace in that room. It had been her sanctuary. Her own space to think, plan, and as she got older, a place to be free of the confrontations and disputes that took over outside that room.

She was alone in the hallway. Madison couldn't resist opening the door of her past and looking inside. She turned the knob, and when the door swung open, she couldn't believe what she saw. It was as if she had never left. The same bed, bedspread, and matching canopy, and even the stuffed pink pony centered on the pillow. On one wall, a white and gold-trimmed mirrored vanity, and along the other wall, the matching dresser.

She walked to where a cardboard-framed photo of Daniel West and her dressed for prom, and another of her smiling brightly in an orange and blue volleyball uniform. It had been almost a decade. This room was a memorial. It was as though she had died, and they couldn't bear to lose what memories they had.

"You can stay here if you'd like." Her mother stood behind her. "You can be in your old room," she said, motioning to the bed. "It still has your bed and dresser. Almost nothing has changed."

And yet, everything had changed.

REDEEMED

There is a tomorrow for those who have faith.
Bring me home with heart and arms waiting.
Time and pain vanish.
Giving hope that those broken will be redeemed.

CHAPTER 2

The tiny town of Lindon, Utah, was a short five-mile drive from the city of Orem, and Jenny's condo was nestled high up in the foothills, hidden in a cove of junipers and pine trees. Madison had never been there. When Jenny told her she had bought a place in Lindon, Madison envisioned a small town populated with small minds of her past.

Jenny opened the door, arms wide and face beaming. Madison couldn't remember when she wasn't smiling. Her sunny disposition was perplexing to Madison. They had so many similarities. Old friends usually do, yet Madison couldn't find the patience or resolve to let her anger go. Jenny never seemed to have had any, and yet she'd experienced almost identical rejection, and most of it they went through together. The difference was that Madison had escaped, at least geographically.

Madison found herself with her small suitcase in hand, whisked inside her dearest friend's upscale two-floor condo.

"This is so nice," Madison said, glancing around at the floor-to-ceiling windows that revealed an unobstructed view of Mount Timpanogos, the backdrop of Madison's childhood.

The ridge line of the mountain was said to resemble a maiden named Utahna. The legend was that this mountain was where a young girl's sacrifice to the gods took place.

Madison studied the peaks, and even though she claimed to be able to pick out the nose, cascading hair, and other features of the sleeping woman, she really couldn't quite see it.

Jenny had always been thin and fit. This was obvious from the sleek skirt and silk blouse she hadn't changed from work. She wore large hoop earrings and bright red lipstick, with a shock of short white hair that almost stood straight up. It wasn't a big change from how Jenny looked in high school. She was about the only girl who had the confidence to wear the super short hairstyle, when the rest of them seemed to place their validity as females in the length of their locks.

Sleek but inviting furniture was arranged around the large room to accent the view, and original artwork adorned the walls. It was a far different space than the shake-shingled track home Jenny lived in as a child.

"I have you in the guest room," Jenny said, guiding Madison down the hall. The room was warm and the bed was huge. On the nightstand was a photo of the two of them from high school in a rustic barn wood frame. Madison picked it up and smiled.

"It's usually in my office, but I thought you'd enjoy the throwback. I bet you can't get your hair that big again," Jenny chided her.

"Don't tempt me. All I need is a comb and a can of Aqua Net."

"I'm still jealous of your gorgeous red curls. I'm just glad hair gel was invented, and going gray is now the trend," Jenny laughed and ran her fingers through her short white spikes.

They walked back to the large room, and Madison again admired the view. "The mountains seem so much bigger than when I grew up here."

Jenny smiled and nodded.

"Las Vegas always has something going on," Madison continued, "and I love the heat in December, but I forget how incredible these mountains are. When I think of this place, it's hard for me to remember anything that I like about it. That sounds so petty, like I'm still bitter."

Jenny smiled. "It wasn't always easy growing up here, especially if you don't walk the line."

Madison nodded. Jenny had been Madison's best friend since the sixth grade. They migrated to each other through a shared awareness of being outsiders. It was a complicated friendship from the start because Jenny's family was Catholic. Madison's parents knew they drank alcohol, so they never allowed Madison to stay at Jenny's house overnight. Madison knew her parents' hesitation to have her spend too much time with her non-member friend, which only solidified her desire to be with Jenny.

Saul and Darlene were kind to Jenny initially, but when she showed no interest in attending or learning about the L.D.S. church, they encouraged Madison to make friends with the girls in her ward. It was hard enough raising a child in that day and age without having them influenced by those who weren't of their faith.

Jenny had been there the night Madison's brother, in order to protect his own secret, revealed something about her that had the family convinced would send her straight to hell. Her parents blamed Jenny and banned Madison from contact. Jenny's rebellious nature had already formed her parents' discontent concerning the friendship, their concerns only confirmed when Madison disavowed their beliefs and turned against them.

"Thank you for letting me stay here. It was pretty uncomfortable at my parents', and I'd just be depressed at a hotel."

"Of course!" said Jenny. "I would have been so mad if you didn't stay here. Do you want something to drink?"

Madison looked at her watch. "Is it too early for a glass of wine?"

Jenny laughed. "It's never too early. Sit, and I'll grab some. White or red?"

"Whatever you have open."

Jenny laughed. "Red it is!" She went around the corner but called back to Madison. "So, you've already been to see your dad?"

"Yes. I didn't stay long because he fell asleep, and I'm too tired right now to handle being one-on-one with my mom."

Jenny returned with two glasses of dark red wine and handed one to Madison. "So, how is Aretha?" she asked with a lilt.

They both laughed. And in unison, mocked her mother's angry tirade when they were young. "Respect! Is that too much to ask? Respect? Respect?"

Madison had to steady her glass for fear that her laughter would cover Jenny's beautiful floor with merlot. "I'd be getting that same lecture today if she knew I was here. That woman is a master at holding a grudge."

Jenny's face fell a bit, and Madison apologized.

"Sorry, I meant when it comes to me."

Jenny sighed sadly. "That terrible night... I'm sure they still feel I was the cause of everything."

Madison held the glass up and studied the wine. "Well, you certainly weren't the cause of everything," she smiled at her friend, "but you did teach me to drink. Remember the red wine that night?"

"Wow, that's right. I hid the bottle in my pillowcase. I took it from the back of my father's cabinet, where I thought he wouldn't notice it was missing, but it was super expensive. We drank that when I would have preferred Boone's Farm!" She gave a wicked giggle. "When we decided to cause an uproar, at least we did it up right!"

"I'm not so sure I've ever done anything so thoroughly scandalous ever again!" Madison laughed.

"Here's to good friends," Jenny said, and the glasses clinked.

Madison smiled. She loved Jenny and felt like she was finally back home for the first time.

"I can't believe I haven't seen you since your wedding. How is Taylor?" she asked.

"Good. Wonderful, actually."

"So, why are you here alone?"

Madison sighed, "This is the busy season for the restaurant. But also the stress of being here, watching my dad dying, and dealing with all the past stuff is too much for me. Having Taylor here would be miserable for us both. I couldn't handle having my family treat us both like pariahs. At least I'm used to it."

Jenny gave a sad but knowing nod. "How long ago was

your wedding?" she asked, scrunching her face in thought. "It was so beautiful."

"Three years last June," Madison answered.

"Has it really been three years? That's crazy." Jenny's eyes suddenly went wide. "Oh! I forgot to tell you. Speaking of weddings, I saw your parents at my sister Darcy's daughter's wedding about a year ago. She married a Mormon kid." She gave a mischievous smile. "They were shocked to see me there."

Madison huffed. "Seriously? Isn't it funny how they can attend a wedding of someone they probably don't even know, but when their own daughter gets married, they don't even send a card?"

"I'm sorry," said Jenny. "I shouldn't have said anything."

"Why are you sorry? It's their issue."

Jenny leaned back and took a sip of the wine. "It probably will never change. Not much does around here."

Madison shook her head. "I just don't get it." She turned to her friend. "How are you not angry? You never seem to let it bother you. I don't see how you live here right in the middle of Happy Valley. My only solace is that I live away from this place."

Jenny shrugged. "It's not the place; it's the people. I have my circle of friends, and with my work, I don't feel it or see it as much as before. You'd be surprised. With the growth in this area, and the number of new people moving in, it's changed...a little."

They both laughed and shook their heads.

"What would I have done without you to vent to all these years?" Jenny asked.

"You and me both," said Madison, and they clinked glasses again.

"I wish I didn't have to run off to Denver. I can't believe that the one week you're here, I have to leave."

Jenny was an environmental law attorney. She loved the outdoors and had always been an avid hiker, skier, biker, and bird watcher. Her career was a perfect fit for the geography of Utah. After law school at the University of Utah in Salt Lake City, she'd taken an internship working on a project involving the Geneva Steel plant and pollution in the nearby Utah Lake. When Jenny completed that assignment, she stayed on with the firm, and she was now saving the scenery and land she loved. She had dated some in college and had a relationship with a colleague that lasted almost a year. Still, regardless of her optimism with the changes in their hometown, even as a bright and successful lawyer, she found the prospects for love were scarce.

For a moment, they sat in thought. Then Madison shot up straight. "I need to tell you what happened with my dad today. Before he fell asleep, he told me the weirdest thing, something about a girl who fell off a cliff years ago when he was young. It was at church camp. Her name was Sara something." She tried to remember but couldn't. "Anyway, he was really upset about it."

"I can imagine. That sounds terrible," said Jenny.

Madison took another sip of wine and nodded. "But get this. He said that another girl at that camp went to *prison* for pushing her off that cliff. And my dad said he knows she didn't do it."

"What?" asked Jenny, flinching back.

"Yes. He said that the girl who went to prison didn't do it. He started to fall asleep, and my mom came barging into the room. He had told me that he didn't tell anyone what he knew, except for my grandpa. Like it's some secret he's never told. He has this photo album and was showing me pictures of both these girls. I brought it with me," she said, tugging it out of her large tote bag. Madison found the picture and pointed out the two girls, and told Jenny what her father had said about each of them.

"If he knows she didn't do it, why didn't he say something?" asked Jenny.

Madison shook her head. "I'm not completely sure, but he did say he told his father, and my grandpa told him to stay quiet. I guess he's kept it a secret all these years. My mom didn't know anything about what he told me. He obviously doesn't want her to know. Maybe his illness shook something loose that he had forgotten."

"Seems like a huge thing to keep secret." Jenny gave a long sigh. "And what if he's right? What if that poor girl spent years in prison for something she didn't do?" She turned to Madison. "Is she still in prison?"

Madison shrugged. "I have no idea."

Jenny got up from the sofa. "Come to my office. I'll look her up on the inmate roster at the prison website. Do you remember her name?"

"Yes. Amelia Johnson."

"Birthdate? Year?"

Madison shrugged. "It would be around the same as my dad, I'm guessing. So, in 1964?"

They went to the small bedroom that Jenny had turned

into an office. A dark, cherry wood desk and a matching bookcase filled almost the entire space. She opened the laptop on the desk and began typing. "Amelia Johnson," she said as she punched in the letters. Then she sat back, and she and Madison gave a collective gasp. A photo slowly appeared of a woman with shoulder-length, dark graying hair and a face that held no expression. She wore a light blue prison top, and her dark eyes were empty. "She was sentenced in February of 1981." Jenny did the calculation in her head. "Over forty years," she said, staring at the photo. Then she turned to Madison. "My God, that's a long time."

Madison sighed. "Yes, but she *was* convicted of murder," she said, pointing to the conviction in the boxes under the photo.

"Second degree," Jenny corrected. "Even so, I think the actual time spent in prison for someone sentenced to life is usually around twenty-five years. Being that she was so young, I can't believe the parole board hasn't considered that."

Madison nodded in thought.

"And if what your dad says is true, that's unimaginable." Jenny looked down a moment and then took a deep breath. "I hate to ask you this, but..." she paused.

"What?"

"Do you think he called you here so he could make a deathbed confession?"

Madison's face dropped along with her stomach. The stunning tingle washed over her as the realization of what her friend said hit her. She shook her head. "My dad? You think he was the one who pushed that girl?"

Jenny shrugged, but her eyes were large. "Why is this such a secret if he knows that Amelia didn't do it? Why didn't he say something until now?"

Madison put her hand to her mouth and thought. It seemed plausible and also horrible. "And if that is the case, what does he want me to do?"

CHAPTER 3

The plush bedding and cloud-like mattress did nothing to help Madison sleep. Too much wine, unanswered questions, and the stress of being back with her hostile family had Madison wide awake, buried in blankets, and wishing she had a job that was calling her back. It was hours before she fell into a light, disturbed sleep.

In the morning, she awoke groggy. She wandered into the kitchen and found a full pot of coffee and a plate with two pastries covered with plastic wrap. A note from Jenny apologized again for having to leave and travel for work. She also wished her luck with her dad.

"My dad, the killer?" Madison said to herself, remembering Jenny's initial assertion regarding her dad's revelation. She scoffed at the thought, but the more coffee she drank, the more the idea grated at her.

She dug her small laptop from her tote bag and typed the names of both girls into the browser. Several old newspaper articles appeared. She clicked on one dated in early February 1982.

On Thursday, February 5, 1982, 16-year-old Amelia Johnson of Orem, Utah, was sentenced as an adult in the murder of her classmate, 16-year-old Sara Lynn Voorhees, also of Orem, Utah. Johnson was found guilty of pushing

Vorhees off a cliff near Camp Aspen Veil, where both were part of a youth outing in August 1981. Johnson was originally charged with first-degree murder for stalking and killing the victim. However, she pleaded guilty to a lesser charge of second-degree murder and was sentenced to life in prison. Defense attorney Jerry Alford represented Johnson, but because Johnson pleaded guilty, there was no trial. Johnson did not take the stand and had no statement during sentencing.

Phil and Glenda Voorhees, the victim's parents, were in the courtroom during the sentencing and, in emotional testimony, talked about their daughter, how she was a kind and devoted girl. They also addressed Johnson and told her they forgave her. Johnson did not acknowledge anyone in the courtroom, but when her mother, Martha Johnson, spoke during sentencing, the defendant wiped tears and appeared to be affected by the testimony.

Life in prison, Madison thought, rereading the sentence. *It's been over forty years.* Sentenced at sixteen . . . more than twice her life had been spent in prison. Amelia Johnson was a juvenile at the time, yet she was sentenced as an adult. If what Madison's father said was true, why did she plead guilty?

Madison had so many questions to ask her father, but it was too early to go back to the house. She continued to skim through search results on the computer. There weren't many.

But then she came across a story that made her sit back against the kitchen chair, stunned. There weren't just the two girls involved in this tragedy, but a boy as well. As she read furiously through the grainy newspaper copy on the screen, she realized this wasn't just a case of one girl killing another, but of a supposed love triangle.

The article named the girls, leaving the boy anonymous. The only identifying description of the boy was his age—a seventeen-year-old male. Madison scoured through other articles, but it had been years. In the few entries she was able to uncover, nothing ever identified the boy by name. *Could his name have been Saul Woodruff?* she thought.

The 17-year-old male witness reported that the two 16-year-old girls began to fight after the accused came upon him and the other girl at the overlook near Echo Lake. He states he tried to break up the fight, which is when the accused pushed the victim off the cliff. Sara Lynn Voorhees died after falling approximately sixty feet. Rescue crews retrieved her body from the ledge below.

Madison stopped reading. She took a deep breath. What did her father see, and what did he do? Was Saul's dying wish to confess that he was the one who killed that girl? What other reason could there be?

She sat, thinking, and shaking her head. Even with the pain she had experienced because of her father, she couldn't believe he had the capacity to do something like that. The hurt he caused her wasn't just something he inflicted but also came from something he had taken away. Her choices not to follow the teachings and wisdom he had impressed upon his children weren't negotiable. You were either in the church, or you were out.

For Saul and Darlene, the choice was as important as life and death for Madison, as well as the rest of the family. They told her that if she couldn't see that and didn't want to work toward what they knew to be "right and true," they couldn't pretend to condone her decisions. Accepting her would have been accepting her bad choices, and they refused to do that.

Saul saw it as his duty to stay true to his beliefs and not falter. And it wasn't just his children that he saw his actions affecting. As the bishop of his ward, others were watching. They looked to him for guidance in their own family struggles. He told her over and over again, if he were to bend the gospel's teachings for his daughter and tolerate her actions, how could anyone respect him as a true believer?

When she looked at her watch again, an hour had slipped away. It was time to go and see him. She decided to leave the photo album. She wanted more time to peruse it when she returned.

She quickly showered and dressed and realized when she stepped outside, the temperature had dropped significantly overnight. Even with the dry cold, her breath crystallized, and she pulled her gloves from her tote. Inside was her laptop, making it heavy to lug around. She usually carried a purse but had used the larger tote as her personal item on the plane, packing her belongings into it and one small carry-on, not being able to afford to check a bag. After all, she was unemployed.

When she arrived at the house, she parked in the same spot and made her way to the door. In the early morning light, the silhouette of the Wasatch Range made her pause.

The sunshine spread across a vast blanket of red and gold that covered the foothills of the enormous mountains. While so many things had changed since she had lived at that house, those peaks and valleys never did. With only two days left, she was already looking forward to seeing them grow smaller in the distance.

"Would you like some breakfast?" her mother asked when she got inside. "I can make eggs, toast, and I think I even have some ham leftover from Sunday."

Madison shook her head. "Thank you, but I'm fine. I had something at..." she caught herself. "...the hotel."

She sighed inwardly at the silliness of her parents and their continuing beef against Jenny. Like it was her fault that Madison had turned her back on them. Jenny was simply a scapegoat, which was why she didn't tell them about being at Jenny's condo. She was a twenty-eight-year-old woman who couldn't tell her parents where she was staying, let alone anything significant about her life.

"How is he this morning?" Madison asked. She stood at the breakfast counter while her mother used a familiar yellow and green sponge to clean the stove top. It was the same brand of sponge she remembered her mother using years before. She was sure it wasn't the exact one but still marveled at how embedded in the walls of that house was her childhood.

Darlene finished wiping the counter and then removed the yellow latex gloves and laid them next to the sink. "He's good. But it was a rough night. He is like a newborn baby. Sleeps during the day and keeps me up all night." Her mother turned toward the hallway. "I'm sure he's awake now if you want to go in." She then realized she had forgotten a glass on the table and reached for it.

"Here," Madison said, handing it to her. She moved to go and see her father, but then paused. Leaning on one of the faded yellow kitchen chairs, padding emerging from the cracks in the vinyl, she asked, "Did he tell you *why* he wanted me to come?"

Her mother placed the glass in the soapy water in the sink and then turned slowly. She shook her head. "He just said he needed to see you. He's your father and still wants what's best for you."

Madison refused to let what her mother said inflame her. What's best? What about disowning and turning against her all these years? She took a deep breath. "Is there a plan in place?" she asked. "I mean, for you?"

Her mother stood up straighter. "Plan? Plan for what?"

Madison shrugged and struggled for words. "For what you're going to do. Are you going to stay in this house? Did he put money aside to take care of you?" Darlene had never worked outside the home, and Madison knew that a seminary teacher's pay was barely enough to support their basic needs. She could see by the house's condition and just about everything in it that money was tight.

Her mother gave her a skeptical nod. "Money?" she asked. "Is that what you're worried about?"

"For you, yes. You've never worked outside this house. I'm worried about you and how you'll..." Her words petered out. There were so many things her mother had never done on her own. While she was like a drill sergeant in her role as a mother—brusque and unbending—once out from under the

42

sheltered role of housewife, the real world could be cruel.

Her mother studied her severely. She cocked her head to the side. "I'll be fine," she said, sharply.

"Will you?"

Darlene nodded. She started to speak and then stopped.

"What is it?" Madison asked.

"What did he tell you?"

A guilty chill swirled in her stomach. "About what?"

Darlene's face fell in frustration. "About why he wanted to see you. Why did he ask you to come here?"

Madison felt the heat rise in her face, and the prickle of sweat begin to form along her hairline and base of her neck. She swallowed and tried to keep herself in check. "I came because he's my father. I'm just worried that...."

"You're worried about me?" Darlene snapped, wiping her hands on the dishrag. "I didn't think you cared."

Madison groaned, started to reply, but then stopped. *She* didn't care?

Her mind played back the last and final phone call she had made to her childhood home.

Back when she was eighteen and her first year in college had ended, she'd stood in the dorm and watched the last of her roommates leave with packed boxes and suitcases, heading home, promising to stay in touch for the summer. Madison had no home in which to return.

Overwhelmed by loneliness and fear, she'd broken down and called her mother.

"You made a decision, Madison. We tried to help you, and you lied to us." On the phone, her mother's voice was unfaltering, and Madison knew that stance hadn't changed.

"What about free agency?" Madison had debated.

Darlene scoffed. "I believe completely in free agency. You are free to choose, but that doesn't mean those choices don't have consequences."

Madison often wondered why she hadn't just denied her brother's accusations. They may have never found out.

"Don't you even care what happens to me?" Madison cried out.

Her mother explained stoically that caring often meant doing things that were hard but eventually for the best.

Now, standing in her mother's kitchen, staring at the dark green phone on the wall, Madison swallowed back her ire. "I do care."

Her mother paused and then simply lifted an eyebrow. "I'll be just fine. Syd is taking care of things. Don't you worry." She walked past her and down the stairs to the basement, leaving Madison alone in the kitchen, her eyes blinking and her chest pounding.

"Syd," Madison grumbled.

Of course, her mother's brother was the consummate hero in her mother's eyes. She wondered if her father felt inadequate when her mother espoused about her gallant older brother. Madison's Uncle Syd. *What a joke,* she thought. 'Uncle' had never been a term of endearment, any more than the title of niece was for him.

As she thought back to the worst time of her life, he was there, stepping into their family crisis and delving out unwanted and self-righteous advice. Her mother was crying into his shoulder rather than her own husband's. The vision still made Madison shudder with disgust.

Madison felt if her mother wasn't so entrenched in the church, she would have held onto her maiden name. It wasn't that she thought her mother didn't love her father, but the consuming admiration she had for her esteemed brother cast a shadow on just about any relationship she had with anyone else. In her eyes, no one measured up to the accomplishments and accolades of the great Syd Wallace.

Part of her wanted to follow after her mother and point out her absurdity, but instead, she remembered the pep talk with herself and refused to go there. She went to the cupboard and found a glass, got water from the sink, and calmed herself. Peace didn't last for long.

The sound of a loud clang, as the washing machine lid slammed shut down in the basement, was a signal that her mother was upset. The house was always cleaner when Darlene wasn't happy.

Madison debated leaving the house and driving straight to the airport, but instead, she set the glass down and went to her father. He was the one she was there to see, and if things continued to heat up, at least when she stormed off, she would have spent the time with him as she'd planned.

When she entered the room, he was awake and watching a small, archaic television set on the side dresser. His eyes widened when he saw her, and then softened. It was as if he had forgotten that she had been there the day before.

"How can you even see that?" Madison asked. "It's so far away."

"It doesn't matter. None of it is worth watching anyway," he grumbled.

She stepped around a wheelchair at the end of the bed

and took a seat in the same spot on the bed that she had yesterday. "Mom said you had a rough night."

"I guess. I don't remember." He seemed tired. His voice strained.

"Can I get you anything?"

"A ticket out of here."

She gave him a sympathetic grin.

"I know what's waiting for me. I believe in the afterlife and in eternal families," he said softly. Tears filled his eyes and started to roll down his cheeks. He cleared his throat and continued to speak. "I also know that Jesus died for our sins."

"What sin did you commit?" she asked. "And why are you telling me?"

He seemed to steady. He looked at Madison and wiped his eyes. "Because you're the only one who will understand."

"Understand what?"

"Why I need to repent. I believe in the power of repentance." His voice cracked and again he began to cry. His guilt and regret came pouring out.

Madison felt a twinge of irritation. Was he comparing what had happened to her and why she left to what he had done? Was he still trying to prove that her soul needed saving?

"Dad, please don't do this," Madison said.

She wanted to tell him that she had nothing to be ashamed of, nothing for which to repent. And yet, she knew his beliefs. She'd been reminded repeatedly of the disappointment she had caused both her parents when she exposed her true feelings and disavowed the church's teachings. She could have done just about anything else, and it wouldn't have crushed and embarrassed them the way this had, but even hearing how wrong and how hurtful this was over and over again, she still felt her decision was a good one, the right one for her.

"I have to do this," he said weakly. "If I don't, I'll let your mother down. When she arrives in the celestial kingdom, I won't be there."

Madison shook her head in frustration, feeling the weight of how they blamed her for their failure as parents. "Dad, your salvation isn't determined by what I believe or what I do. Just because I'm not what you expect doesn't mean you're not going to heaven."

He started to speak, but she kept going.

"I can't change to please you and mom. We've talked about this before. I can't change who I am."

He put a hand up to silence her and then took a weary breath and sighed. "Madison, I didn't ask you to come here so I could change you."

She tipped her head unconvinced.

His face fell into sorrow. "I asked you to come so I could apologize."

CHAPTER 4

as it an apology? Madison thought as she ran the words over in her mind. She was driving back to Jenny's after a long day of mainly watching her father sleep in-between daytime talk shows and game shows. He was absorbed in the tacky programs and kept looking over at her when a contestant scored a point or one of those "liberal ladies" said something he considered to be a bit scandalous. He'd lift his eyebrows, searching for some shared interest, and Madison simply smiled.

She waited for a chance, a break in the programs, where she could ask him more. There were so many questions, yet his weak and confused state made her hesitate. He drifted between this and the father she remembered, with his soft, humble voice, but staunch, unbending views.

"I should have told you years ago," he said. "But there was so much anger, and I didn't want to cause you even more pain. I see now I was wrong. I'm so sorry that I waited until now, but..." his words trailed off.

He said the word *sorry*, but was it for what she had hoped or something else? The terrible but vague story he told about the girls and the cliff pricked at her repeatedly, but even with the intrigue of what part he had played, it troubled her that it was the thing he wanted to be resolved rather than what had torn them apart. She wasn't surprised, just sad. Maybe that was the reason she hadn't pressed him on it. She didn't want to confirm her disappointment.

It was a break away from the stuffy room and depressing situation that brought her back to the condo. She was also planning on one, maybe two, glasses of wine, before returning to her parent's house. That night was a family dinner. Her three older brothers and their wives would be there. They hadn't spoken to her in years, and while she knew they were busy with careers and kids, it wounded her. She rationalized that she too could have reached out, but hearing that her very presence could be detrimental to their children, why would she even try? She wondered if they would bring their children tonight or if they, the adults, would even speak to her. And that was the reason she did not bring Taylor. The embarrassment of her family's pettiness freely paraded as if to prove a point was too much to imagine.

She had debated whether even to attend the dinner. She was there for her father, to be with him one last time. The issues with her siblings were low on her list of priorities, and attending that group meal would simply give them the chance to remind her of their rejection. She knew her mother felt obligated to invite her, making Madison feel even more like an outcast. She wasn't sure if it was stubbornness, pride, or curiosity that made her accept the invitation.

As she drove back over that evening, she imagined the conversations and practiced her responses to their ignorant or sarcastic comments. She smiled a bit at the mature and well-thought-out comebacks she had ready to use. She was a far different person than the tongue-tied and crying girl that stormed out years ago. Her out-of-control emotions only solidified their feelings of pious indignation.

Their cars were already there when she arrived. Madison looked at the car's clock. She was ten minutes early and wondered if they hadn't had a family meeting to prepare before she got there. The nervous, almost nauseous feeling began to set in as she approached the porch.

It was her oldest brother Troy who answered the door. "There she is," he said with a grin. "Come in!" The auburn hair and smiling blue eyes she remembered were still there but now also with thin lines and a thicker waist. When she stepped into the foyer, he patted her gingerly on the shoulder, as if tacks covered her. "How are you?" he asked, as if he had practiced each word.

"Good," answered Madison. "And you?"

"Good. Really good."

They both stood and smiled as the noise of children filled the house. Nieces and nephews she didn't know. She pondered what to say. *Do you still think hell is my destiny? Am I still a miscreant and unwanted in your life?* It's what she had heard from him while they stood in that same house. He had just become a father and didn't want his child raised around someone like her.

He led her to the kitchen, where her mother and two other women stood at the sink. Her two sisters-in-law were wiping their hands on kitchen towels.

Madison saw how comfortable they were there in the family home and wondered why that surprised her. Ever since her brothers brought them home to meet her parents, the family immediately accepted them, even after just a few weeks of courtship. Taylor, however, would never see or feel that. An icy grip was on her heart as she watched them. As if they could see her resentment, both gave her tentative smiles.

Madison recognized Vanessa, Troy's wife, who stepped forward and extended a hand. It was contrived and awkward, but Madison took it. The woman was uncomfortable even touching her. Then Stacie, her brother Vince's wife, came forward and did the same. The two women could have been actual sisters with their similar heights, shapes, and muted features. They stood, heads bobbing and searching for words, and then Madison heard a familiar voice behind her. "It's been so long, but I remember that gorgeous red hair of yours." It was Natalie, her brother Ben's wife.

Madison turned, relieved. She had known Natalie in high school. She was two years older than Madison, the same as Ben. The two had dated from the time they were sixteen. Natalie grew up just a block away, had been in their ward, and was always kind to Madison. After her fallout with the rest of the family, Natalie tried to keep her apprised of family happenings. Madison wasn't sure if her friendship on Facebook constituted truly staying in touch, and often the updates only made her feel worse. Still, she did appreciate the effort. Natalie sighed and gave her a genuine hug, and Madison returned the embrace as the rest of the family shuffled and swayed uncomfortably.

A young girl entered the kitchen timidly. She had long auburn hair, and Vince grudgingly introduced her as his oldest, Bethany. "She's almost nine. She wanted to have a sleepover, but she was forced to tag along with us," he explained. Madison ignored her brother's brusqueness, and reached out her hand to the girl. Bethany looked at her father first before accepting it.

"It's nice to meet you, Bethany. I'm your aunt," Madison said with kindness. She was surprised anyone had brought their child, especially Vince.

The girl gave her an apologetic smile. "My aunt?"

Madison shrugged. "I live in another state. That's why you don't see me." *Plus, no one in this family wants me here. That is the real reason,* she thought.

Madison could tell the poor girl was bored. She tried to engage her by asking her about school, but this seemed to cause distress with Bethany's mother, Stacie, and since the others seemed uncomfortable about talking to Madison past the point of small talk, she made an excuse and slipped away to the back bedroom to see her father.

Again, he was watching television. When she came into the room, he tried to sit up and greet her but couldn't. He laid back, defeated.

"Relax," she said. She had hoped he might be able to come out and sit with them at the table, but seeing him unable to even sit up in the bed, she realized that family dinners at the table were a thing of the past. So many parts of her childhood memories were coming to an end.

"You were my youngest and only girl. Once you came along, I knew our family was complete," he said, as she took a seat on the edge of his bed.

It was a yarn Madison had heard so many times before she had it memorized. As a little girl, her father would sit on the edge of her bed and recite the story of "when Maddie was born." Wasn't it ironic that it was Madison who now sat on the edge of his bed while he told it? From the time she could remember, it was repeated at the dinner table, with neighbors, and from the pulpit from which he often spoke during church services. And while she knew each word, inflection, and pause of the story, she sat and let him tell it, even though now every utterance was a struggle to get out.

"After your three brothers were born, your mother said we only knew how to make boys and was ready to give up, but I wasn't. I knew that you were in heaven, waiting. I prayed so hard and asked the Lord to let you join our family here on earth. When your mother was pregnant with you, I had a dream. God told me that if I had faith, I would have a daughter, and this would fill me with joy."

By the time he ended his story, he had sunk into the pillows, eyes closed, and was speaking so softly, Madison wondered if he wasn't talking in his sleep. She watched him for a moment and then drew the covers over his chest.

Her mother came into the room and whispered that everyone was at the table, waiting. Darlene peered down at her sleeping husband's face and gave a sad and weary smile. She then led Madison out to where the rest of the family sat, encircling the large oval table. When she came into the room, they fell silent and looked sheepish.

As the oldest grandchild in attendance, Bethany was the only child seated at the table for dinner. Madison was surprised to see more children scattered around at card tables or TV trays in the family room. Not everyone had kept their kids away.

Madison took the only empty chair. She reached for her fork, and Troy nodded at her and then bowed his head. The others followed, and Madison quickly put her fork down and instinctively did the same. As her brother blessed the food, she stealthy looked up at her siblings, all bowed and eyes closed. Then she felt young Bethany staring at her. When their eyes met, Bethany realized she was caught and quickly put her head down. Madison smiled, and when Bethany glanced back up, Madison winked to let her know she wouldn't tell. Then she felt the glare of her sister-in-law. Madison quickly dropped her head and closed her eyes.

During the dinner, Madison was mostly quiet. She answered mundane questions about where she lived and her job, but noticed they avoided anything too personal and certainly didn't ask about Taylor.

When they finished with dinner, there were mentions of work the next day, followed by shuffles toward the door. Madison watched as her mother handed out foil-wrapped leftovers.

"Thank you for coming out," Troy said to her as they were leaving. "Maybe we'll see you again in the next day or two?"

She nodded.

When Vince and Stacie began to gather their things, Bethany quickly left first, and Madison waved to her. Stacie waited until her daughter was almost to their car before giving Madison a stern glare. Madison sighed, knowing why.

"I'm sorry I smiled at your daughter during the prayer," she said, feeling it was ridiculous to apologize for a smile but also knowing how her family felt about such things.

"Smiled?" Stacie shot back. "You didn't smile. You winked at her," she said and then turned and gave her husband a knowing smirk.

"You did what?" Vince snapped. "What does that mean? Why would you wink at her during a prayer?"

"It's not a big deal," Madison defended. "I caught her with her eyes open and was just playing around."

"Playing around. That's exactly what you said when I caught you back in high school: 'We were just playing around'," he said, his voice high, mocking her. "And nothing has changed," Vince continued. He shook his head, disgusted. "I don't need you teaching our daughter how to be disrespectful and irreverent."

Madison flinched. Here it was, the argument that started over ten years ago and never resolved. "What? Teaching her? I winked at her because she didn't have her eyes closed. This is ridiculous."

"We don't think it's ridiculous," Vince shot back.

"Not having your eyes closed?" Madison gave a sarcastic laugh.

"That's the problem, you have no respect for our beliefs, and you'd just love to have that rub off on our daughter," said Vince.

Stacie nodded.

Madison took a step back and shook her head. "Rub off on her? You act like she's going to hell just because she had her eyes open during a prayer."

"It's a good thing you're not having kids," he grumbled.

The comment stabbed, but Madison refused to let him think his words had hurt. "Who says I'm not?"

He smirked at her.

She returned a scowl. "I think you're mad because I'm actually happy and doing fine without all this crap. Don't worry. I won't bother your child and try to drag your perfect little family to hell with me. I'll be leaving soon, and you won't have to deal with me, just like before." Everything she had practiced came spilling out in one long rant.

Vince scoffed. "I don't care what you do. I wish you'd never come in the first place. We all know why you came."

Madison bowed up. "I came because Dad wants me to be here."

Vince huffed. "He doesn't know what he wants. But we all know what you do."

"Come on, guys, not here. Not now," said Ben, trying to lead Vince and the rest of the family out of the house.

"Oh, quit trying to play counselor Ben!" snapped Vince. "You know you feel the same way. You told me yesterday you didn't want to bring your kids because she'd be here."

Madison looked over to Ben and Natalie. Her heart stung.

"Only because I knew this would happen!" said Ben, trying to refute Vince's claim.

"What's going on out here," Darlene said, rushing toward them from the bedroom. "I could hear you all the way back there. *He* could hear you."

"Good!" shouted Vince. "He won't listen to us or even see us, but he wants to see her?" He pointed at Madison with a look of disgust.

Madison cringed at the thought of Vince learning about her father's hidden shame. Her brother had never owned up to his own guilty secret, one Madison knew but had never revealed. Even after all that happened between them, she refused to retaliate. "Don't worry. I'm leaving," she said, sneering back at him. "I'll call first before I come over tomorrow to make sure I don't rub off on any of you."

"Madison, wait," called Natalie, but Madison had already walked out the door and to her car.

The chill of the night air hit her like a slap, and she again felt the salty rise of tears. She sank hard into the seat and started the car. She wiped the red hot sting from her eyes, then looked over and saw Bethany sitting alone in the family car staring back at her. In the glow of her headlights, as she backed out of the driveway, she saw Bethany give a small wave. Even though the girl likely couldn't see her, Madison gave her a wink.

BLOOD ON MY HANDS

My chest heaves with the roiling anger as it rises.
Clenched fists but nowhere to throw the punches.
Time has brought hatred to the one staring back.
Alone with my pain and my love for one lost.
Gone and yet still so alive in this broken place.
I scrub, and yet my hands remain with blood.
Will you forgive the one who lays the blame?

CHAPTER 5

Amelia Johnson was sixteen years old when that tragic day happened. She was now fifty-eight. She never rebuked the accusations, and because the witness claimed she had hidden and then ambushed Sara, they charged Amelia as an adult. She had spent over forty years at the Timpanogos Women's Correctional Facility. The prison was located in Draper, Utah, over thirty miles north of the actual Mount Timpanogos, which was blocked from view by both distance and other range peaks.

Madison continued to search the web for more about the case. It seemed like an exorbitant amount of time to spend locked up for someone sentenced when they were a teenager, especially if what Madison's father said was true, and Amelia didn't do it.

Because Amelia pleaded guilty, there was no trial. They sentenced her, sent her away, and wrapped up the entire incident neatly. All the ends were tucked away tightly and put away forever.

What ate at Madison was her father's role. She hoped he was simply the witness that was mentioned and not the perpetrator. But his response to the photos and recollection of events had Madison thinking the worst. It wasn't just his obvious dismay with what he knew, but also his timing. A deathbed confession isn't usually a minor revelation.

She sighed, noticing the time. She picked up the photo album and considered whether or not to bring it with her. She wanted time to peruse it more closely, and if she brought it back to her father, she might not get that chance. However, the album spurred his memories, so she tucked it into her tote bag and headed over to the house.

She had planned to call beforehand, especially after the scene the previous night, but figured none of her brothers or sisters-in-law would be there in the middle of the day, so she took the chance and decided just to show up. She wondered what her mother's attitude would be, knowing her siblings must have had a heyday after she left, talking about her and her terrible influences.

Taylor had called soon after she arrived back at the condo, and while Madison wanted so badly to vent about how her family had treated her, she didn't want Taylor to worry. She kept the incident to herself, with only a vague mention of how nothing had really changed except for how much older everyone looked.

However, when Jenny called later to check in, the gloves came off. Madison unleashed the pent-up anger and frustration. She felt a bit guilty keeping it from Taylor, but with so much of it directed at them as a couple, why lay that bitterness and rejection on the one she loved?

Natalie had sent a text later that night apologizing. Madison wasn't surprised, since Natalie was one of the few who seemed to have always tried to reach out. However, the revelation that she and Ben may have felt uncomfortable about having their children there hurt her. But Madison also knew that much of that was probably due to pressure from the rest of the family. Madison didn't respond to the text, feeling she needed time to gather her thoughts first.

When she arrived at her parents' house that morning, her mother was pleasant, putting Madison on guard. She asked how her father was doing and how his night was, and Darlene gave her a play-by-play of his sleeping, waking, and other events that made Madison sorry she asked.

"Did you bring that photo album?" Darlene asked.

Surprised, Madison nodded and retrieved it from her tote.

When Darlene saw it, she gave a relieved sigh. "He's been asking about that thing since you left yesterday."

"What has he told you about it?" Madison asked. She knew her father was hesitant about her mother knowing his confession, but Madison hoped she could glean something to help her with what seemed a pensive revelation.

"Not much. Ever since he took a turn, he's been talking or rather weeping about things in the past. Sometimes, I don't think he knows what he's saying. He's confused and keeps talking about how he needs to find something that he's lost. He doesn't accuse me of taking his things, but he is constantly saying that something is missing."

The truth, maybe? Madison thought.

"It was around the time he started asking for you. That's when he kept obsessing about things that happened years ago. He brings up the good times we all had. It's what you do when you know your life is ending. That's what the hospice nurse says. You want to remember happier times. But I was surprised how adamant he was to see you." Then Darlene looked down. "That didn't come out right. What I meant was..."

"It's okay, Mom," Madison said, seeing her mother stumble over her words. "Things *were* happier."

Darlene gave a sad smile and nodded. "He's glad you're here. So am I," she added softly.

Her mother squeezed her shoulder and quickly went to the kitchen. Madison tried to swallow, but it was difficult. Just that tiny spark of affection sent her emotions reeling. She was almost thirty years old and still longed for her parents' approval and love. That would probably never change regardless of what disagreements they had, and she knew they wished things were different, yet they knew that was not to be.

She made her way down the hall, scanning the photos covering the walls as she passed by. She paused a moment and stared at the large family portrait taken when she was still in braces. That was such an awkward and awful time, but at least she was part of the family. It was one of the last photos of them all together and smiling. Her father stood tall and proud with an arm around Darlene. He was young and healthy. She sighed and turned to the bedroom door, knowing the shell of that man was behind it.

As she walked into the room, her father smiled from his bed, and when he saw the album in her hand, his face turned to relief.

"I thought I'd lost it," he said. "I keep losing things."

She smiled and took a seat on the bed. "I took it with me to look at it more closely."

"What did you see? Did you find the proof?" he asked, with more vigor than Madison had seen in him since she was back.

Madison shrugged. "It looks like a bunch of kids at a

camp. Is there something else I should be seeing?"

He took a deep breath and sank into the pillows. His words were broken and weak as he turned and studied the pages. "I can't find it. There is more. I know it was here, but it's missing."

She shook her head. "What's missing?"

"The proof. Ah, come on, Dubby, think," he said, knocking his head with his fist.

Madison cocked her head and smiled, remembering her parents talking about how her father only started using his real name, Saul, during his church mission when he was nineteen. Until then, his family and friends referred to him by his middle initial—W or Dubby.

"Dubby is such an odd name," said Madison, seeing the frustration over his forgetfulness.

Her father nodded. "It came from my middle name—William. It started with just *W* and then Dub and then Dubby." He smiled. It was the brightest she had seen him.

"It seems we all had nicknames," Saul continued. "No one was called by their given name. Making up those nicknames seemed harmless then, but now..." His eyes turned sad. "It feels like we knew we would eventually have something to hide."

Madison's stomach clenched. "Dad, tell me what happened that day. How do you know that Amelia didn't kill that girl?"

"Sara was her name." He sighed, a long, yearning sound.

"Yes, and you said Amelia wasn't the one who killed her."

He nodded as his eyes dropped to his hands. He seemed to slip back into a half-conscious state.

"If Amelia wasn't the one, who was? You can tell me."
She really didn't want to hear it if what she suspected was
true. But she sat and waited for his reply.

He squirmed a bit in the bed, with his gaze diverted.
"Without the proof, no one will believe me."

"I'll believe you."

He looked up at her with a weary face. "But will you
forgive me?"

Her brow pinched. Her father worried about her forgiveness for something that happened decades ago and had
nothing to do with her. What about his shunning of her?
Where was the apology for that?

"It will cause more pain. I'm not sure anyone will ever
forgive me. And I don't think I deserve forgiveness."

"You always taught us that if you're truly sorry and
repent for what you've done, then God will forgive you."

He nodded. "Yes, but if you can make it right, you must
atone for your sin."

"Atone?"

"If I don't tell what happened and set Amelia free, I hav-
en't truly repented."

"So, tell me what happened. What did you do?"

"I was a coward. I was angry, and I didn't want to
believe that..." he started to weep.

"Why were you angry?"

He sat a moment, tears slowly inching down his cheeks.
He looked up with eyelids lowered in shame. "I was confused. I didn't understand. I thought she..." He paused and
shook his head. He became oddly stoic. "I should have listened to the still small voice. I knew what was right. I was

64

wrong, not just about her, but about many things." He slid down a bit in the bed and grimaced.

"Dad," Madison called to him, seeing he was beginning to weaken and fall back into his lethargic state. "What happened that day? What did you do?"

His eyes were nearly closed, but he cleared his throat to answer her. "I told you. It's what I didn't do."

She watched as he drifted off to sleep, unconvinced that he wasn't the one who pushed that girl, but the frail and fragile breathing of the man she once thought could talk directly to God, tore at her heart and kept her from asking him the question. She looked at the photo on the wall. The curiosity of what was hiding in that safe struck her. She wondered if that heavy paper bag held the proof about what her father was so adamant about telling. And if that was the case, why was he so insistent that she leave it alone?

She contemplated the combination he had given her. Eight, eight. Or was it seven? And then seventy-one, or was it eighty-one? She sighed and watched as his weak and diseased lungs filled and released.

She couldn't make herself take the leap and open the safe.

CHAPTER 6

I t was early morning. Madison was getting ready to leave the condo and head back to her parents' when Jenny called her cell phone. She wouldn't make it back in time to see Madison before she left on Wednesday. Her client had to postpone some meetings to the next week. Madison was disappointed. It had been years since they'd seen each other, and she missed her familiar and comfortable friend. She had friends in Nevada, but her years of friendship with Jenny, not to mention the past they shared, was something she'd never found with anyone else.

"So, what's the latest with your dad and the murder mystery?" Jenny asked.

Madison had wanted so badly to tell Jenny what she'd learned about her dad and figured she'd do that once Jenny was home. Now she realized over the phone was as good as she would get, at least for a while.

"According to online articles, Amelia was jealous of Sara when she found out she was dating a boy. The reports say she followed them up a path, got in an argument with Sara, and then pushed her off the cliff."

"Oh my god, over a boy? Do you think it was...?" Jenny hesitated. She gave a nervous giggle and then apologized profusely. "It's so scandalous. I can't see your father—you know, Mr. Woodruff—being involved in something like this." Then she asked the question they both were thinking. "Do you think your father is the boy they were fighting over?"

Madison scoffed. "I'm not sure. The name of the boy isn't listed in any of the articles I've found."

"A juvenile," said Jenny. "That's probably why his name isn't listed. Your dad was only what, fifteen or sixteen?"

"Yes," said Madison. "But why list the names of the girls and not him? They were juveniles, too."

"The reason is most likely because they charged Amelia as an adult, and as for Sara, the law says you can't defame someone who is dead, so why protect her name?"

Madison felt her heart sink. "He must have really liked Sara. He gets weepy and moony every time her name comes up."

"Or is he feeling guilty about what he did?" Jenny countered.

"I just can't believe he would ever do something like that. If he liked her, why kill her? Plus, if Amelia didn't do it, why did she plead guilty? None of it makes sense."

"Maybe her confession was coerced? She was so young, and who knows what the investigators said to her. Is your dad certain that Amelia wasn't the one who pushed her?"

"He's adamant about it and says he has to atone for his sin. He says he has proof in that photo album, but I've studied every photo, and I don't see anything except a bunch of kids doing camp stuff and some photos of the trees and the lake."

"If it's his sin, why does he need proof? Why not just confess and tell what happened?" Jenny asked.

Madison thought a moment. "I don't know. I gave him every opportunity today, but he just kept quoting scripture.

The only thing he says about the incident has something to do with the proof that is missing and wanting me to help set Amelia free."

Jenny paused. "This reminds me of the Nancy Drew books we used to read."

"I wish he would just spit it out and tell me what happened."

"Why not ask him point-blank? Were you the one who pushed her?"

Madison thought a minute. It was hard to explain why she was unable to confront him and ask him, "Dad, did you kill that girl?" He was so ill, and her time with him seemed to be broken into waves of lucidness and lethargy.

"Have you considered talking to her? I'd be curious what Amelia has to say."

"You mean I should go to the prison and tell her what my father said?"

When Madison gave in and agreed to this trip home, it was to spend her father's last days with him, hopefully giving the two of them a happier set of memories that they could both keep. She'd wanted to get in and out and be able to go on with her life, feeling like she had done right by him, even if he had not done right by her. She wanted as few regrets as possible. This confessional and subsequent mystery was complicating and prolonging her plans of appeasement.

"Yes. You're a reporter. Go ask her what happened."

"What would I say?" asked Madison. "Hey, my dad says you didn't kill that girl, and you shouldn't be in prison, so why did you plead guilty?"

Jenny scoffed. "This should intrigue you."

"You're the attorney. Maybe you should look into the case?"

"I'm not that kind of attorney, but I do know people at the Utah Justice Center who might help. Still, they'd need more to go on. Why don't you stay longer and look into it? You don't have a job to go back to, and you can stay at my place as long as you want."

"I'm not sure Taylor would be too happy about that."

"It's not like you'd be away for months. And what if your dad is right? You could be helping someone wrongly accused of murder."

Madison paused and let what Jenny said sink in. "Even if that means condemning my own father?"

"He's the one who wants this to be right. And even if he is the one who did it, he's dying. What's going to happen if the truth dies with him?"

Madison groaned. "It's bad enough that my family is ashamed of me. If I start investigating my dad for murder, this will bring a whole new meaning to the word outcast."

"I'm sorry. I shouldn't be pressing you to do this, but..."

"Here it comes," Madison chided.

Jenny laughed. "I'll say it, and then I'll shut up. You are out here because it was your father's last wish to see you. He had a reason and wants your help to relieve his mind and what he feels will save his soul. You'd be doing it for him, not for the rest of them. Not even for you."

Madison pondered what she said. "I hate you."

Jenny laughed. "That's because I'm right."

They hung up, and Madison sat back in the solitary condo and mulled over Jenny's suggestion that she contact

Amelia directly. A dread came over her, a trepidation of what this information might set in motion. She knew her father wanted her to find the truth. But that was because he would be gone soon. Madison would be the one left with not only the real story of what happened that day but also the questions of what to do with it. She imagined the wrath from her family if she brought the shameful event to light. She shook her head. Why did she care? How much more pain could they inflict?

She pulled up the Utah State Prison website, scrolled to the section regarding prison visits, and saw a media section. The sad fact that she was technically no longer part of the media made her stomach drop, but she still had her press credentials and business cards, so she decided to try that route anyway. The time frame given for access, if they accepted her request, was five days. Madison sighed loudly. She had planned to be in her hometown a total of three days, no more, and the only reason she'd given herself that long was because she had secured the sanctuary of Jenny's home and could escape there if things turned tumultuous. The thought of an extra five days facing the awkward and often scornful scrutiny of her family without any guarantees the prison visit would prove fruitful or even take place was painful. She wondered why she was even considering the idea of meeting with Amelia. But her journalistic curiosities were strong, and she knew that if she tried to disregard her instincts, the lost chance at truth would eat her alive.

Not surprising, Taylor was concerned yet supportive. The idea of possibly incriminating her father while on his death-bed would be a chore with no positive outcome. Yet, Taylor understood when Madison explained why she needed to pursue her father's wishes.

"Take as long as you need," Taylor reassured her. "It's important. I miss you, but I can handle it. Barney may not forgive you, though."

Madison laughed. Barney was their Boston terrier. They had adopted him a year after they married, and he quickly became spoiled. He made their house feel even more like home.

Madison felt so lucky to have someone who wanted the same things she did in life. But with that happy thought, she cringed inside. What Taylor wanted was a child. This wish was something that gave Madison pause. It wasn't that she was unsure of their relationship or how they would be as parents, yet she was hesitant.

Losing her job factored into it, but Taylor's job paid well and was stable, plus provided them both with insurance, so it seemed like a feeble excuse. Was she continuing to let what had caused so much pain in the past affect her deci-sions today? She thought about it a lot, but the topic felt even more pronounced in her mind since she returned home. She wasn't sure why. Maybe being home also reminded her that having children was what her parents had taught her was her fate—to be a mother.

From the time she was very young, being a mother was what she was supposed to want in life. Nothing was more important than a family. That and being with the family in the afterlife—a forever family. For that to happen, it meant being worthy members of the church. Without that, entrance into the celestial kingdom, the highest level of heaven, was unattainable. The vision of a bright and forever home that she would never be able to enjoy was a scab she continued to pick at, despite not believing in her parents' vision of an afterlife. They would be there together and happy, looking down on her as she spent the afterlife in outer darkness.

When Madison left home and the church, she not only lost her chance at that special place in heaven, she deprived her family of an eternity of being whole. She also laid a veil of shame over her parents. How could a faithful and staunch member of the church, and a seminary teacher no less, raise a child who could take that path and turn her back on their beliefs?

She had thought that when they saw that she was doing well in life, graduating from college, having a successful career, traveling the world, and finding love, they would change their views or at least tamp down their unwavering stance against her. But it didn't make a difference; in fact, it emboldened them, as if it was their mission to prove that no matter what she did, it wasn't real happiness and would never lead to what was most important.

And now, with her father soon on his way to spend eternity in that exclusive paradise, she felt the weight of his disappointment and wondered when it would surface during their talks. It had to at some point. His desire to make a decades-long secret known couldn't be the only reason he summoned her home. One last attempt to bring her back surely had to be his dying wish.

She watched him sleep. She argued internally about whether or not she should plan to stay longer and drag out this awful endeavor he'd asked of her. She opened her computer, and even though she felt the information she'd already found regarding the murder and sentencing was lacking, something tugged at her to continue to dig.

She put her father's name, Saul Woodruff, into the search engine, and to her dismay, one of the first items listed in the results was a death notice. She clicked the link to find it was the obituary for her grandfather. He, too, was named Saul Woodruff; however, she noticed that her father was listed in the survivors with his full given name, Saul William Woodruff. It was the name William, not Woodruff, from which his nickname W or Dubby arose. It reminded her of what her father had said earlier about almost everyone having nicknames, as well as secrets.

What a horrible and heavy chain to have around your neck for so many years, she thought.

She entered his full name into the search engine, and several unrelated results to the murder case appeared. Her father was an amateur photographer, and his entries into several local contests had garnered mentions in the local newspaper. She scrolled through until nothing else in the list had any significance to her father. Nothing was jumping out as connected to Amelia Johnson or that day in 1981.

Eighty-one. She looked at the photo that hid the wall safe and then back to her father. His breathing was labored but steady, and he seemed deep in sleep. She lifted the notebook from her tote, the one on which she had written the date of the murder. Convinced it was the combination, she quietly rose and went to the photo. She carefully removed it, set it on the floor against the wall, and then turned and set the dial with the numbers corresponding to the date of that horrific event. It was no surprise when it opened.

Madison continued to look back at her father with each step in the process. What would she say if he woke up and found her in his safe?

Gingerly she reached in and removed the brown bag. There was nothing else left in the safe. Again, she was surprised at the weight of it. The rustle of the paper made her cringe. She closed the safe, quickly replaced the photo, and then brought the bag back to the bedside chair. She swiveled so that the back of the chair shielded her from his view, in case he awoke. She carefully unrolled the top of the bag and reached in. The first item was a torn and crumpled piece of paper. She put it aside. Her interest was the weighty object. She took a deep breath and grabbed something rolled in a white handkerchief. She unwrapped the thin material, and then flinched back. It was an unmistakable form—cold, heavy, metal. Hidden in that white handkerchief was a small handgun.

"I'm not afraid to die."

Madison jumped and turned to her father, though continuing to shield her find.

He was looking up at the ceiling, unaware of what she had in her hand . . . or was he?

"What?" she asked, wondering what he meant. She

looked back at the gun. Then she realized what she'd found. It was *the* gun, the pistol that had started the unraveling of her lurid secret and the beginning of her last days as a member of both her church and her own family.

She never intended to be the irritating little sister, and at sixteen, she was happy most of the time to avoid her brothers' taunting and just enjoy being the only girl. She got a room to herself, as well as her own bathroom, and when she began her sophomore year, Ben and Vince, who were still in school, rarely paid her any attention. That's why the urge to spy on Vince was unusual, but the pull had her standing at his bedroom door and quietly pushing it open just enough to see that something horrible was about to happen.

She was supposed to be at her piano lesson, but the teacher was ill, so she'd come home early. Even though she had her driver's license, both her parents needed a car that day, so she had to walk the two blocks. When she arrived at the house, she was surprised to see Vince's car in the drive. He usually wasn't home until late due to football practice or being with his girlfriend, which piqued Madison's interest. Had he skipped school? It was the one thing her seminary-teacher father never allowed. Teachers spent precious time to prepare their lessons and be there, so the children of the Woodruff household would respect that and be there as well.

The voice whispering in her ear was that of the irritating little sister. Deep down, she hoped to catch him sloughing school. It would feel good to have that small piece of ammo tucked away in her back pocket. His age, size, and quick temper were things she couldn't compete with, along with his place as her parents' golden boy. He was never very brotherly or kind to Madison. His treatment of her ranged from accusing her of being adopted, due to her bright red hair, to sticking a dead mouse down the back of her shirt, to simply ignoring her completely.

Gingerly, she padded down the stairs to the basement bedroom he shared with Ben. Troy's room had been across the hall and was actually a storage room. It was much smaller and had no window, but he claimed it just to be on his own because he was the oldest. When he left for college, they turned it back into storage.

Madison took a deep breath and peered through the small crack of the door. It was technically closed, but one of her brothers' raucous fights over nothing had damaged the doorjamb, and this left the slightest bit of a gap for her to see through. Vince sat on his bed, his back to the door. In his hand were papers and a thin plastic wand. A pregnancy test. She couldn't see his face, but from the sound of his breathing and the heaves of his back, she could tell he was crying. She felt the urge to ask him what was wrong but knew he would only yell at her for spying on him. Then she saw the gun. He looked at it, turning it over several times in his hand. The sight startled her, and she stumbled backward, tripping on an ironing board stored near the washer and dryer nearby. It clattered to the floor. Before she could run, he was out of the room and glaring at her.

"What are you doing here?" he growled.

She felt her breathing catch. "My piano lesson got canceled, and I didn't know who was home."

"Did you just get here?" He studied her for any evidence she had been watching him.

She nodded. "Is Mom here?" she asked, trying to act nonchalant.

For a moment, he stood contemplating her. He stayed silent and shook his head.

"Why are you home so early?" she asked. "It's Friday."

"So what. Mind your own business." He turned and went back inside the room and slammed the door. It didn't latch, and he let out a spiel of swear words. It was obvious their parents weren't home.

Madison made her way back upstairs, trying to breathe, and called Jenny. While she whispered to her what she had seen, she heard the slam of the front door and a car's engine rev. She peered carefully through the blinds of her window to see Vince driving away. Her breath released in a loud gush.

That evening, Madison and Jenny sat in the large metal porch swing in Madison's backyard. It was around the side and in the shadows away from the porch light. It was the place they had always gone to hide away and just be alone. Almost every summer weekend, Jenny stayed over, and they sequestered themselves, scooting the large, heavy swing to the place that was out of view of the sliding glass door and other windows. There as they sat on extra cushions from the lawn chairs and wrapped in sleeping bags, the girls were able to hide. Unlike the other nights when they whispered wickedly about other girls or shared stories about controversial books they'd read, this night, Madison was filled with an anxious dread.

Saul's eyes closed, and he slowly drifted off again. She waited a moment watching him, then turned back to the gun.

Madison wondered why he still had it. She figured he would have gotten rid of it years ago. It was the source of so many painful memories, but he had an open distaste for handguns even before that dreadful day. "Why does anyone need a handgun? They are used for one thing—shooting people. I do not need anything like that."

It was a contrary feeling living in the small conservative valley. And while he hunted and allowed her brothers to shoot BB guns out in the field, there was little more than that when it came to firearms. So, why keep a handgun? The fact that it was that specific pistol made it even more disturbing. She felt beads of sweat above her lip as she wondered what he might have planned. And with that gun. She wondered if he kept it, knowing his secret, like hers, would eventually be his undoing.

She wrapped it back in the handkerchief and placed it back in the bag. Then she remembered the crumpled and worn paper. Even though folded neatly, it showed the signs of age.

Madison unfolded it, and written in large, rounded cursive was a note. The top had been ripped off and missing, and at the bottom, was signed with just the letter *S*. She stopped and then went back and began to read from the beginning.

I don't know what to do. Some days I want to die. I'm scared, but the one thing I know is that I love you. That will never stop. But I'm so afraid about what will happen if they find out what we've done. No one can find out. If I act weird, please don't think I am mad or that I no longer love you. It's because I don't want anyone ever to know. Someday we will be together. Remember, I will always love you.
Love, S

Was this signed by Saul? Or could it be Sara? she thought. *After all, the note was stored with the album. Was this another clue?* Either way, the words were so grim, and knowing what soon followed, struck Madison in a rush of sorrow. *Some days I want to die.* They loved each other and were regretting what they'd done. She assumed it was sex. Going too far would have them both facing the bishop and the consternation of their family and peers. Even possibly a dis-fellowship from the church. No wonder her father didn't want her mother to know. He had kept his love and sin a secret all these years. Imagining what they were facing, her thoughts went back to her own brush with the accusations of being unclean.

CHAPTER 7

On the Utah State Prison website, Madison found the email form to request an inmate interview. She filled it out using her invalid press credentials, hoping they wouldn't call the newspaper to verify them. Using her married name to fill out the documents, Madison was relieved she didn't have to use her maiden name of Woodruff. She felt certain that Amelia would recognize it and would then refuse the meeting.

When she got married, she had decided to officially take Taylor's last name of Moore solely because of the anger she held toward her family for shunning her. Why keep something that only reminded her that she was an outcast? It was an unusual thing to do for someone who prided herself on being an independent and liberated woman, but it was undoubtedly advantageous for this particular function.

A message from an attorney's office on Madison's phone informed her that Amelia's original lawyer, the public defender, had retired from practice more than a decade ago. They offered a forwarding email, and Madison made a note of it and decided to send him an email directly. She had seen his name in the initial court documents and wanted to speak to him first to glean information about Amelia and the case. She also hoped to learn anything she could regarding her mindset and how open she might be to the conversation.

Madison later contacted the prison, only to discover there had never been another attorney assigned to Amelia, because she had never asked for one, and that she had not been granted parole—the main reason being she simply never applied for it. It was as though she had disappeared into the prison's complex and indifferent system and was living in anonymity amongst its vast population. Madison wondered if anyone even knew Amelia was still in there.

What really happened? Madison repeated the question in her head. After all, no one but her father had ever said anything different than the scenario that put Amelia behind bars. There was no trial, no appeals, and no application for parole. Either she was not worthy of freedom or not attempting to attain it.

She sent an email to Jerry Alford, Amelia's original defense attorney, asking if she could speak to him about the case and specifically about Amelia. She didn't mention anything about her father's confession, just that she was a reporter looking into the case.

Madison sat back and contemplated the reasons why Amelia had never spoken up, never fought for her release, and whether or not what her father was telling her was true. Maybe what her mother had said about his medications and delusions was correct. His illness could be affecting his memory. His story of Amelia spending years in prison for a murder she didn't commit was beginning to seem like the fantasy of a dying man, and Madison worried she would appear like some senseless wannabe crime writer who was wasting everyone's time.

But then her father's request and Jenny's words surfaced

in her mind. It was her father's wish to give Amelia his confession. Whether Amelia would use that information to her benefit or not was up to her. Madison's only duty, as she saw it, was to offer what her father had given. What he felt was the proof of who really killed Sara Voorhees. But what proof? She had nothing to offer Amelia but her father's vague confession. It wasn't anything that could help to set her free. There would have to be something more before she stuck her neck out and asked to meet with Amelia.

The moon was large and so bright it gave a luster to the valley. Madison stood at the large windows and peered into the darkness, feeling exposed as if part of a display in a brightly lit storefront. There could be so many things going on in the black depth of the foothills, but she wouldn't see it. Yet, whatever or whoever might be there could see every inch of her.

She stepped back and looked for blinds or some sort of shade to pull for privacy, but there were none. She smiled to herself, knowing that Jenny would scoff at the idea of obstructing that view, regardless of what might be lurking in the dark. But Madison still felt the need to guard herself, even against things she imagined.

She had left the house before six that evening, knowing her oldest brother Troy had called a family meeting after he got off work. Her father was fading quickly, and the decisions about prolonging his life were a point of contention. Madison felt his wishes to keep him at home should be honored. She thought he should be kept comfortable but was against extending his life. What was the value of time when you are lying in bed all day with no hope of recovering? But she knew her ideas and opinions, regardless of how reasonable, would be dismissed, so she didn't see the point of staying. She also had no desire to be the object of whatever snide comments or innuendos they tossed her way again.

When she told her father she was leaving but would be back in the morning, he clutched her wrist and pulled her back to sitting on the side of the bed.

"I'll be back tomorrow," she reassured him.

He tried to smile, but only his eyes showed any emotion. "You're the only one that can understand," he said. His voice was so low and raspy, she could barely hear him.

"Understand what?" she asked him. The lack of details and her need for answers was increasingly frustrating.

"You are the only one who will understand why I didn't do what I should."

"What do you mean? Why only me?"

He took a labored breath. "I was wrong. I was a coward."

Madison flinched back, unsure if he was directing this at her. Was he calling her a coward? Did he think that her leaving and staying away for so long was cowardice?

"I let pride direct me. Even when I knew that I was wrong." He coughed, and his entire body shook.

Madison sighed, disturbed that he still felt her reasons for staying away were just a form of defiance. She became impatient. "Dad, why can't you tell me exactly what happened?"

"I should have been there for you, but instead, I turned my back."

A chill went over her. Was this the apology she had hoped for all these years?

He cleared his throat, and Madison leaned forward, wanting to hear more.

"In Proverbs 14, verse 24..." he whispered.

Madison's shoulder sank. *Is he going to quote the bible to me?* she thought, discouraged.

And then, as if rehearsed, her mother came into the room, and his words ceased. Madison looked over at her with annoyance. She felt she was finally getting somewhere with her father, but when he turned to scripture is when she tuned out.

"Your father has a visitor," Darlene announced. "It's your uncle."

Madison sat up and smiled. "Morey's here?" she asked.

Darlene sniffed and pursed her lips. "No, it's your Uncle Syd. He's been coming by to check on him almost every day. He's so busy with his position, but he makes time."

Madison inwardly rolled her eyes. Syd. Darlene felt her older brother walked on water and lauded it over everyone, even her husband. Sydney graduated top of his class at BYU. Sydney married Katie, a former Miss Utah. Sydney was a real estate developer and lived in a massive house in Cottonwood Canyon.

Madison stood and turned her mother toward the door to keep their conversation quiet. "I didn't think Dad wanted to see anyone right now," she whispered.

Darlene lowered her head sadly. "He doesn't, but it seems he wants to see Syd." She lifted her head and smiled. "Syd's doing great things for the state. He's also a bishop now, and your father has always looked up to him."

This time her eye roll was evident.

Darlene stiffened. "I'm not sure what that means, but at least he's always been there for us."

It was Madison's cue to leave. She went back and looked down at her father. His eyes were wet and filled with regret. It was something she saw in his face almost every time she was with him now. "Dad, it's okay. I'll be back tomorrow, early," she assured him.

As her mother went to fetch her revered brother, Saul pushed the photo album toward Madison. "Proof" is all he could manage to say.

She gave him a reassuring nod but inwardly groaned. There was no proof in that album, but she took it and held it to her as a show of affirmation.

As she turned toward the door, her mother ushered in a tall man with dark hair and smiling eyes. Madison recognized him, and even though he had aged over the years, he looked young and robust compared to her father. He scooped his dark hair away from his face. It was dyed to remain dark, and shined from the gel he used to slick it back. She remembered how much he fussed with it.

When he saw Madison, his expression turned to weary sympathy, obviously forced. She could see in his face that he remembered the tumultuous past between Madison and her parents. He bit his bottom lip and dropped his brow to give the impression of genuine concern. Madison knew that inwardly he was thankful that his children hadn't disappointed him in the way she had with Saul and Darlene.

"Madison. It's so nice to see you."

"Hey, Syd." Madison had never called him uncle, even as a child, and unlike Morey, the connection with him was always uncomfortable and tense. It was likely due to her mother's over-the-top admiration. Madison wondered if maybe she was unfair to him because of that, which is why she relented when he reached out to embrace her. However, instinctively, she held the album between them almost as a shield.

"What's this?" he asked, releasing her and seeing the album clutched to her chest.

"Saul found an old photo album," Darlene answered. "It has his photos from that camping trip from years ago. You know the one?" She raised her eyebrows.

Syd nodded as he looked down at the album with interest. "And these are photos from that trip?"

Madison nodded and clutched the album close.

He whispered, seeing that Saul was asleep. "Did he tell you what happened on that trip?"

Madison gave an uncommitted shrug.

"We were so young, but I remember it," he said. "Why is he bringing that up now?"

Madison hesitated, answering him. "You were there when it happened?" she asked.

"Yes. Well, kind of. What did he say?" Syd asked her the question as he looked over her shoulder, where Darlene had gone and taken a seat on the bed. She sat and watched her husband sleep.

Madison shrugged but then directed him toward the door, wanting to speak more, and away from her parents. Syd followed, and they stepped into the hall. He closed the door, shutting Darlene in with Saul and away from their conversation.

"What's he been telling you?" Syd asked again.

Madison felt a strange pang. "Not much. Just some things about the girl who was killed." She wasn't about to reveal her father's confession, even to the man who her father seemed to trust.

Syd sighed and nodded sadly. "It shook the entire community. I don't think either family ever recovered from it."

"Are they still around here?" she asked.

He thought a moment. "Amelia's parents lived right down the road from here for years. Martha, her mother, stayed in the house, but she moved to a smaller home on the other side of town after her husband died. As for Sara's parents, they moved soon after it happened. I'm not sure where they are now. They were older. It was a long time ago, and they may have already passed."

He paused, rubbing his chin. "I remember the police arriving. The camp advisers kept us in the lodge and the dorms until our parents could pick us up, but we watched out the window. I saw the helicopter fly overhead. They weren't able to get Sara's body off that ledge until the next day."

He shook his head slowly. "I can see Amelia's face looking out the back window of the police car as they took her away. We stood there at the window, watching. We were numb. We couldn't believe it. If she hadn't confessed, I still wouldn't believe it."

"Why do you think my father is thinking about it now?" she asked him, hoping to glean some clues.

"I don't know. I think it affected all of us. We were friends. Close friends. But we had no idea what was going on that would lead to that."

Madison swallowed and picked her words carefully.

"Do you know who the boy was that Amelia and Sara were fighting over?"

Syd leaned back, and then his face turned pained. "He didn't tell you?" he asked.

Madison shook her head.

He took a step back, obviously uncomfortable with the position he found himself in. "It doesn't matter now. There is no point in bringing this up again. It was such a long time ago."

And a long time to spend in prison, especially if you didn't do it, Madison thought.

He opened the bedroom door and tried to back his way into the room and away from her.

"Yes, but ..." She tried to stop him. "Please just tell me."

He shook his head.

When Madison saw her mother looking toward the open door, her face pinched with annoyance, Madison acquiesced and let him go. She was discouraged, and his uneasiness only intensified her suspicions that it was her father at the center of it. Syd didn't have to say the name.

She left the house without saying good-bye and went to her car. Her brothers would be arriving soon, and she wanted to be gone before they did. She hoped that Syd was also leaving soon. She worried that he would expose her queries to them and raise their ire even more.

Glancing back at the house as she drove away, she wondered what other secrets Syd held and if pursuing answers from him would prove fruitful or frustrating.

That night, as Madison sat propped up in the massive bed, the glow of her computer casting a blue hue across her, she typed in the name of Amelia's mother, Martha

Johnson. She gave a surprised grunt when she easily found the address and phone number from the name and city. She recognized the number as a landline, with the same three-digit beginning as her parents' home number. It was far too late to call, and again she was faced with that perplexing question. What would she say? She imagined several scenarios, but they all felt odd and clumsy.

Madison glanced at the time and saw that it was creeping up on midnight. Sleep would be unlikely as the copious questions continued to swirl in her mind.

CHAPTER 8

The breeze as she jogged made the brisk morning air feel even colder. She needed the run. She was going to confront her father with the truth of what happened that day at Echo Lake. The muscles in her neck and back were tight with stress, so she'd found a paved path near the library and set out for a short jog.

The path took her down toward the park and swimming pool. The area had been completely renovated and updated, but the old Scera Theater was still a fixture, and Madison smiled as she remembered her first real date there. They sat in the very back of the theater, no one behind them, so they could hold hands and sit with shoulders touching. She hardly watched the movie. She was so aware of every touch, breath, and look. It made her smile thinking about how awkward and sweet it was. A memory of someone she never saw or heard from again, but who Madison had heard was still living in town. From what Jenny had told her, many of her classmates had never left.

Back at the car, the fleeting thought she'd had when she left the house came back and stuck in her mind. She tried to talk herself out of it but soon found herself making the drive across town to the address she found listed for Martha Johnson, Amelia's mother.

She had planned to call her in the morning. It was time

to start setting things straight. But then she decided a run first would be good. Maybe it would clear her mind and help her plan what to say. But as she pulled away from the condo, the urge to drive past the address she had found kept picking at her, and, back in the car, she found herself going the opposite direction of her parents' home and toward Martha Johnson's.

I'm wasting time, she thought, as she navigated her way through the numbered streets and to the area called Lakeview. *It's not like I'm going to walk up and knock on the door.*

Needing a shower back at Jenny's before going to see her father, she would surely be over an hour later than what she had planned. She had planned on leaving tomorrow. She hadn't mentioned anything to either of her parents about staying longer. Now she was wondering if she had made the right decision to continue with this caper.

She made her way down to the Lakeview area. It was a part of town she wasn't very familiar with, even when she'd called that area home. Anyone who lived in that part of the city went to the other high school, and up until Madison left home, she hadn't associated with anyone outside her neighborhood, ward, or school. It was a thought that made her cringe. A place less than ten miles from her home was like traveling to a different state.

She found the street and turned onto it. House numbers painted on the curbs made it easy to navigate, and when she came upon Martha's home, she slowed the car and studied the small white brick house. Even though the cold weather of late autumn had settled the plants into dormancy, the entire yard was full of color, from the red and gold of the fallen leaves to the dark green of the junipers lining a small path to the door. Madison stopped the car and wondered if Martha was inside and what she would do if she were.

The buzz of her phone startled her with an email notification. She looked at the screen and was surprised to see it was a reply from Jerry Alford, Amelia's former attorney. Her heart gave a leap.

> *Good Morning Madison,*
>
> *Regarding information about Amelia Johnson, I'm afraid I will be unable to do much to assist you. I've been retired since 2009, and I haven't spoken to her in years. When I was representing her, she was unwilling to help in her defense and never talked much about her case. I believe she is still incarcerated at the women's prison. I'm unaware of anything past that.*
>
> *I'm sorry that I'm unable to help you further. If you would like to reach me by phone, the number is 801-555-2341. Good luck with your project.*
> *Best, Jerry Alford*

Madison's shoulders sank. Amelia was unwilling to talk to her attorney, the person who could have made a difference in her case, so why on earth would she be willing to speak to her—someone who had nothing to offer but questions?

She dialed the number, and a gruff voice answered. It was Jerry Alford.

Madison thanked him for getting back to her and asked if he had any notes or records from the case.

"That was a long time ago, and even though it was a big

case, you're asking a lot of this old brain," he said. He told her he would send a request for the court documents at the county courthouse. "I'll give them your name, and you will need to go to the records department to pick them up."

Madison thanked him.

"All right then," he said, sounding tired and eager to end the call.

"Can I ask you one more thing? Can you tell me the name of the boy the girls were fighting over? They don't list his name in any of the items I've found online."

He thought a moment. Madison could hear him grunt a few times while he pondered her question.

"I don't remember. Though I think he went by a nickname—not his real name."

Madison's stomach clenched. Another checkmark against her father. She thanked him again, and when she hung up, she sat back against the seat of the car in dread.

Then she saw something move from the corner of her eye. She looked up to see an elderly woman in a long beige sweater, slowly making her way down the driveway toward the mailbox. She was using a cane and studied Madison's car quizzically.

Madison felt the need to duck but knew that would look suspicious. She pretended to look at the house next door but slyly continued to observe who she assumed was Amelia's mother.

She had a gray braid down her back. It went almost to her waist, and there were clips on each side, just above her ears, drawing up her hair in silvery swoops. A long nose and big dark eyes cemented Madison's recollection. "Sister

Johnson?" she whispered to herself. Could it be? The name Johnson was so common; of course, she didn't consider a parallel before. But here it was. Martha Johnson was not only Amelia's mother but Madison's childhood Sunday school teacher.

She never knew Sister Johnson's first name and had no idea the history of what the woman she saw each Sunday morning had endured. She also was oblivious to any connection this woman had to her father's secret past. *Didn't any of these people leave town? Did they all just grow up and stay in the same place?*

The woman turned when she heard the car door open.

"Sister Johnson?" Madison called to her as she stepped onto the curb.

Martha stopped in the middle of the driveway, envelopes in hand, and peered over skeptically. "Yes," she said. Her voice was soft but guarded.

"It's Madison Woodruff. My parents are Saul and Darlene Woodruff. You taught me in Sunday school."

Martha stood up straighter. "Madison?" she asked, surprised. "My goodness, it's been years. What are you doing all the way over here?"

"I'm in town visiting my father. I just wanted to stop by and see how you were." The lie felt especially cruel, seeing how frail and vulnerable the old woman seemed.

Martha's expression showed her hesitance, but she eventually smiled.

"My father isn't doing well," Madison said, trying to change the subject of her surprising visit.

"Yes, I've heard. I'm sorry to hear that. I've known your

family for a very long time. I lived in that neighborhood for so many years," she said, and then her eyes saddened as though a hidden sorrow surfaced. She leaned harder on the cane.

"Here, let me take that in for you," Madison said, reaching for the stack of envelopes and offering her arm.

Martha looked up and nodded. She appeared confused by Madison's presence but softened and invited her inside. "I should have recognized that beautiful red hair of yours," she said as they stepped into the tiny living room. "I remember thinking about how much it fit with your personality when you were young. You were always full of questions."

Madison smiled and wondered if Martha would mind the questions she had for her today.

Stepping into the house, the smell of baking brought back warm memories of coming home from school to the sweet and comforting aromas that her mother created.

Shelves filled with books covered the walls of Martha's home. The sight made Madison pause and stare in awe. There must have been hundreds of them. Stuffed into every nook was everything from large voluminous hardcovers to thin colorful paperbacks. Even the end tables and other surfaces had stacks.

Martha noticed her gaze and sighed. "They're not all mine. My late husband liked to read, as well. I try to give them away, but it seems actual books aren't as popular now. How about you? Do you like to read?"

Madison nodded. "I love to read."

"Feel free to borrow whatever you'd like." Martha took off her coat, hung it on the hall tree, then motioned for Madison to do the same. "Where are you living now? I'm sure your mother has told me, but it seems I can't remember much of anything anymore."

Madison cringed inside, wondering just how much her mother had told her. "I'm in Las Vegas...or actually a small town just outside. But I work in Vegas." It just came out. She started to correct herself, but the woman didn't need to know that Madison was unemployed.

Martha's eyebrows lifted. "That's quite a distance."

"Yes," Madison said, feeling the breadth of those miles both physically and in her heart. "And I wish it was a happier occasion that I'm here now."

Martha took Madison's hand and patted it. She gave a sad smile, started to speak but then just nodded.

Madison hung her coat next to Martha's, then rubbed her hands together and pulled her shirt down as far as she could over her spandex running pants.

"What took you to Las Vegas?" asked Martha.

"I went to college there, and then I got a job and have been there ever since."

Martha nodded. "What do you do?"

"I'm a reporter." She was still a reporter, she rationalized in her mind, just in-between actual jobs.

This made Martha smile. "That's not surprising. Like I said, all those questions."

Madison was reluctant to believe that Martha really did remember her, but now she could see there was a glimmer of memory, and she was relieved it wasn't about the conflicts that had sent her away just a few years later. She was almost certain the entire ward was aware of Madison's fall from grace and the pain her parents had endured because of it.

"Can I get you some water or cocoa? I just made peanut butter cookies." She lifted an eyebrow and smiled.

Madison tried diligently to stave off her sweet tooth, but she gladly accepted the offer, and then as Martha went to the kitchen, Madison continued to look around the room. There were a few framed photos, one of the church's prophets, identical to the one hanging in her parents' house, and a couple of a man she assumed was the late Mr. Johnson. Madison didn't remember him and again was surprised at how the turn of events had happened with her now sitting in Amelia's mother's front room.

She noticed a small book displayed separately and distinctly on a metal stand. The title read *Sorrow's Keeper*. It was a book of poetry. The cover showed a pair of hands covered in blood. Madison leaned in and scrunched her brow in question. It didn't seem like the type of book her elderly Sunday school teacher would read, let alone display so prominently.

"I haven't quite got to that one yet," Martha said, coming back into the room and seeing Madison's interest in the book. She held a steaming mug and a plate full of cookies.

Madison took the mug of cocoa and a single cookie and thanked her. She nodded toward the book. "It looks ..." She grasped for words. "Interesting."

Martha carefully picked up the book and looked at the cover, and then turned to Madison. "Will you read it and then tell me what you think?" she asked. "It was written by someone I know."

Taking the book, Madison looked at the author. Millie Juarez. "Sure. I'd love to read it," she said. Since she didn't currently have a book with her, it would help her pass the time, and it was thin, so she figured she could finish it quickly and have a plausible avenue to continue her contact with Martha.

As she drove toward the condo, she pondered the fortuitous coincidence of her past connection with Sister Johnson. Was this something her father figured into his plan? Was it just another piece in his odd puzzle? The reasons he wanted her to come home were still a mystery to Madison, but she hoped he desired to make things right with her.

It was becoming more apparent that his intentions in bringing her home were part of a final grasp at absolution, but it was someone else's daughter for whom he desperately wanted to seek forgiveness.

SORROW'S KEEPER

There is a love so sound and true,
but lives alone in shades of blue.
No longer here to feel the pain,
of shattered hearts and endless bane.
The rage inside condemns to hell,
who holds the truth and will never tell.
Hands covered with her lover's blood,
the fallen angel who rises above.
The one left behind is sorrow's keeper.
Who prays in earnest for the day of the reaper.

CHAPTER 9

Madison sat back in the small, cushioned chair that had been placed at her father's bedside. She read the last line of the poem again. *Who prays in earnest for the day of the reaper.* She's wishing for death, she surmised. So dark and sad. *No wonder Sister Johnson hadn't read this book,* she thought. It surprised Madison that she even had it in her library. Talk of hell and death. She turned back to the cover. The bloody hands made her cringe. *Sorrow's Keeper.* She contemplated the title.

It didn't seem like something an active Latter-day Saint woman would read. And why would she encourage Madison to read it? "So strange," she said, softly, as she contemplated the book and Martha. Of course, everything felt strange at that moment. This just fit with all the bizarre happenings with her visit home.

She looked over at her father, and realized he was awake. It seemed he did nothing but sleep anymore. He was getting weaker, and although his eyes were able to speak volumes, his voice became but a whisper. Madison had so many questions, but was either interrupted by her mother, or her father was so drained and unable to do much but sleep. When he did speak, most of it was regretful and melancholy.

"I sent you away," he said, weeping.

Madison shook her head. "You didn't send me away.

I left for school." It was only partially true, but Madison didn't have the energy right then to prove anything to him or make him feel guilty for her pain. She had felt pushed out, but she was the one who made sure she was going somewhere far enough away that her anguish could be pushed into the past.

He shook his head. "No. Before. That place we sent you." His breaths were short and shallow. "I thought it would help you. I was so worried."

An ominous chill rushed over her. Madison closed her eyes as if to block his words from entering her mind. She knew what he was referring to and so badly wanted to keep that terrible memory from flooding back. It was no use. She stood up and went to the sideboard for a tissue. For a moment, she stood facing away from him and trying to gather herself, but the tears were relentless.

"It was wrong," he mustered.

Madison turned. She nodded. "Yes, it was."

The second quarter of her senior year of high school, there were slamming doors, heated tears, and, more painful than anything, were the words. It was Madison who took to shouting, but the simple phrases that her parents were able to sternly and calmly state back left scars. So assured and confident in their remarks. Madison was too young and far too emotional to react with thought or wisdom. How many hours of sleep did she lose over the years, reworking those arguments in her mind?

"They can help you," her father tried to explain, as he loaded her suitcase into the car. "It's only a couple weeks. Maddie, please try. Come back to the fold."

Madison was emotionless, and when she glanced back at the house, her mother's face was both annoyed and disappointed.

"We're just worried that you'll ..." his words trailed.

She shot him a look. "That I'll what? Embarrass you?" she spat.

His eyes turned to sorrow. He shook his head. "No. I just want you to be happy. This path you're on will only bring you pain."

Madison was indignant but didn't object. In her mind, some time away would be a relief, and because she knew none of it would matter, she could then prove they were wrong. Once the therapists saw she would not change her mind, they would see the truth and hopefully convince her parents that there was no reason to try. She was her own person, with her own thoughts and beliefs. She may be young, but she wasn't naive.

Her resolve began to crumble, and on the fourth night, she called her parents' house, begging to come home.

"We're not punishing you, Maddie. We're trying to help you. You need help," her father told her.

"This isn't helping. It's like a prison or a mental institution. Please come and get me," she wept and yet tried to stay as quiet as possible. She had sneaked from her room and found a phone in an empty office.

"Listen to what they're teaching you," he urged. "I know that *you* know what is right."

She simply cried into the phone. There was nothing else she could do to convince him.

"God will guide you if you allow him into your heart. Listen to the still small voice," he whispered.

Madison knew that her mother must be close by. She had called hoping that her father would answer and had been prepared to hang up if it was Darlene's voice instead.

"Please, Daddy," she begged, but then she heard him quietly hang up.

It was exactly two weeks—her entire Christmas vacation—and then she was home. She smiled when they came to retrieve their reformed and redeemed daughter, but behind her bright eyes burned a determination to reach her eighteenth birthday and then escape. Leave it and all of them behind.

Those months, after Madison's time at Canyon Springs Center and before she turned eighteen, were daunting. It was like playing a role. One in which she starred as the mended and happy young woman who had simply stepped out of line for a moment, and quickly saw her blunder.

Upon returning home, she attended church, did well in school, and even got a part-time job. And she made every effort to avoid conflict with her family.

Her bond with Jenny was the escape that kept her sane, but she had to do it without anyone knowing. Her parents blamed Jenny for what they felt was Madison's ill-fated path in life. How could it possibly be something she chose on her own?

The therapists and counselors at the Canyon Springs Center were well-versed and convincing, and although the

Mormon Church didn't run the center, the protocols and treatments were designed with the same goal—bring the fallen back into the fold. Their patients' actions and views weren't part of the eternal plan, so they were tasked with demonstrating how destructive and wrong they were.

Madison knew that to get through it—not just those two weeks, but the entire eight months of her life as a minor—she would have to comply. So, that is what she did. Even now, she was surprised and impressed with her ability, at such a young age, to fool them. She'd survived, and then on the very day she hit that golden age of freedom, she again revealed her true self and was able to shake off the lies like a heavy, drowning cloak. As she announced her intentions and exposed the ruse, she felt their coldness directed at her like a breeze while she stood naked before them.

Her parents were shocked and devastated when they realized what she'd done. Madison thought their reaction would be a satisfying retaliation, but instead, she felt even more ostracized. They accused her of betraying their trust, and Madison shot back at them with allegations of the same.

She had plotted and planned for that day and was ready. With her car packed to the brim, and all the money she could save from her job, she left the driveway of the split-level house and drove to her college dorm two states away. From that point, her life was the beginning of a concerted effort to throw what they opposed about her right back at them, not just the things that had caused their divide, but anything and everything that would show her decision to not comply with their beliefs.

Even Jenny disagreed a few times with Madison's over-the-top rebellion. "Throwing it in their faces isn't going to change anything. It will just make them more adamant that you are the one who is wrong."

Madison would shrug. She knew Jenny was right, but the pain and anger just seemed to fester.

Now, her father was apologizing. It's what she'd desired. She wanted to stand tall and have them admit they were wrong, beg her forgiveness, and feel remorse for the pain they'd caused.

Instead, she stood, feeling deflated, her expectations dashed, as she peered through a blur of tears at her dying father.

"You thought you were helping me," Madison offered.

He nodded sadly.

"It doesn't matter anymore. I'm happy now. My life is good."

He took as deep a breath as he could and let it out slowly. "As it should be," he muttered.

Madison wiped her eyes and took a seat at his side. "You were a good father," she said, trying to ease his pain. She then realized the use of past tense. *You were.* "You are a good father," she corrected.

His brow creased, and his eyes were wet. "I could have done better."

Madison grasped at words. "You did your best."

He looked down. "I could have done more. I could have

told the truth and saved her."

Again, when Madison thought his apology was solely to her, instead, his regret included another. Reminding her again that she wasn't the only one he felt he had left out in the cold.

"How?" Madison asked. "What is the truth? And why did Amelia confess if it wasn't her?"

His eyes closed, and he shook his head. "That's because she thinks she has something to hide." He was slowly lulling to sleep. His voice was so soft and slurred that Madison had to bend down to hear him.

"What did she hide? What happened that day?" she asked. Madison's voice was urgent as she watched him doze off.

"If only we could find the proof," he whispered. "It would show you."

Again with the proof, Madison thought, watching as he drifted off. He was enveloped in the bed as if part of it. The hospice nurse was visiting every day and had told her mother that his time was quickly dwindling. Seeing the toll it was taking on Darlene, even in the few days Madison had been home, had her hoping this terrible disease would be merciful and take him soon.

It was an odd feeling, wishing for his death. Even years ago, when she was angry and feeling betrayed, her thoughts never crossed over into wishing him gone. It was her own life she had contemplated ending. She was so wrecked with confusion and betrayal when they sent her away. She felt nothing would ever be good again and that they would be relieved to have her gone. No more shame, no more embarrassment about a daughter who had fallen away. She saw no future, and with so many people convincing her that her choices were making it even worse, she had stockpiled pills and hid them for when things proved to be too much. The day she left for college is when she flushed them. It was a symbolic gesture as much as anything as she reflected on that time.

Just as those pills had disappeared down the drain, the resentment and dejection she had felt were finally beginning to fade.

"I forgive you," she whispered. He couldn't hear her, but she hoped he would somehow know.

CHAPTER 10

Madison realized as she walked up to the double glass doors of the Utah County Courthouse that she had never stepped foot in that building, even after driving past it almost every day when she lived there. It was on the busy main boulevard of the city and on the way to her high school. She knew it was there but never even considered what it was when she was young. Like so many other parts of her former life, what she saw and understood differed from what actually existed. She would have never imagined working in a profession that would have her consistently in a courtroom.

As a reporter in Boulder City, a small bedroom community just outside of Las Vegas, she practically lived at the courthouse during the cases she was assigned. She didn't only cover the crime and court beat. No one had that luxury at a small-town newspaper. But it was certainly the one she most enjoyed.

She heaved a sad sigh thinking about her precarious job situation, and started wondering about the time she was spending on her father's past regrets rather than looking for work. It may be the last thing she did for him, is what she kept telling herself.

She tugged at the jacket she pilfered from Jenny's closet. She felt the need to look somewhat professional when she retrieved the documents Amelia's former attorney had requested for her. She had only brought jeans and casual tops in her suitcase. Having planned on being there a few days, why would she need her work clothes? She wasn't going to be doing anything but spending time with her father.

The jacket fit but felt tight. Madison had always been taller than Jenny, but now she realized she was a bit wider than her friend as well. The realization was flooring as she had considered herself in shape. She was married to a chef, and that, along with her conciliatory ice cream, glasses of wine, and other favorite foods, had caught up. All that wasn't helping her waistline any more than her ability to find a job.

"Use whatever you need," Jenny told her. "Half the stuff in my closet I haven't worn in years, so if you like something, take it!"

The sleek black jacket would work. She wore her jeans, but with her black boots and dusty pink blouse, the outfit was nice enough but not distracting.

Walking into the court clerk's office, she was relieved to find she was the only person at the counter. A woman with short dark hair and a pleasant smile greeted her.

"I'm here to pick up some documents that were requested by an attorney named Jerry Alford," Madison told her.

"Your name?" the woman asked.

"Madison Moore."

The woman glanced at a clipboard, gave Madison another smile, and then went to the back. When she returned, she carried a large box of files. She checked the label on the box with the clipboard. "Madison Moore," she said, checking off her name. But paused and looked up at her. She smiled widely. "Madison?" she exclaimed.

Madison nodded. "Yes," she answered tentatively.

"Madison Woodruff?" the woman asked.

Again Madison nodded and then became self-conscious because she felt like she should recognize this woman.

"It's Camille Hansen. We went to school together."

The name rang a bell. Madison remembered the girl from her past. They weren't close friends, but they did spend time together while riding the bus to and from volleyball games.

"Camille. I'm so sorry. It's just been so long," Madison stumbled.

Camille waved her off. "I know, and we've both certainly changed a bit. How long has it been?"

Madison didn't have to do much thinking. She could've told her the exact day she left. "About ten years."

"Wow. That long?" Camille shook her head. "Do you still live around here?"

"No. I'm just visiting. I live in a town just outside of Las Vegas."

"Really? What do you do there?" she asked.

"I'm a reporter." Again, the disappointing truth hit her.

"Oh, so is that why you're looking at this? For a story?" she asked, motioning to the files.

Madison began to hem and haw, but then smiled and nodded.

"So, you're married?" Camille asked.

For a moment, Madison wondered how she knew and almost became defensive, but then realized she had used her married name when talking with the attorney. It was the name she had given Camille. "Yes."

"Me, too. I married Trent Bell. We have three little boys," she said. "You?"

Madison sighed. "No." Her throat tightened. If Camille knew, she wouldn't feel Madison deserved children. Why did she care what anyone thought? The brave and defiant young girl who drove out of this town with a finger in the air was now worried about a former classmate she barely knew. She wanted to slap herself. When would she ever shake off the pain of the past and truly move on?

"Well, you look amazing, and it's so good to see you," Camille beamed.

Madison smiled and returned the compliment and then quickly reached for the files.

Camille pointed to the side of the counter. "There is a room back here where you can look at them."

Madison looked back toward the door. "I can't take them with me?"

"Oh, no. We can only check them out and have you look at them here. We can make copies if you'd like, but they're ten cents each." She looked slyly around and whispered. "Or you could take photos with your cell phone."

Disappointed that she wouldn't be able to peruse them back at the condo, Madison shrugged and then followed Camille to a small room. She flipped on the light, and Madison placed the box on one of the two small tables.

"It isn't much, but at least you'll have some privacy," said Camille.

"Thank you," said Madison. She pulled over one of the

metal folding chairs. The room was stark and cold but quiet.

"Oh! I just thought of something," Camille squealed. It made Madison jump. "Go ahead and have a seat, and I'll be right back with someone you'll want to see."

Before Madison could ask who, Camille was gone. She wondered what other Orem High volleyball player worked in the building. She sat her purse on the chair, and while standing, began to look through the tabs to see if anything stood out. She wasn't sure exactly what she was trying to find, but she hoped that the boy's identity would be in there. That was her main objective. Was it her father?

For several minutes, she sorted through the tabs, trying to figure out where to start. Then she saw something that made her sit up and gasp. It was the date of the murder, written numerically. Eight, seven, eighty-one. It came back to her. It was the numbers her father had given her. The weight of what that date meant to her father that he would use it for the combination to his safe. Her breath halted, as his connection to the murder continued to grow. Then she heard a familiar voice.

"Madison?"

The man standing in the doorway made her stomach clench.

"Isn't this crazy?" Camille said, in the same, shrill tone. She clasped her hands together excitedly as she peeked from behind him.

It was Daniel West, and he looked nothing like the skinny, awkward boy from that prom photo. He was tall, and his brown eyes and dark blond hair showed the signs of age, but with positive results. He leaned in and gave her a confident and warm smile. It was nothing like the shock and disappointment on his face when they broke up all those years ago.

"Daniel," she said, both surprised and a bit worried. Their history came flooding back, and she wondered if he saw the same images in his mind. Jenny had told her that he was an attorney, but Madison had failed to remember his position in their hometown. *Doesn't anyone move away from this place?* she thought again. "How are you?"

"Good," he said, staring at her like she was a ghost.

Madison tried to smile. It was painful, wondering what he was thinking. The last time she'd seen him, he was hurt and angry. She had not blamed him for that. However, she didn't see what she did as purposefully deceptive. They were a pair, but she never saw him as anything but a good friend. After all, they were still in high school. And when his tone and advances changed, she knew it was time to shut him down. Madison had been annoyed that she even had to make their breakup that clear to him back then.

"So, where are you living now?" he asked. "Have you moved back?"

"No, I'm still in Las Vegas. I went to school there and never left."

He raised his eyebrows and gave a small laugh. "Yes, I remember."

She felt her face flush, remembering how he had begged her not to leave.

Daniel stepped into the room and peered at the box. "So, why are you here?"

"She's a reporter, and she's looking into a case," said Camille.

Both Madison and Daniel turned back, realizing Camille was still there. Madison tried to break in, but it was too late.

"Really? What case is it?" he asked. He came closer.

"It's the one that happened up at ..." Camille started to say excitedly.

Madison shot her a look, and Camille took a step back.

"Sorry," said Camille with chagrin. "I'll let you two get caught up. Let me know when you've finished, and I'll put it away." She gave Madison a sly smile.

Madison flinched back, perplexed. Did she think some silly high school fling was relevant now? She obviously had no idea how things really were and how they had ended.

Daniel sighed. "Some things never change."

Madison agreed. "Seriously." She shook her head. "I've only been back a couple of days, and I can't believe how many people I've run into that are still here."

"Tell me about it," he said. "Unfortunately, I've seen a few of our former classmates come through my office."

"That's got to be awkward...for everyone. So, Jenny told me you were an attorney with the county," she said, hoping she remembered correctly.

"I am."

She thought a moment. "Wasn't your dad also an attorney?"

He lifted his eyebrows. "Close. My dad was an accountant. My grandfather was the attorney. In fact, he held the same position I do now, but decades ago. I guess it kind of runs in the family."

She smiled. "Now I remember."

He chuckled. "You'd be surprised how many people still remember my grandpa in this position."

"It doesn't surprise me," she said, shaking her head. "So much of this place hasn't changed a bit."

"Well, you haven't. You look great." Daniel grinned at her.

Was he flirting with her? The idea perplexed and somewhat horrified her. She cleared her throat, but before she could respond, Daniel glanced again at the file box.

"So, you're looking into the Amelia Johnson case," he said.

"Yes," said Madison, surprised. "Do you know about it?"

He smiled and pointed at the front of the file box where the name was written. "I didn't become the youngest county prosecutor in Utah for nothing."

Madison laughed and rolled her eyes. "Good hell."

Her reaction made Daniel laugh louder. For a moment, the dark cloud of their past lifted. They both took deep breaths, and as their shoulders relaxed, Madison felt herself lighten.

"So, Camille said you were writing a book?" he asked.

"A book?" She tried to remember what lie she had given. "No, not a book. I'm just looking into the case ..." she hesitated, searching for words. "For a possible story. I'm not exactly sure if anything will come of it."

He walked closer and pulled out one of the first files, and started to flip through it. "I'm not sure I remember this one right off. When did it happen?" he asked.

Madison felt a chill go over her. She pondered how much she should tell him. Was it a risk to reveal her father's confession? "It happened in 1981 at a youth camp up the canyon. Two girls were fighting over a boy, and one of the girls pushed the other off a cliff."

"Of course. The Echo Lake case," Daniel exclaimed.

"Yes. It was at Echo Lake," Madison said, surprised.

"We don't have many murders around here, and besides, this was pretty sensational. Plus ..." He turned the page he had opened toward her and pointed at a line on the document. Utah County Prosecuting Attorney LaVerl West.

"Your grandfather?" she asked. She had read the name while going over the articles on the computer but had never associated it with her old friend.

He nodded. "That was a big case. It may have happened before I was born, but some people still talk about it. It even came up when I was in law school. The girl accused of the murder pled guilty, and it never went to trial. No evidence to prove otherwise and no other witnesses."

Madison cocked her head surprised. "No witnesses? What about the boy they were fighting over?"

Daniel raised his shoulders. "I'd have to look over the case files again, but I'm pretty sure that was part of what made the case so interesting. No witnesses. The accused could have pled not guilty and said it was an accident. Instead, she confessed adamantly, and the case didn't go to trial. I remember reading through the case files and thinking about how it was a slam dunk for my grandpa."

Madison's forehead creased in thought. "But I was told a boy was there and saw what happened."

Daniel shot her an inquisitive look. "Who told you that?"

Madison began to answer but then paused, realizing she had almost exposed her father. "I read that in the old newspaper clippings. They said there was a boy who the two girls were fighting over when it happened."

"As I said, it's been a long time since I looked at this case, but..." Daniel sifted through the files a moment and then handed her a folder. "This looks like the initial police reports and statements. If there were witness statements, they should be here."

Madison took them from him and gave him a distracted thank you.

He scrunched his forehead. "So, tell me again why you're looking into it? What's the story about?"

She shrugged. "It's really nothing. Just something I heard about." Madison pretended nonchalance and began to thumb through the files.

"You came all the way back here for this?" he asked skeptically.

Madison realized how absurd it sounded. She told him about her father's failing health. "He asked me to come home."

Daniel's brow pinched with genuine concern. "I'm sorry to hear that. I always liked your dad. It wasn't that long ago that I saw your parents. I had no idea he was sick. When was the last time you saw him?"

She bit her bottom lip. She began to speak but then saw the realization on his face.

He was lost for words but wanted to fill the silence. "I'm sorry, Madison. And if you need anything, I'd be happy to help."

She nodded aimlessly and stared down at the files in her hand, avoiding his pity.

He stepped back. "I should probably get back to work."

"Oh," she replied, coming out of her thoughts. "Thank you. I really appreciate it."

"It was good to see you again," he said, and he turned toward the door.

Madison tried to smile. "Yes, it was."

He turned back and reached into his suit coat pocket. He handed her a card. "Here's my contact info," he said, as he took a pen and began to write on the back of it. "My personal cell, if you need it."

Madison took the card and considered giving him her cell number. But she decided against it and instead just nodded and smiled. She had at least learned something from their relationship long ago. He couldn't accept that she wasn't interested in him. That is why she hadn't even kept up a cordial friendship.

When he left, she let out a long and burdened breath. There was so much to process in the short amount of time she had been back. So many memories, so many people that had her mind spinning with emotions she had done so well to shutter away.

Once she was alone, she sat and began to read through the police reports. They were stiff and technical, but what she found was that Daniel was right. There was no mention of the boy witnessing Amelia pushing Sara, only that they were fighting, and that a boy had gone to get help. Madison realized then that it was her father's confession that had her imagining things differently.

She continued to read, to see if there was anything more that she hadn't already found. She located a witness statement and grimaced to herself. A witness statement from someone who didn't see it happen? And then what she'd been searching for was right there in front of her. Madison felt her chest tighten, and a hushed breath rush from her. The one thing she hoped she wouldn't find. The proof that her father was there in black and white. The witness statement transcribed from the boy's interview had numerous blacked-out areas. It wasn't his name, but his identity was there, listed with the initials S.W.

"Saul Woodruff," Madison whispered. "Oh my god, he *was* there."

She put a hand to her mouth and felt her lips tremble. His urgent pleas to find the proof and his assertions that Amelia didn't do it repeated in her head. He had never actually admitted to her what had happened, but his adamant declarations that he needed to repent and his desire to free Amelia were a sure sign that he did know. He may have told the investigators that he didn't witness it, but Madison now knew better.

As he faced death, he wanted the truth to come out. If Amelia didn't push Sara, and her father was the only other person there, it was apparent to Madison who did, and he had waited all these years and was ready to spill it while expecting her to clean up the mess.

She pulled out her phone and snapped as many photos of the documents as she could. When Camille appeared at the doorway, Madison was placing the last folder in the box.

"They still talk about this at the camp," she said, motioning to the files. "I remember hearing about it when I went to camp, and my nephew was up there several years ago and heard the story. They call her the leaping lover and say she walks the forest around the camp, and at night you can hear her calling for her lost love." She raised her eyebrows. "Is that part of your book?"

Madison rolled her eyes. "No, I'm not..." She finally gave up. "Do they allow kids to go by that cliff where it happened?"

Camille shook her head. "Oh, no. I think they cooked up that story to keep them from trying. But you know kids, it made it even more tantalizing. They've blocked the trail, and I know the rules are very strict about it. They told us they would send us home if we left the camp boundaries."

Madison nodded.

"I wasn't eavesdropping on you two, but I thought I'd tell you what I knew." She gave Madison an affirmative nod. "To help you with your project."

Madison thanked her for her help and then left before Camille could ask her anything else.

In the car, again, she found herself filled with disturbing visions of what happened at that cliff. From the police reports, it was so steep there was no chance Sara could have survived that fall. And the description of the quick drop gave Madison the chills. Her fear of heights and the idea of falling from that sheer and unforgiving ledge made her wince. And now a ghost story to go with it. No wonder her father had refused to let her attend that camp.

She wanted to go to him and confront him with what she'd discovered, but she also dreaded the idea. It was what she feared she'd find, and now with proof, she couldn't deny it any longer. The more she contemplated what he might have done, the more she wished he had taken it to the grave.

CHAPTER 11

Jenny wasn't answering her cell phone, and Madison paced the condo, desperate to tell her what she had found. It was clear to Madison there was substance to her father's dying plea. But now what? He summoned her home on the pretense that he was dying and wanted to see her one last time, but in reality, what he wanted was to remove his heavy guilt and place it solidly on her. He wouldn't go to prison or even to court. He waited, knowing that what he gave her would be what she needed to expose his secret and give his conscience relief. He would die divested but leave his burden for the rest of them to shoulder. *Bastard,* she thought. As if shunning her for the last decade wasn't enough.

Her heart was heavy, and her mind a blur. Again, she paced, thinking about the scenarios. All she could envision was her brother Vince screaming at her for again bringing shame upon their family. They would blame her for this, not the weak and dying man unable to even sit up in bed. And again, she wondered why she cared what they thought or did. They hadn't even given her a thought for a decade. If she had died as a teenager, it would have been less of a heartache than what she had done. At least they could have been the grieving family, instead of the one with a daughter like Madison.

She opened a bottle of wine and poured a glass. She thought of Sister Johnson, alone in the tiny house. This could bring her daughter back to her. After all these years, she might finally have Amelia home.

Madison thought about driving over and telling Sister Johnson, but then decided she needed to give herself time to come up with the right words. This news would surely shock her, and just blurting it out wasn't the way to do it. She needed a plan.

After two glasses of wine, her body was slack and folded into the creases of the sofa. Her mind wandered back and forth between confronting her father and calling the police. That's when the phone rang and sent her body and emotions hurdling.

"Finally," Madison answered.

It was Jenny. "What? Is everything okay?" she asked, hearing Madison's desperate tone.

Madison took a mental step back. "Sorry. It's just that I need to talk to you. I can't believe what I've found, and I don't know what to do."

"Tell me," said Jenny.

Madison unloaded her angst and information.

"You're not obligated to turn any of this in," Jenny said hesitantly. "You do realize that?"

Madison hadn't, but even if she had, she couldn't imagine just tucking it away and being able to go on with life as usual. "How can I not bring this forward? What I've found shows that my father was there. What if what he's saying about Amelia is true?"

"I don't want to throw a wet blanket on this, but as an attorney, I think the evidence is really weak. You have some initials and a vague statement from an unreliable source.

Don't forget that Amelia confessed to pushing that girl. If you're hoping to set her free, it sounds like a steep uphill battle. And even if it's all true, are you sure that's what you want to pursue?"

"Why wouldn't I? If it's true, then yes," said Madison, emphatically.

"Really? You want to be the person who exposes the possibility your father is guilty of murder?"

"He's the one who is practically begging me to do this."

"I get that. But even if it's what he's asking you to do, are you sure this is what you want? To be the subject of this kind of scrutiny is not going to be pretty. Besides, a police department and prosecutor's office revealing that they got a murder case wrong is not something they are going to take on with glee."

"But it wasn't them. This happened decades ago," said Madison.

"I know, but..." Jenny paused and then gasped. "Oh, my god. It's Daniel West. This is his county. Did you know he was the prosecutor who inherited the case?"

Madison huffed. "I didn't until I ran into him at the courthouse today."

"You saw him?" Jenny gasped.

"It was a total shock. I had no idea he was the county prosecutor. No thanks to you."

"You've never wanted to know anything about him," Jenny defended. "Don't tell me he was holding a grudge."

Madison sighed. "No. But it was so awkward."

Jenny gave a knowing huff. "I'll bet. So, did you talk to him about this?"

"Kind of, but not really. He saw that I was looking into the case, but I didn't tell him anything about my father or what he had told me. He just thinks I'm working on a story. However, what I did learn was that his grandfather was the county prosecutor at the time. It was *his* case."

"Wow," Jenny said softly. "This whole thing gets even more strange and twisted. Imagine your old boyfriend right in the middle of this."

"He wasn't my boyfriend. We just dated," Madison grumbled. "You know that."

"Ha!" Jenny quipped. "Tell him that! I remember how broken up he was." Then she gasped again. "Does your father know that Daniel's the prosecutor?"

Madison thought a moment. "I don't know. Probably. Daniel said he had seen my parents..."

Jenny cut her off. "Do you think this is the reason your dad is telling you all this? Some strange attempt to get you and Daniel back together?"

"What? Oh, hell no," Madison said, annoyed. "That's ridiculous."

"Is it?" Jenny asked. "Your parents were more upset about that breakup than anyone. Is this your father's last-ditch effort to bring you back? Everything started spiraling when you ended it with Daniel. That's when everything came to a head. Is he hoping to bring you two back together? Get you back where you belong?"

"I truly think you've lost it."

Jenny laughed. "This whole thing is pretty messed up. I don't think I'm that far off base."

"Whatever. I was hoping you'd help me," said Madison,

regretfully. "Even with all the crap between my dad and me and the past, I feel there is more to what happened with that murder, and unfortunately, I believe my father was involved. It's not like I want to get mixed up in this or even want to do it for him, but I can't stop thinking about that woman in prison for decades and the possibility that she's innocent."

Jenny sighed. "I'm sorry. I'm being so insensitive, but when you called me and said you were coming to town to see your father, I never expected it to turn into this."

"I certainly didn't either! But I can't just dismiss it." Madison paused and contemplated where to go from here. "So, what do I do? Should I talk to Daniel about this?"

Jenny let out a long and loud lament.

"You said this was his jurisdiction," Madison defended.

"It is, and that's why I doubt he'll want to touch it."

"Why not? He could help an innocent woman get out of prison. Besides, it's his job."

Jenny gave a weary chuckle. "It's not that easy. There is a lot more to this. It's a case that was technically solved and closed. That girl confessed to the murder." Jenny cleared her throat and then spoke to someone, telling them she would be there in five. She needed to end the call and get back to her meeting.

"But what about my father's confession and the documents I found? And the photos. They show he was there." Madison was desperate to keep her on the phone.

Jenny sighed. "They were photos of the camp, not of him. It's still not enough evidence to prove anything. And even if you can prove he was there, is your father going to take an oath and say he did it?"

"Besides," Jenny continued. "Unless you have concrete proof, they aren't going to be keen on making themselves look like they dropped the ball during the original case."

"But that was decades ago. I doubt any of those people are working anymore. Some are probably already dead."

"True, but it's still their agencies, and it has the possibility of making them look incompetent, even though they didn't work on the case. Daniel is not going to want that negative attention. Not to mention the dark cloud this could throw over his grandfather's legacy as the prosecutor," Jenny tried to explain.

Madison thought about Daniel and how proud he was of his grandfather's position, but she sighed. "I just don't think Daniel would be like that. I think he would at least look into it. Regardless of how he feels about me."

Madison could hear Jenny's weary reluctance. "It's also a matter of time and resources. He would have to assign someone to open the case again and look into everything that happened before. It's very unlikely they would do that from what you have. But I'm not telling you what you should do." Then she laughed. "Even though you're asking me for advice."

Madison huffed.

"I don't want you to be disappointed. I'm afraid you'll get your hopes up, and all he'll do is pat you on the head and then shove that information away in a forgotten file."

When she hung up, Madison tossed the phone on the sofa and went to the kitchen. She was feeling dismissed and frustrated. Before the call, she felt that Jenny would bolster her findings and encourage her to see them through.

Instead, she felt brushed aside like a child telling an out-landish tale.

As she poured another glass of wine, she took a deep breath and continued her self-shaming. She was drinking alone. It was something she rarely did. In fact, she rarely drank at all. Even through her rebellious departure from the church's strict anti-alcohol rules, she seldom had more than a glass or two and only on the weekend. However, the glass of cabernet in her hand was more of a comfort than a craving.

She continued to ponder the happenings of the day as well as her entire visit. That initial call from her mother was what began the odd sequence of events, and then it snowballed. When she first saw the familiar number on her phone, she thought it was a cruel joke, but then the disbelief turned to terror. Something horrible must have happened. There was no other reason for her parents to call her. Granted, hearing that her father was close to death wasn't a pleasant thing to hear, but she already knew her father was sick, so it wasn't a complete surprise to learn that his condition was dire.

The call was short, and afterward, Madison thought about the reasons her father wanted to see her. Her thoughts turned to daydreams of his tearful apologies and desperate pleas for forgiveness. It never occurred to her that his reasons were instead to rid himself of regret and to use her as his means to that end.

The idea bothered her, but the thought of a young girl spending decades in prison when she was innocent disturbed her even more. The case was so buried; it had evolved into a fabled tale of a ghostly aberration haunting the woods. She had forgotten to tell Jenny that part of this continually twisting story.

Madison trusted Jenny. She was the only friend she had from that awful time in her life. It was understandable, given Jenny had had similar struggles. However, she had been able to make amends to the extent that Madison was unable to accomplish. Being back, Madison realized how the bitterness had never subsided and was simply waiting to boil to the surface.

Could this be the reason Jenny felt the case was weak? Did she see Madison's passion as revenge rather than reprieve? Her bond with Jenny was strong, but she seemed more worried about Madison's fragile connection to the past rather than making a terrible wrong right. And while Madison appreciated her concern, she knew that simply ignoring what she'd uncovered and going on with life was unimaginable.

She wasn't drunk. She wasn't even tipsy. She was merely relaxed and had thought about it enough to feel good about the call Jenny cautioned her not to make.

"So, are you up for grabbing dinner?" Daniel asked. "We could go to that Mexican place on State Street that you always liked."

Madison wasn't sure a dinner date was the way to go. She had planned to speak to him over the phone, but then the idea of telling him her father most likely killed someone made a phone call seem insufficient. She could have invited him over to the condo, but it wasn't really her place to do that, and it almost felt like inviting him to her hotel room, so she decided otherwise. "Okay," she agreed.

"Great! Do you want to meet me there?"

"Oh," Madison hesitated, wondering if she was okay to drive. "I..."

"Or I can pick you up?" he offered.

Pick me up? That would be awkward and unnecessary, she thought. "No, I'll meet you there. In an hour?"

Madison hung up the phone and then slumped back into the leather sofa. What had she just done? She thought about how she could retract agreeing to meet him, but then thought, *why not*? She needed someone to talk to, and he might actually have some insight into what she should do.

Her thoughts then turned to Jenny, and a twinge of guilt picked at her. She shook her head. There were so many emotions and conflicts she had faced in the last few days.

Walking to the large windows of the condo and looking out at the Rockies' daunting wall, the weight of what she carried seemed even more onerous.

CHAPTER 12

As Madison drove up to the restaurant, the skies were brilliant with radiant pinks and oranges, as the sun set hovered in the western sky. She checked herself in the mirror and saw smudges of black under her eyes. She quickly licked her finger and wiped away the evidence of her despair. For several minutes, Madison sat and tried to bring herself back from the pounding angst in her head. Then her thoughts turned toward the man waiting for her inside, and she began to regret accepting his invitation. It would be an awkward conversation, looking across a table at the person she dumped years ago.

He had been friendly at the courthouse, but was this his chance to tell her how he really felt, or was she being paranoid? They were both adults. Surely, he wasn't still harboring a grudge. Madison began to consider his position. As a prosecutor in the county where the murder took place and a grandfather who was the person in that position when it occurred, it was incredible luck for her investigation. Meeting with Daniel could mean the accessibility she needed to find the truth and see her father's desire for Amelia to be set free.

She had "dated" Daniel for two years in high school, and yet she had rarely given him a second thought since she left. Was it awful to ask for his help now? And was that really what she wanted if it led to the finger of guilt pointed directly at her father? She sighed—it most likely wouldn't make a difference to him. Madison didn't think he would live long enough to see his confession come to light, let alone go to jail for a murder conviction.

When she walked into the restaurant, she looked around and marveled at the rush of nostalgia, as though it were yesterday, and they were back in high school meeting for lunch. The thrill of knowing they weren't supposed to be off campus made Madison roll her eyes and smile.

The room was large, with pink adobe walls. Colorful piñatas and bunches of bright red dried peppers hung from the ceiling. The booths were high-backed and painted with suns, cactus, and howling coyotes. She spotted Daniel. He was sitting in a back corner and talking with an older man who stood while his wife patiently waited at his side.

Madison removed her coat, draped it over her arm, and went to where he was waiting. The heels of her shoes clicked loudly on the tile floor as she walked toward him, and when Daniel saw her, he beamed and stood up.

The couple saw that his "date" had arrived. They gave a knowing smile and nodded as they walked off toward the cashier.

"Perfect timing," Daniel said when they were out of earshot. "No one's ever happy with a sentence. I'm too lenient or too harsh, depending on what side of the aisle. That is unless it's their friend or relative, then I should take into consideration that they come from a good family."

Madison gave a huff. "Because if you come from a good family, you never do anything wrong."

Daniel pulled out her chair, and she sat, thinking how odd that was in her life now. She never gave Taylor the chance to open doors or pull out chairs. It wasn't that Taylor wasn't kind or considerate; it was that Madison never expected it. In their relationship, Madison enjoyed their marriage of no labels or roles. A true partnership.

Daniel was ingrained with the gentlemanly courtesies of the past. He was pulling out chairs and opening doors even before high school. His consideration and manners always impressed Darlene. He would have been the perfect choice in her parents' eyes. And now, with his graduation from BYU, a two-year church mission, and his prominent position, Madison was sure they were still shaking their heads at her decision to end it. Even at age sixteen, they didn't hesitate to encourage a future between the two. Madison felt they would have been happier if she got pregnant and married Daniel as a teenager rather than ending up in her current situation. Sadly, she was sure of it.

When she settled into her seat, she realized Daniel was staring at her. She felt exposed and self-conscious. She gave him a small smile in hopes of keeping things light, but inwardly she was regretting that she had agreed to meet him. She intended to use his position to get the information she lacked, yet she could tell he was hoping for something else.

The waitress came to the table. "Can I get you something to drink? Or are you ready to order?" She was young, chipper, and made Madison feel even wearier.

Madison clasped her hands and leaned forward on the table. "I'll have a margarita on the rocks, please." She looked at Daniel.

"Water for me," he said with an apologetic raise of his eyebrows.

The waitress shifted from one foot to the other, uncomfortably. "We don't serve alcohol here."

Madison's eyes shot open. "You don't have margaritas at a Mexican restaurant?"

"Is that a game-changer?" Daniel asked. "We can go somewhere else if you'd like."

"Is there somewhere else?" she asked playfully.

He shrugged apologetically. "I'm sure there is, but I..."

She stopped him. "No, this is fine. I'll manage." She turned to the waitress. "Water for me, too."

The girl scurried off, and Madison rolled her eyes at Daniel. "I should have known, but I still forget. It surprises me how much nothing has changed here."

Daniel raised his eyebrows. "I know. It can be frustrating at times."

It made Madison giggle.

"What?" he asked.

"How's it frustrating for you? You've always been part of the group here. And I know you don't drink."

"How do you know?" he asked. "You haven't even spoken to me in years."

He looked injured, and she apologized.

"I'm sorry. I'm not trying to be rude, but come on."

He shrugged. "Just because I still live here doesn't mean I'm a prude."

She tried not to laugh again and relented. "I know. I remember I made you drink a beer in high school."

"You didn't make me do anything. I think I liked it."

Madison laughed, and it felt good. She glanced around the restaurant. "Even after all these years..." she sighed. "I keep repeating the same thing everywhere I go, but it's so true. Some things never change."

"You're right. You look like you did in high school," he said.

"Minus the big hair?" She was trying to keep things light.

He laughed. "But still that beautiful red."

She blushed. Seriously?

Daniel adjusted himself in the booth. It was a tight fit for someone with long legs. "I see Jenny once in a while at the courthouse, and she gives me little updates on you." He put up his hands. "Not stalking you. I promise."

Madison laughed but inwardly worried that he was pining for what would never be. She also found it odd that he even acknowledged Jenny or would speak to her after what had happened. He, too, had blamed her for Madison's descent.

"Yes, she told me you were an attorney, but I didn't realize you worked on cases together," said Madison.

"We don't. Our cases are completely different, but we do have some common circles. Jenny knew my wife when they were both in law school."

Madison sat up, surprised. "Your wife? You're married?" Was it something Jenny failed to mention, or did Madison fail to remember? And now she felt utterly ridiculous in wondering if he was trying to rekindle something from long ago.

Daniel looked down and then gave Madison a sad smile. "*Was* married. My wife died two years ago."

"Oh god, Daniel, I'm so sorry. I had no idea." How could

she not know this? Why didn't Jenny tell her?

He smiled. It was something he was used to explaining. "It was skin cancer. Melanoma. She was only twenty-six. We'd only been married a year. We had both just graduated from law school and were..." he paused and looked down again.

"That's terrible. I can't even imagine."

He nodded and took a deep breath. "Sorry to drag this all up. I was looking forward to a fun night catching up, not bringing you down by telling you about my sorry life."

Madison shook her head. "Don't be silly. What are old friends for? I just feel terrible that I wasn't there for you."

He laughed at this.

"What?" she asked, confused.

"It reminds me of when you broke up with me. We'll still be friends. I'll still be there for you. Remember?" He sighed and then smiled at her, but Madison could see that the hurt had never gone away.

She didn't know how to react, feeling chided.

"I'm sorry," he said, shaking his head. He reached over and took her hand. "It sounds like I haven't gotten over our high school breakup. That's not it. I think I just feel bad that we didn't stay friends. It was like you were so eager to get away from me, and I didn't know why or what I'd done. I didn't understand everything back then."

Madison retrieved her hand and then cocked her head in question. "But you understand now, right? It would have been worse if I'd stayed and lied to you."

He threw up his hands in defense. "I know. I guess I'm still puzzled. It caught me off guard."

"We were so young. Neither of us had a clue of who we were or ..."

He sighed. "I'm sorry. I didn't mean to do this tonight. I just wanted to talk and catch up more. I wasn't trying to make you feel bad."

She looked down and adjusted the fork and knife on the napkin in front of her. "It wouldn't take much right now. This whole trip has been one big downer. I appreciate you asking me to dinner. I needed the distraction ..." Madison cringed. "I don't mean that you're just a distraction. I ..."

Daniel laughed. "Hey, I'm happy to try and distract. Otherwise, I'd be sitting at home watching the news with my dog or working late on something to kill time. Speaking of being married, I heard you got married?" he asked hesitantly.

Madison sat up, surprised that he knew. "I did."

"Happy?"

"Very. Taylor is amazing," she said and then sighed. "We've been together since college. I take it Jenny told you."

Daniel shook his head. "No, I ran into your parents at the courthouse a couple of years ago."

Madison groaned inside. She could only imagine what they told him and how they acted. She envisioned her mother fawning over him and her father slapping Daniel on the back and calling him "Son." After so many years, they refused to accept that she was with someone else, married, and happy.

That feeling had been confirmed when Madison saw the prom photo of her and Daniel displayed in her old room. Daniel, with a big smile, standing behind her, one hand on each of her hips. Madison looked uneasy and cold—literally.

She'd refused to wear the long-sleeved baby blue dress that her mother had picked out and instead wore a sleeveless red sequin gown. The gym's temperature was frigid and she'd ended up wearing her jacket most of the time, but at least the photo showed she wasn't going to turn into a sister wife.

"Young ladies from good families don't wear things like that," her mother argued when she saw the glittery gown Madison had bought and hidden in the back of her closet.

"I must not be from a good family," Madison shot back with venom. Seeing her mother's face turn pained was satisfying, but she soon felt guilty. She didn't necessarily like the dress. It was merely another of her attempts to prove she wasn't going to acquiesce to their archaic and flawed beliefs.

When Daniel had arrived at the house to pick her up for the dance, her parents weren't eagerly waiting to take the typical pre-prom photos. Instead, they smiled at Daniel apologetically when Madison came down the hall. Daniel's expression appeared to be one of surprise, which only proved to Saul and Darlene that the dress was inappropriate. After a few moments of awkwardly pinning flowers to each other's chests, Daniel made a sweeping motion toward the door. "Your carriage awaits," he announced, having obviously practiced the line.

There were no words from her parents of "have fun" or "you look beautiful." Instead, her mother handed her a jacket. "You'll probably need this," she said.

Madison almost balled it up and threw it at her, but instead, she handed it over to Daniel and rolled her eyes as she left the house.

Arriving at the dance, it was apparent she stood out. There were no girls in sleeveless, let alone red sequined gowns, and Madison silently cursed her mother for trying to save her from the raised eyebrows and whispers.

She was surprised when she saw the photo of the two of them displayed at her parents' house. After fifteen years, it seemed they were still hoping and waiting for her to come around.

He smiled at her, and she came out of her stupor and smiled back.

"So, tell me what it is about this case you're working on?" Daniel asked. "It must be pretty important to bring you back here."

Madison took a deep breath. She felt the sadness of her father's illness come over her and the exhaustion from his overwhelming assertions of regret. *Where do I start?* she thought. She sat a moment working over everything she had taken in over the last few days.

"What is it?" he asked.

"It's my father. I think he did something terrible. I haven't seen or spoken to him in years, and then I get this phone call from my mother telling me he's dying and desperate to see me. When I got here, he told me he needed to repent for something. I think he wants to clear his conscience before he dies."

Daniel's brow creased, and his eyes squinted in thought. "And you think it has something to do with the Amelia Johnson case. What did he say?"

Madison took a deep breath and hesitated.

"You don't have to tell me."

"No, I want to. I need your advice. I don't know what to do."

He gave her an appreciative smile and nodded. "Of course. I'll do whatever I can to help." Daniel leaned back as the waitress brought two large red plastic tumblers with water and set them on the table. They both quickly ordered, and once she was away, Daniel clasped his hands on the table and leaned in.

"So, what do you think your father did?"

Madison shook her head in angst. Her shoulders relented, and then she let the story spill out. There was no other way of doing it. She started with the photo album and his need to confess and her short and awkward talk with her Uncle Syd.

"I had forgotten that Syd Wallace was your uncle. What did he tell you?"

"Nothing," she scoffed. "He practically ran away and hid in my father's room. He knows who the boy is, but he won't tell me."

Daniel flinched back. "Hmm. I'm betting he wishes your father would just let this die." He then realized what he said and looked up apologetically. "Sorry, what I meant was..."

Madison shrugged. "You're fine. It seems there are a lot of people who feel that way." She proceeded to tell him about her meeting with Amelia's mother. As the details poured out of her, she realized how incredibly tragic it was and how incomprehensible—a deathbed confession about a horrific murder and the youthful love triangle that had caused it all.

Daniel sat, hands clasped in front of him on the table, and carefully listened, nodding as he absorbed the strange and intriguing information. When she finished, he sat back. He blinked and was stunned into silence.

"I know," Madison groaned. "And today, while searching the files, I found one that identified the boy at the center of the conflict. Up until now, I didn't know for sure it was my father. None of the old newspaper articles ever listed his name."

"A juvenile," Daniel pondered.

Madison nodded. "Yes, but it was in the court records."

"His name? They didn't redact his name in the court documents?" said Daniel, surprised.

"They did, but what I found wasn't his entire name, but his initials," Madison explained. "S.W."

Daniel cocked his head. "That does add to your argument that it was your father, but it doesn't prove it's him. There are always a ton of kids at those camps. You remember, don't you?"

Madison shook her head. "I never went to youth camp."

"You didn't? Why?"

"My dad was worried about me being up there overnight with boys. At least, that's what he told me. Now, I think it was other reasons. I also wondered why he didn't chaperone up there. He loved to camp and do things like that."

Daniel took in a deep breath and sat up in his seat. "Well, all I'm saying is there were a lot of kids who went to that camp. There could be others with those initials who were there." He thought a moment and then smiled to himself. "What about my dad? Stuart West—S.W. He was there at that camp, too."

Madison lifted her eyebrows. "Was he?"

Daniel nodded. "Yes. In fact, I remember asking him about it when it came up in my class at law school. My grandpa, the prosecutor on the case, died when I was young, so I asked my dad if he remembered the case. That's when he told me he was actually there."

"What else did he say?" she asked, urgently.

"It was a long time ago. He didn't say too much other than it was a tragedy. He didn't know the girls involved." Daniel put a finger to his chin as if contemplating a riddle. "Or at least he said he didn't." He laughed.

Madison couldn't help but laugh, too. "My father more or less confessed," she said with a shrug. The very idea that she was trying to sleuth out her own father was both comical and tragic. "This is nuts," she said with a disgusted click of her tongue. Then she sat up straight, unable to let it go. "But if your father was there, he would know who the girls were fighting over, right? He could tell us if the boy was, in fact, my father."

Daniel frowned. "Most likely, but only if you can speak to the dead."

FATHERS IN HEAVEN

Hazel eyes, calloused hands,
and the musky way you smelled
Nothing left but memories and stories you would tell.
Left too soon. An empty chair now sits along with two.
Wishing I could have the chance to say that I miss you.
It's still so hard not to be sad you weren't allowed to stay.
My only hope is that I'll be with you again someday.
I tell myself I'm fortunate for the time that I was given.
And now, each night, I say a prayer
to both my fathers in heaven.

CHAPTER 13

Daniel's father had died years ago. Madison vaguely remembered hearing about it but had forgotten. The news probably came from one of Natalie's Facebook messages, updating her on the continuing saga of life back home. Some of it she appreciated, but most of the updates only needled at her. No one there cared about her life; why should she care to know about theirs? However, her brooding curiosity overwhelmed her at times. Like driving by a car crash and being unable to look away, she found herself searching for signs of agony. Did it really make her feel good to see those who had hurt her in pain? It was usually fruitless, but it didn't keep her from looking.

The meeting with Daniel wasn't what she had hoped. She thought he would somehow give her the answers about what to do and where to go from there. Instead, it was two hours of her venting her frustrations about what she felt tasked to do and her conflicted feelings about her father's involvement.

The release of what had been pent up inside her, along with another glass of wine once she was back at the condo, didn't help and only had her feeling discontented.

She had considered asking him to keep the conversation between them but then wondered why. Even after a painful adolescent breakup and years of no communication, she remembered him as a friend and felt he was someone she could trust. Besides, as Jenny had told her, he probably wouldn't want this type of publicity.

"I haven't told anyone except Jenny about any of this," she told him as they waited for the check.

"It will certainly cause some issues if it does get out," he said.

"Yes, but why would he tell me this if he didn't want me to find and expose the truth?" It was the question she had mulled over so many times since first hearing his revelation.

"It's not just your father who would be facing scrutiny."

What he said didn't hit her until later. As she sat and pondered their meeting, she wondered if his statement was one of concern for her or himself. And yet, as their conversation continued, she felt his unease with her father's confession.

"Sometimes, I feel he's told me this as a way to fix the past—both his and ours. And other times, it feels like another punishment. Why me? He kept it hidden all these years, and now he decides to tell me?"

"It is an incredible burden to place on anyone, let alone your daughter. I wouldn't blame you if you decided to let it go," he said.

She cringed a bit, hearing Jenny in her head telling her that he wouldn't want the burden of the case. "It's not like I haven't considered that, but I feel there is something to this." She stared at Daniel with purpose. "What if this woman really is innocent? Would you as a prosecutor do something about it?"

He looked confused. "If you're asking me if I'd reopen the

case, that would be a long shot. I'd need a lot more information and evidence. You said he had photos. What do they show?"

"Not much, but he claims they are the proof or that the proof is somehow in there." She was beginning to see how weak her case was.

"Have you spoken to her? She confessed. What does she say now?" he asked.

Madison shook her head. "I haven't spoken to her. I put in an interview request but haven't gotten a response."

"Is there anyone else that can corroborate what he's telling you?"

Madison shrugged. "There was no one else there when it happened. You were right about the witness. I went through the reports, and it says the boy didn't see it happen. I'm assuming that boy was my father and that he lied to investigators. I think he was there and either witnessed it or..." she shook her head. "Or was the one who did it."

"I could come over and get a statement from your father," Daniel offered. "I'm not sure what else I can do."

She shook her head. "I could ask him if he'd be willing, but... I don't know. He doesn't want my mom or anyone else to know what he's told me. And besides, he is barely giving me any details. And even though I know he likes you, I don't think he'd talk to you about this. It's like he wants to draw it out until the last moment, so he can die without ever really revealing the truth. If he weren't so sick, I would think it was a cruel game he was playing on me."

"We could get an official statement from you, but it's hearsay. I want to help, but I also don't want to give you false promises. I can only do so much unless we have real concrete evidence." He shrugged and sighed. "Don't forget that the girl, Amelia Johnson, confessed."

Madison huffed. "I know. I know. But why would he say that she didn't do it and be so adamant about wanting to repent?"

Daniel walked her to her car, and they stood in the cold, both wondering what to say and do. Madison finally stepped forward and hugged him. It was oddly familiar, and she even recognized the faint smell of CK One. *Things really haven't changed,* she thought, but it warmed her inside.

"Thank you," she said, feeling tears begin to sting her eyes. She slid into the car before he could see her weakness. She was genuinely appreciative of his willingness to let her vent, and she was optimistic he was at least open to helping her. Although he mostly listened, he said he would ask around about the case and see if any of his colleagues had involvement or knowledge that might uncover more information, including the boy's identity.

Daniel bent down, and she opened the window of the car.

"Stay in touch. And let me know what you find."

"Of course," she said.

"Are you staying at your parents' place?"

"No. At Jenny's, but no one knows." Madison rolled her eyes. "It's so stupid that I feel I have to hide things from my parents. They still blame her. It's silly that I have to keep it from them, but I have enough conflict just in being here."

Daniel raised his eyebrows and gave a regretful grin. "Sometimes it takes a while to get over stuff. When your entire life revolves around the church and what you're supposed to believe, that can be hard to change. I know I thought differently about Jenny back then. Good thing I've matured since high school." He raised his eyebrows and laughed. Then he stopped and took a reflective breath. "She sent a nice note when Steph died. Tell her I said hello."

Madison appreciated his candor and ability to be reasonable, a trait her family could learn from Daniel. "I will when she gets back. She's actually in Denver on business. I've been going crazy there alone in her condo trying to come to grips with this stuff."

He smiled and stood up from the car window. "Well, if you need another distraction, let me know."

As she drove off, she felt her heart break for him. He had been blindsided by her when they were young. She saw now how much it had affected him. And then to lose his wife at such a young age. *We were friends*, she thought, and no reason that couldn't have continued. And yet, she knew why it didn't. She wondered if things would have been less painful had she not wholly distanced herself from everything and everyone. Even Jenny, one of the only people who understood and supported her, was pushed away for a time.

Was she too quick to rush to judgment? Her parents may have rejected her and made her feel that hell was her destiny, but she hadn't given friends and others a chance. She closed them off and left before she could be hurt any longer. She just assumed because they had the same beliefs, that they, too would reject her. Had she been as closed-minded as she had accused them of being?

She paced the quiet and sparse rooms of the condo. She paused at the window and could see the dark wall of clouds that signaled a storm. The wind brushed through the tall, sturdy pine trees, and a streetlight below flickered on. For a moment, she thought she saw someone duck behind a tree in the distance. She stepped back, behind the window casing, turned off the light in the room, and watched in the dark.

Soon the outside light went off. It was a motion sensor, but was that a person hiding in the dark that set it off, or was it just shadows and the movement of the wind? And what if it was someone out there? They could be walking a dog or simply going from the parking lot to their condo. However, the parking lot was on the other side of the building, not where the large picture windows looked out over the foothills. And who would be out walking in this weather? Again, she cursed Jenny for her lack of sense when it came to privacy. If she lived anywhere else but Happy Valley, she would know the importance of blinds.

Madison continued to watch and see if the figure appeared again or if something else may have tripped the light, but after several minutes, she decided to go back to the bedroom and read. She was allowing her paranoia to creep in. The discussion of murder and illicit secrets had her on edge. She was missing the comfort of Taylor and feeling incredibly alone in the town she once called home.

Her phone rang. "Shit," she gasped as it sent her heart racing.

Grabbing the phone, she saw it was Taylor, and she put her hand to her chest, relieved.

"I must be telepathic because I was just thinking about how much I miss you," Madison said. She was so relieved that she could talk about what her day of investigating had revealed. She went through all the details, the court records, the initials, and the meeting with Daniel.

"A date with another old flame," Taylor said, teasing her.

Madison scoffed and then sighed. "It was actually pretty sad. He lost his wife to cancer a couple of years ago, and he seems lost. I'm not sure if he can help me with any of this, but I think he's at least willing to try."

"Have you told anyone else about what your father told you?"

"Just Jenny, and that was over the phone because she had to go out of town for work."

"What about your mom? Does she know what your father is saying?"

"No," said Madison, imagining her mother's dismay.

"She's going to find out."

Madison knew that was true, but she felt it was better to keep it from her for now. "Eventually, yes, she'll find out, but I can tell he is trying to keep this from her. At least until ..." She sighed heavily. "I think he knows she would get in the way of me looking into it. She'd also tell my brothers, and then they'd be accusing me of trying to dig up dirt."

"Sounds like you've already been dreading the scenarios of what will happen once it comes to light."

Madison huffed. "I feel like my father has put me into this situation to punish me all over again. Seriously, why me? Why call me back here to unload some terrible regret from the past? Why didn't he just tell my mom or my brothers or Morey? He has shut out almost everyone except my mom and ..." She thought a moment about her other uncle. Why not tell Syd? Her father seemed to trust him.

"What is it?" Taylor asked.

"My mother's brother, Syd. I've never been close to him, and he did something the other day that was strange. My father has refused to let anyone into his room except me, my mom, and Syd. And when he came by the other day and saw the photo album, we talked privately about what happened. I didn't tell him what my dad said about Amelia being innocent, but I did ask him about the boy who was there, and he acted weird and wouldn't tell me who it was." A rush of unsettled skepticism fell over her. Or was she being unfair and judging him harshly because she knew how he felt about her?

"Maybe he knows more than you think. Is he trying to protect your father?"

Madison contemplated Taylor's question. She had never felt that Syd worried about anyone but himself, but maybe what Taylor asked was true.

"You okay?" Taylor asked after the long pause.

"Yes," she blurted, coming out of her muse. "I'm just annoyed. I feel like my dad waited until he knew he was dying, so he wouldn't be able to face the consequences. If he weren't so sick and weak, I'd tell him to do this himself and leave me out of it."

"It may be his way of telling you that you're the one he trusts and that he feels bad about things he did in his life."

It was a stretch, but she appreciated the attempt Taylor was trying to make. Madison thought for a moment. Would he ever feel bad for casting her aside? Love the sinner, hate the sin. She sighed, wondering if his feelings about her had softened.

"He did say he needed to apologize, but he rarely says more than a few words, and nothing is specific." It is what she had hoped was the case, but even now, she didn't want to admit it out loud. "And even if that is the case, comparing my situation to committing a murder is messed up."

Taylor chuckled. "Yes, it is. But this may be as close as you'll get to him admitting he was wrong in the way he's treated you."

She took a deep breath and sighed. Is that what she wanted, even if it was misguided? "Maybe I should just come home. What am I trying to accomplish? All I'm doing is running around here, reminding myself about how painful and disturbing my life used to be. My brothers treat me like a pariah, my mother acts like I have ulterior motives, and here I am trying to dig up information that could prove my dying father is a murderer."

"Wow. And I thought I was having a bad day because a guest complained about my cioppino tonight."

Madison gave a weary laugh. "Your cioppino? How could anyone complain about that? Oh, how I miss your cooking."

"Well, I'm glad to hear you miss my cooking. But I miss you."

"You know I miss you, too. Should I come home?" Madison asked.

"That's not my decision. You need to do whatever you can to get some closure so that you can be happy."

She scoffed. "I'm not sure any of this will ever make me happy."

"Well, then do what will make you satisfied after all is

said and done. Whatever decision you make, I'll support you. However, I can't speak for Barney."

Madison's heart sank with longing for her sweet dog. "I've only been gone a few days, and it feels like weeks."

When she hung up the phone, she sank into the large overstuffed chair in the guest room and dug out the notes from her tote bag. She scanned them and then again flipped through the old photo album. She tried to decipher any strange or out-of-place elements in the images. She studied the ones that showed Amelia and Sara. Oddly, there were no photos in which the two girls were apart.

Nothing seemed out of place. They looked like best friends, arm in arm in every frame. Even when other campers were present, the two seemed detached and in their own little world. The betrayal of finding out they both wanted the same boy would be especially devastating for two girls who seemed so close. It must have been particularly vicious when the confrontation happened.

She wondered which girl the boy chose and who had felt the sting of rejection, not only by her crush but also her best friend. She had assumed Amelia was the one scorned, but even in the police reports and news articles, nothing alluded to that. She had no proof that the boy had chosen one of the girls over the other, only that there had been a fight between the two.

Again, imagining her father as the object of their desire seemed outlandish. She realized that because it was her father who was in question, that alone would keep her from seeing him as sought-after, but she had seen his high school photos and knew that back then he was short, somewhat scrawny, and his light brown hair was cropped, while the other boys wore theirs long. And his fair skin was dotted with the red and angry burst of late-onset puberty.

Maybe it was her father they rebuffed? Did the girls laugh at him, anger him in some way? Was that what he wanted to confess? At that moment, that scenario seemed much more logical.

CHAPTER 14

t was time to reveal what she knew to Sister Johnson. Madison would never find the truth without going straight to the source, and it was apparent the only person who had contact with Amelia was Martha, her mother. After being charged with murder and spending years in prison, Martha was still the person Amelia had on her side. The idea made Madison's heart hurt. She thought about the strained and basically nonexistent relationship with her own mother. *Imagine if I had confessed to a murder?* she thought. Then she wondered if it would have really been worse.

Madison called Sister Johnson, but instead of telling her over the phone, she asked if she could stop by. Martha was pleased, and the optimism in her voice made Madison dread what she planned to tell her. Even if the news could generate hope, she was sure it would also bring up the sorrowful feelings from the past. Regardless, she knew there was no choice but to let her know what her father had said. It would be shocking and confusing for the elderly woman, but she had to do it.

The day was warm for Utah Valley in the late fall. Madison regretted wearing the long-sleeved shirt but wondered if it wasn't nerves that were also making her sweat. Martha met her at the door before Madison even had a chance to knock, and a plate of cookies waited for her inside.

The woman's enthusiastic smile and eagerness to whisk her into the house had Madison feeling rueful. She needed to get to the point. Dragging this out would only be cruel to them both.

"I'm glad you're here. You said you needed to speak to me about your father?" Martha asked. "How is he?"

Madison looked down. She pulled in a deep breath. "He's hanging in there. But it's only a matter of time."

"I'm so sorry to hear that." She patted Madison's arm. "Just remember, you'll see him again one day."

It was a familiar comfort for those in the church to remind and enforce the plan of eternal life. How Madison wished she had at least that much of her former faith. To believe in that would be an incredible relief, even if she felt it was misguided. Madison looked up and gave her a small smile.

"Would you like some cocoa or ..."

Madison shook her head. "No, thank you. I just need to talk to you."

"Yes, of course. What is it?"

"It's about your daughter."

Martha leaned back and took a deep breath, as if bracing herself. "What about?" she asked.

"Did she ever talk about boys she dated?"

Martha shook her head. "She never dated. She was so shy."

"Really? Has she ever talked about the boy that may have seen what happened that day?"

She cocked her head and studied Madison. "No. I told you she never talks about it. Why are you asking?"

Madison felt the room grow cold. "I have no idea how to tell you this, but..."

Martha made her way to the sofa. She eased herself slowly into the earth-toned cushions as if the weight of that day was pushing her down. With her hands in her lap, she took a deep breath and settled herself. She reached for a tissue, prepared for the reminder of sorrow.

"I'm sorry, Sister Johnson, but my father has been talking to me about what happened that day when Sara died; he said something that I think you should know."

Martha shrugged. "I don't want to know more. What I've already heard about what happened that day is hard enough. We all suffered through that horrible time, and I don't want to bring it up again."

Madison took a seat beside her. "I know it's hard to think about, but my father told me that Amelia didn't do it. He says she's innocent." Her entire body shuddered as the words lingered between them.

Martha shot her a look of confusion. "Your father said that?"

Madison continued. "He was there at that camp."

"There were a lot of boys and girls at camp that day."

"But he says he has proof that it wasn't Amelia that pushed that girl off the cliff."

Martha's brows furrowed, and Madison could see the doubt in her face.

"He is so adamant that he can't stop talking to me about it. He says he should have said something years ago and now feels he has to set things right."

Martha shook her head. "But she confessed. Sara was

156

her best friend. If she didn't do it, she would have said something."

"What did Amelia tell you?" Madison asked.

"When she confessed, I didn't believe it. I asked her if she did that to Sara, and she nodded. She said yes. And then she cried. She's always been so ashamed of what she did."

"Is that all she told you? What about why she did it?"

Martha shook her head. "She won't talk about it. All she's ever said or told me of that day was that it was her fault and how sorry she is."

Madison thought a moment. "Maybe she just thought it was her fault. What if my father does have proof that it wasn't her? I filed a request to speak to her at the prison, but I haven't heard anything. Do you think you could help me?"

Martha sighed. "I don't think she'd agree to speak to you. She's hardly said a word about it even to me."

"Even if there's a possibility she could get out of prison?"

Martha sank back into the sofa. "How could that be? Why would she say she did something so horrible if she didn't? It makes no sense." She sat for a moment in thought. "Amelia had some behavioral issues. She was angry and hanging around people who weren't good for her.

"We tried to get her help. I had her talk to our bishop, and I put her in counseling. We did everything we could. When we moved here from Idaho, Amelia wasn't happy about it at first. She was so shy and was scared about starting school. We went to church that first Sunday after we moved in, and Sara was the first to come over and befriend her. It was summer, and Amelia was just turning thirteen.

"Sara made all the difference. They were together

constantly. I thought Amelia was finally herself again. When they told me what happened, I didn't believe it. I still can't believe it." She raised her shoulders, and for a moment, she stared off in thought. "What did your father say?"

Madison paused as his vague and unspecific ramblings went through her mind. "He says he has proof. It's just that he's been so sick, and with the pain medications, he's been unable to tell me much more than that."

The skepticism and disappointment spread over Martha's face. "If he has proof, he should have said something when this happened. Why didn't he?"

Madison could only shrug apologetically.

Martha thought a moment and then sat up straighter. "All those years, we lived just two streets over. I saw him every Sunday at church." Her face was both pained and confused. "He is a good man. He was a seminary teacher. If he knew something, he would have said something."

"From what I can see, whatever it is he knows has been terrible for him. I think he's been tortured by the guilt."

Martha blotted her eyes with the tissue. "If he says Amelia didn't do it, do you think he's the one who did it?" Her voice cracked.

Madison's shoulders fell, having thought precisely that many times in the past few days. "I don't know, but..." She hesitated. "I do know he's going to die soon and asked me to help set Amelia free. He keeps telling me he has proof that she didn't push Sara."

Martha took a long and labored breath in. She looked down with her thoughts and then gathered her hands in her lap and raised her head to address Madison. "What proof?"

"There's an album with photos that he took during that camping trip. He keeps telling me the proof is in there, but I've looked at every one of those pictures, and I can't see anything. Maybe if I showed them to Amelia, she could see something I don't."

Martha sighed. "Old photos?"

Madison nodded. It was true. The photos were decades old, and they seemed meaningless. "I'm sorry. I wish I had more to tell you, but I felt I should at least tell you this much. He wants to make things right, and I want that, too."

Putting a hand on Madison's to comfort her, Martha leaned in. "There's nothing I'd like more than to have this be true. But what if your father just thinks he remembers things? It was so long ago. I can't imagine getting Millie's hopes up for nothing."

"Millie?" Madison asked, confused.

Martha gave Madison a sad smile. "That was my nick-name for her. It wasn't until after the adoption that we started using her real name—Amelia. I think Jeffrey wanted to start new, but I called her Millie."

"Amelia was adopted?" asked Madison.

Martha shook her head. "No. Amelia is my child. I married Jeffrey two years after my first husband, Jorge, died. Jorge was Millie's father. He was killed in a farming accident."

"I'm so sorry," said Madison.

Martha nodded. "It was a long time ago when we lived in Idaho. Even after I married Jeffrey and moved here, Amelia visited Jorge's family for a week or so during the summers." She paused and looked at Madison sadly. "Until that summer."

Madison felt her skin prick.

"Jeffrey adopted Millie, and after that, he wanted her to use her real name. I think she wanted a new start. Since we moved from Idaho, no one in Utah knew her as anything but Amelia. Jeffrey tried to be a good father, but Amelia was almost fourteen, and it was hard on her."

"What about the family in Idaho? Do they have contact with Amelia?"

Martha took a deep breath and shook her head. "No. I think I'm the only one who visits Millie. I think they tried to stay in touch, but Millie didn't want to speak to anyone." She shrugged. "I should have tried harder to help her."

Madison began to refute Martha's guilt, but then something struck her, and she pulled the borrowed book from her tote. "Wait. Millie Juarez," she said, motioning to the book. "The author. Millie. Is that Amelia?"

Martha gave a sad smile and nodded. "Yes."

A chill rushed over Madison.

"She didn't want to use the name people would associate with what happened to Sara. With all of her writing, she used this name instead." Her face showed the years of sadness as she stroked the book like it was a child's head. "I'm curious about what you think. As I said, I haven't been able to bring myself to read it. The cover is so dark. It reminds me of how Millie was. Have you finished it?"

Madison shook her head. "Not yet. I've been busy with the stuff with my dad, but so far, it's really...interesting." There was that word again. "And as a writer myself, I'm even more impressed that she was not only able to write it, but get it published, especially while in prison."

Martha raised her eyebrows.

"How long ago did she write it?" Madison asked, holding the book as though it was on fire.

"It's been years. I don't think she's written anything since." Martha turned to Madison. "She used to write all the time. Her poems were published quite often. She even got her degree in prison and won some awards for writing, but she stopped after this book came out. I'm not sure why. I'm her mother, but I think she's very talented. And she's a good person. She was so young when everything happened. It's not an excuse, but she took her punishment, and she's repented."

Madison sat for a moment, taking in what she had learned. The poems she had been reading at night came directly from the mind of the person she was having the hardest time understanding. She wondered how someone creative and expressive could live for decades behind bars. "I'm surprised Amelia is still in prison. I know that she confessed, but usually, there is the possibility of parole after all this time. Is there a reason they haven't granted her parole?"

Martha was undaunted by the question, as though she'd heard it before. She answered simply. "She's never been paroled because she's never wanted to be."

"That's what the old articles say . . . but why? Why wouldn't she want that?"

"I don't think she feels she deserves it. I'm not sure she ever will."

"But you said she had repented. What does she tell you?"

Martha shrugged. "As I told you, she doesn't tell me much. We don't talk about it when I visit." She expelled a long and weary sigh. "I used to try, but then she stopped wanting me to visit. I didn't want to lose her completely, so I stopped asking. I've come to accept that if she wants it, she'll say something."

Madison shook her head in disbelief. "I just can't imagine anyone wanting to stay in there. It's been over forty years. It would be terrible."

Martha nodded and shrugged. "It's been her life for a very long time. She doesn't know anything different. When I visit, we talk about books, and that's about it. If I could help her, I would, but she doesn't seem to want it or even care."

Madison looked down at the book she held. "Maybe she feels like no one else does, either, other than you."

Why do I care? Madison kept asking herself. Amelia's mother and her former attorney had made it clear that Amelia was unwilling to talk about what happened that day. She had confessed, pled guilty, and showed no interest in being free after decades locked away. Her father's claims of Amelia's innocence began to sound more like tirades than testimony, and Madison was starting to wonder if anyone in the system cared if the woman rotted in prison even if she was innocent. And with Amelia's own seeming disinterest, the entire situation was becoming an exercise in futility.

"Millie's been through so much, and unless there is more solid evidence, I think it's best that she not know what your father told you. I don't think that anything will ever come of it. And telling her, I feel would be cruel."

Madison sat silently, wondering where to go from here. She wanted to reply, to deliberate what this might mean for

Amelia, but instead, she relented. She knew from her own life experiences that some discussions can't be resolved. Continuing to try and argue her point would only turn things worse. Until she had something concrete to show Martha, she would have to find the answers without Amelia.

As she waved to Martha and drove away, she pondered why Amelia would stay in prison rather than try to be free. If she was truly innocent, maybe her confession was coerced. And with her young age at the time, she was probably made to feel like a monster with the accusations. The prison walls might feel like a barrier to most, but with the fears of what the outside world could hold, the confines might be a comfort for her. Regardless, Madison felt the overwhelming weight of what her father wanted her to do and the reality of what it would mean to the woman he thought he'd wronged.

Even with her daughter's confession of murder, Martha had stayed vigilant in her role as a mother, visiting and worrying about the daughter she loved. Madison's thoughts turned to her father. Up until now, she'd wondered if he ever thought about her. He was more determined to make things right with someone he barely knew. Yet, he made no effort to make amends with his own daughter until he wanted her help. *And what if it's all just smoke*, she thought. She had no evidence to prove anything. Amelia confessed and had never tried to prove otherwise. So why was Madison?

She glanced over to the book sitting in the passenger seat next to her. "Oh, Amelia," she sighed. "Why should I care about proving you're innocent when you seem happy to take the blame?"

TOMORROW'S MEMORIES

Dreams of soaring turn to falling
Light as air then crushing weight.
What was real and bright is now absent.
The wistful regret of tomorrow's memories.

CHAPTER 15

Madison dug her laptop from her tote and propped it in her lap. Her father was wrapped in the sheets and simply slept while she sat, knowing her questions for him would again be unanswered.

The meeting with Sister Johnson was both frustrating and enlightening. Madison didn't understand Martha's reluctance to pursue her father's claims or even share them with Amelia. Or was it Millie? She typed the name from the book into her browser. Millie Juarez. Amelia's dark skin and hair now made more sense, considering Martha's fair skin and light eyes. Of course, Madison knew this dichotomy well. Her scarlet waves looked nothing like her mother's straight, dark hair. The red came from her father's side, yet his hair wasn't red but brown. Her brothers all sported the thick dark locks of Darlene. As a child, she fought with the curls and hated her fire-red color. It often made her feel even more of an outsider.

When her computer loaded, she typed in the words of the new name she had discovered. She wasn't sure why she was surprised, but her breath caught when the screen listed several hits for the author, Millie Juarez. Most were bookseller websites, but one link caught her eye. It was a feature article written for Utah's largest newspaper, and the reporter actually interviewed Amelia.

Quickly scanning the story, she found nothing referring to Millie as Amelia Johnson or anything specific regarding what happened at Echo Lake. It did state that Millie was an inmate at the prison and was serving a life sentence for murder, but that was it. Nothing about the crime itself that might identify Amelia. Instead, it listed her accomplishments while in prison, including a college degree and success as a published writer and poet. The quotes were short, but it was apparent Amelia was proud of what she'd done while incarcerated. The byline was a reporter named Teresa Skilling. The tenor of the article focused on Millie's triumph over tragedy, and the story was part of a series focusing on people who had made terrible choices but had risen above them.

In the quotes from Amelia, it was evident she was hesitant to say much about her life. However, when asked about her writing, Madison felt she could actually hear Amelia come alive. The story's date was almost fifteen years old, but Madison wrote down the reporter's name and then went to the paper's website to see if she was still there. Her eyes lit up when she saw that Teresa Skilling, the features reporter was now Teresa Skilling, Editor-in-Chief. If Teresa Skilling had convinced Amelia to speak to her, maybe she would consider talking to Madison as well.

Her father began to stir, and she quickly composed an email to Teresa, asking to speak with her regarding the case of Millie Juarez. She put Amelia Johnson in parenthesis in hopes this would give her inquiry credence. She worried that a busy Editor-in-Chief at a large paper wouldn't even have time to open her email, so she also mentioned the possibility of a story regarding new evidence in Amelia's case as a lure to get a reply. She gave an unconvinced shrug, hit send, and then closed the computer and placed it back in her tote. She had to adjust the spacing with the album, the book, and the gun to make it all fit. She shook her head with the odd combination of items she had acquired in just a few days, not to mention her father's confession. She felt the enormous weight of lugging it around with her. To think she had planned just a quick visit to say good-bye.

She watched him mumble weakly and then return to sleep and wondered why his frail and ravaged body refused to surrender. He had told her numerous times he was ready to go, and yet his chest continued to rise and fall. He wasn't afraid to die. He had made that clear. In fact, it was as though he welcomed death, knowing what and who awaited him on the other side.

More than once, as Madison sat and wondered if that weary breath was his last and contemplated her own life and death. Did she believe in an afterlife? She wasn't necessarily scared or worried about that part of death. It wasn't the idea of heaven and hell or even if her death would be drawn out or painful. Her real fear as she witnessed her father facing death was the idea of doing it alone.

Who would be there when it was her turn? She had Taylor and the few close friends she had made since living in Nevada, but she was unsure if there would be a child in her future. The idea of having someone at her bedside, like she was for her father, was a comforting thought, although it was a terrible reason to have a child.

She loved children. That wasn't the issue. The problem

was fear. Her angst and doubts about her own childhood always tainted her view. She was grown and comfortable about her life, yet her past had her feeling unworthy of creating a family of her own. She worried that fear would have her miss out on something wonderful for both Taylor and her.

The crippled chime of the doorbell roused her from her book. Her mother had gone to the store, so Madison quietly and quickly made her way to the foyer. When she opened the door, the warmth and brightness of the sunlight made her squint. There stood Natalie.

"I thought you might need a break," she said. "I brought some things to make lunch."

Madison smiled uncertainly. She was surprised to see her sister-in-law, especially after the family argument, and realizing that they had wanted to leave their children at home because of her. Natalie had apologized and tried to explain how that wasn't the case, but Madison doubted her sincerity.

Madison stepped back and motioned for her to come in. "Thank you," she said, tired of the continued hurt and rejection.

As Natalie brushed by, the fresh air that followed her had Madison realizing how stuffy the house had become, especially in that back bedroom.

"It's been so nice of you to help like this. I know Darlene was about worn out."

Madison shrugged. Everyone seemed so surprised that she was staying to help in her father's care. She wondered if it would be so out of the ordinary if she had toed the line, remained in the area, and within her family's moral guidelines.

Madison checked on her father, and seeing that he was still sleeping, she went to the kitchen where Natalie was making sandwiches and placing salad into two bowls. "Nothing fancy," she said apologetically.

"I don't need fancy," said Madison, retrieving two bottles of water from the fridge.

"I'm sure you're used to those fancy restaurants in Las Vegas. I bet it's so different from here."

Madison smiled. "There are some pretty great places, but I don't eat out that much. Taylor is a chef, so I'm pretty spoiled."

"Is that right?" said Natalie giving her an interested lift of the eyebrow. "I've only ever driven through there, but I see the photos you post. It looks exciting."

"You've come through Vegas?"

She nodded. "We took the kids to Disneyland last year. We could see the lights from the freeway."

"Why didn't you let me know?" Madison asked, injured. A stab of pain hit her, realizing her brother and his family had come through her town and never bothered to tell her.

Natalie's brow lowered in question. She thought for a moment. "We didn't think you'd..." she paused, searching for words. "I'm sorry."

Of course, why would she expect that? They had made no attempts to connect with her outside of Natalie's messages through Facebook. She'd come to accept that they were uninterested in her life and in staying close. And after the altercation at the family dinner, Madison knew that would never change. She shrugged, defeated.

Natalie stepped closer. "You're right. It's silly that we didn't stop and see you."

Madison gave her a doubtful sigh.

"No, really. This is all ridiculous. We're taught to love everyone regardless of what they do. Where is their belief in free agency? It's your life, and no one has the right to judge you—whether they agree or not."

Madison nodded in agreement but was annoyed that her suspicions were confirmed. Her family continued to believe she was a moral delinquent who needed to be brought back into the fold, in order to assume her position as daughter and sister. However, she appreciated Natalie's attempt to at least reach out and declare her private defiance.

As they took their seats at the table, Madison's phone rang. She glanced at it and saw that it was Sister Johnson's number. She quickly put the ringer on silent and let it go to voice mail. She'd call her back after Natalie left. She didn't want Natalie overhearing what they might say.

Madison found it ludicrous that she would have to hide what she was doing, especially since she was certain Natalie was there on the sly.

Again Natalie expressed her admiration of Madison's time and willingness to help with her dying father. It grated a bit. Madison was his daughter, and regardless of the past, that hadn't changed. While he hadn't been there for her, she refused to let that stand in the way of her being there for him.

"It seems these times in life are what bring out the best and the worst in people."

Madison nodded in agreement.

"When my grandpa died, I couldn't believe how my relatives acted. And he didn't have anything to fight over. I really hope that people will just accept what Saul wants and honor his desires."

Was the statement pointed? Madison thought. Did Natalie know why her father wanted Madison there? "I agree," said Madison.

"Do you?" Natalie asked.

"Of course. That's why I'm here. It's no secret there have been some hard years between us, but he's still my father..." she felt the stifling sting of tears.

"So, he's told you what he wants?"

Madison gave her a tentative shrug.

Natalie scooted closer. "A couple weeks ago, he told me what he had done, and I've felt so guilty not speaking to Ben about what he said. He told me he wanted you to be here but to keep it a secret. I think he knows that you and I are in contact. I've been going crazy not knowing what I should do."

Madison felt relief, knowing she was no longer the only one in the family who knew his regret and was keeping his secret. "He told me, too. I've been so torn. I want to do what he asks, and yet I also don't want to stir up a bunch of crap from the past."

"Oh, I feel so much better knowing I'm not the only one he told," said Natalie, leaning back against the chair.

"Me, too. But what now?" Madison took a bite of the sandwich and looked back toward the front door, wondering how long Darlene would be gone and they could talk in private. "When this comes out, it's my mom I worry about. She's the one who will have to deal with most of this once he's gone."

"Well, that's if you agree to what he wants," Natalie said. She struggled to say the words. "I think it will be an issue the entire family will have to deal with. I'm surprised he decided to do this now. Why did he wait so long?"

Madison gave a huff. "Because it's a terrible thing, and he doesn't want to deal with the aftermath."

"So, what do you plan to do?" Natalie asked.

Madison thought a moment and then took a deep breath and told her sister-in-law the few things she had already done and learned about regarding the murder. Natalie sat silently listening. Her eyes grew large as Madison explained what she'd found. A few times, she squirmed, looking anxious and confused. When Madison stopped, Natalie sat up in the chair and shook her head. "But..." she hesitated. "Oh my. This is terrible."

"And it could be worse, especially if it's true and the person who actually killed that girl is..."

"No! It can't be," Natalie spouted.

"I hope not. But why would he tell us this?"

Natalie twisted in her chair. Her face was pained. "This isn't what he told me," she confessed.

"It isn't?" Madison reeled back, wondering what other terrible confessions her father had made. "Then what did he tell you?" She was surprised but also hoping it might reveal something new.

Natalie's shoulders sank, and she swallowed. "He told me he wanted you to be here because he planned to make things right. He said he was tired of living with the lies and said you deserved to know what he'd done."

Madison nodded. "And was that all he told you?"

She cocked her head from side to side. "More or less. I thought he was talking about the will."

Madison flinched back. "The will?" Aside from their home, Madison couldn't imagine anything more than a small retirement Saul may have scraped together from his teaching job. The idea of a will was something Madison hadn't even considered. Not only did he have no money, she assumed anything he did have would go to her mother.

"It feels like everything has changed since the land sold. All of a sudden, everyone seems to be on his doorstep with their hand out." Natalie gave a slight shiver of annoyance. "When he told me he wanted to make things right with you, I thought he was talking about leaving the money to you."

Madison's head was spinning as she remembered watching the bulldozers leveling out her grandparents' old orchards. "Do you mean grandpa's land? Where Morey lives?"

Natalie nodded, looking perplexed that Madison wasn't aware.

"I thought Morey was selling part of the farm because...." She thought a moment. She had just assumed it was because the farm wasn't making ends meet. Madison took a deep breath. "It's just some farmland. How much can it be worth?"

Natalie raised her eyebrows. "A lot. He sold it to Dynamap, that big computer company. They owned the land on the other side of the orchards, so they bought it and plan to build more offices there. They paid a fortune for it."

"So, my dad and Morey are now wealthy men." She pondered the odd reaction Morey had while looking out over the new construction at the homestead. It wasn't the response she expected from someone who was now rich.

"Well..." Natalie waffled. "Actually, it's just Saul." She stopped and groaned. "I feel awkward being the one to tell you all this. I feel like a gossip."

Madison ignored her angst. "Just my dad? Why? Didn't Morey sell his part?" It didn't surprise her. As much as she loved her uncle, she knew he had never been very good with money. It wouldn't strike her as odd to hear that he sold his piece because he needed some quick cash.

"Well, not exactly. Your grandfather left it all just to Saul."

Madison shook her head, confused. "He cut Morey out? Why?"

"I don't know. Your father never talks about it, and when he got sick, he quit talking to anyone. When he told me he wanted to talk to you and make things right, I figured it had to do with the will. I think Morey was expecting Saul to leave him some of the proceeds from the land when he passes, but now I wonder if he's giving everything to you?"

Madison sat in a daze, remembering what she had heard that first day she sat with her father. She recalled him telling her that the only person he had told about what he knew regarding the murder was his own father. She wondered if there could be a connection to the will. Had her grandfather used the land as a bribe to keep her father quiet? Had he worried about the shame it would bring on the family if Saul said what had really happened? Or did her grandfather have some other connection to that horrible event?

"I had no idea about any of this. Why would he give anything to me? He's barely spoken to me in years."

Natalie sighed. "Maybe he feels guilty about shutting

you out? He's obviously guilty about what he told you."

"I didn't come here for money. I came because my father said he wanted to see me. I didn't know about any of this. The money or the murder."

Natalie nodded dubiously.

Madison could see her resistance. "So, is this why my brothers are acting like I'm a parasite?"

"They don't know what your father told me. Saul told me to keep it a secret."

"They don't know about the will?"

Natalie shook her head. "I don't think anybody does—well, except maybe Syd."

"Syd," she grumbled. "Why him?"

"He's the one who your parents seem to trust, especially with these types of things."

"Which means my mom has to know."

Natalie shrugged. "She doesn't say anything about it, at least to any of us. But she seems confused and worried about what's going to happen. It's hard to believe that Saul would leave her nothing, but who knows."

Madison thought about her mother's odd response when she asked her about her plans for the future. It was apparent now why she reacted oddly to Madison's questions. If she thought Madison knew about the money and the will, no wonder she responded strangely.

"This is crazy," said Madison. She sat pondering what connection the will had to her father's regrets about the murder at Echo Lake. And why giving money to Madison would make a difference. *It's Amelia he should be giving the money to, not me*, she thought.

Then a stunning rush went through her. His request was to help Amelia gain freedom. He wanted to make things right for her and had asked Madison to help him do that. Was his desire to put his money toward that end? Again, the conversation about his confession to his father came back into her mind. Was her grandfather also feeling the weight of guilt in keeping his son quiet about what he'd done? The implications of all this coming to light made Madison's stomach clench.

"God, my brothers already hate me. This will only make it worse," she said with a groan.

Natalie started to deny the claim but knew it was useless. "After the family dinner, I heard the confrontation and the accusations and complaints they already had against you. They don't hate you. They're just confused and worried. Saul refuses to talk about things." Natalie licked her lips and looked down. "After hearing what he told you, I can see why. It's so awful."

"It is. He's been a coward. He should have taken responsibility years ago, and now he expects me to make it right. It's messed up."

"What do you plan to do?"

Madison took a deep breath and then looked back toward the room where her father lay sick. Her plan had been to come in, say her good-bye, and then wrap her painful past into a neat little bundle that she would toss and move on. She would then go back to her home with Taylor feeling complete and resolved. Plan. It was the one thing she had always been so good at, and now she was back in the thick of her past life, reminded of her estrangement and the reason she continued to feel like a pariah. She wondered if she would ever not feel that way. Would she spend her entire life continuing to let it make her feel unworthy and an outcast?

She sat up straighter in the chair, squared her shoulders, and told Natalie precisely what she hoped to do.

"I plan to find the truth."

CHAPTER 16

Madison was tired, her inquiries about what happened at Echo Lake futile. She sat at Jenny's kitchen table with her second cup of coffee and opened her laptop. The first unread message was a notification that she qualified for unemployment benefits. That was bittersweet news. The extra money would be helpful, but it was something she had never had to do before. Even when she was young and without her parents' support, she had always found a way to pay her bills.

As a full-time student, she'd worked several jobs, applied for grants, and Morey sent regular checks to cover what he called "the extras." The checks weren't much, but it always felt like a windfall when they came.

Now she had no income. Taylor had assured her that it was a non-issue, a chance to see what other opportunities might be out there. She smiled, feeling again how lucky she was.

She scrolled down, and another email jumped to her attention. It was a reply from Teresa Skilling, the reporter who did the story with Amelia years ago. Her heart leaped, hoping this might reveal something new.

Dear Madison,

Your inquiry about Amelia Johnson is intriguing. She is a promising writer, and I enjoyed her poetry in the Iron

Post magazine. That publication is also owned by the same company that owns our paper. That is how I learned about Millie's story and her life as an inmate. It's been years since I've seen anything from her, but I would love to talk to you more about Millie and the information you mentioned in your email. I can pull what notes I have regarding her and see if anyone at the magazine has any information. I'd be happy to help if I can. If you'd like to set up a meeting, please call the number below. Thank you for reaching out. Best, Teresa Skilling, Editor-in-Chief

Madison felt her spirits rise. Teresa Skilling had information and was willing to share it. Without hesitation, Madison called the number, and a woman answered and told her Teresa was in a meeting. Madison told her about Teresa's email. She also explained she would only be in the area for a short time and was surprised when the woman offered an appointment for that afternoon.

"You mean today?" Madison asked.

"She has an opening today at three. Otherwise, it will have to be next week," the woman explained.

Madison jumped at it. She would have to miss seeing her father that day but felt confident he would want her to follow this lead.

It was a forty-five-minute drive to Salt Lake City, but with new hope, Madison dashed off to the shower. It was the break she felt she needed—someone outside the tiny box that she seemed to be stuck inside.

A newsperson should have more information on Amelia's background, and she was hopeful for Teresa's amiability to discuss what happened that day. She needed an in and hoped to find a kindred soul in Teresa. Putting herself in her shoes, she would surely be willing to help however she could.

Dressed casually again in the black jacket, jeans, and boots, she practiced her questions on the drive up. The parking garage was large, and she marveled at the size of the building. She hadn't realized Salt Lake City's growth, having only distant memories of her rare trips to Temple Square with her family to see the lights during the holidays.

The newspaper's headquarters were located in a tall brick building in the middle of the downtown. It was an operation nothing like her own—the one where she used to work. The large lobby was filled with framed accolades and awards, and the receptionist sat behind a wall of windows, keeping her visible but inaccessible. Madison was on the list of appointments and was quickly buzzed back to the news-room, where she found rows of desks and reporters busily chatting on phones or working on computers.

"Can I help you?" asked a young man with shoul-der-length hair and a Fang Island t-shirt.

"I'm here to see Teresa Skilling," she answered, in awe at the size of the room and the number of people employed there.

"Is she expecting you?"

Madison nodded, and he directed her past the desks and down a narrow hallway to a large office. The door was open, and Madison could see a smartly dressed woman at a desk. The backdrop behind her was a wall of windows with a view of Salt Lake City's downtown.

Teresa Skilling had short bobbed blonde hair and looked more like a television news anchor than a newspaper editor. She was on the phone but waved Madison in.

"Sit. Sit," she said, after she wrapped up her call. "Tell me about the story you're doing about Amelia Johnson, alias Millie Juarez." She rolled her *r* and raised her eyebrows. She spoke quickly, and her face was animated. "I haven't thought about her in years."

Madison shifted in the chair. "I'm not really sure of the angle yet," wishing she hadn't used that ruse. "But I think I may have found some new evidence..."

A young man came into the office and took the chair next to Madison. He held a pad of paper and a pen. "New evidence?" he asked.

Madison looked at him strangely, then turned to Teresa.

"This is Evan Nelson. He's one of my I-team reporters," Teresa said with a lilt and another raise of her sculpted brows.

Madison cocked her head in question. "I-team?"

"It's our investigative unit. I asked him to join us and see if there's a way we can work together here." Then she smiled with another lift of just a single brow.

Madison took a deep breath and started to object, but Evan cut her off. "I did some research on the case, and it's fascinating. Millie Juarez is the pen name of Amelia Johnson, who is still in prison. She pled guilty to pushing another girl off a cliff. She was only sixteen when the murder happened."

"Yes, I know," said Madison, annoyed.

"So, what new evidence do you have?" he asked. "Is she now claiming she's innocent?"

Teresa sat back and grinned with pride, like a mother watching one of her children at a piano recital.

"I don't think it's ready to be released," Madison said coldly.

Both Evan and Teresa tensed at Madison's dismissal.

"We thought you'd appreciate the help. We have resources that smaller papers don't, plus we're here where it happened," explained Teresa. "We'd, of course, give you the byline, too."

A story in that large Utah paper? Madison thought, horrified. It would be carried throughout the state and other parts of the region. That was the last thing she needed on top of the dispute she already had with her family. "I'm not looking at doing a story at this time."

"But I thought that's what you told me in your email. You said you were a reporter," Teresa snapped.

"Yes, but this is all preliminary. I may have some leads, but I came here to see if you had information that might help me talk to Amelia. If I can speak to her, I may be able to see if what I've been told is true."

"What have you been told?" asked Evan.

Madison turned to him with a glare.

He put his hands up in defeat. "Why am I here?" he asked, annoyed, and then looked to Teresa for permission to leave the office.

"Yes, go. I'm sorry I wasted your time," she said.

He stood up and walked off without acknowledging Madison.

Madison sighed. "I'm sorry. I didn't mean to lead you into thinking this meeting was anything other than just talking about Amelia."

"You told me you were working on a story about her. And now you say it's not a story. So what is it?"

Madison looked at the floor. "I've learned some things that may have a connection to Amelia and what happened that day. Someone..." she picked her words carefully. "Told me that Amelia may be innocent."

Teresa flinched back. "Really? How do they know? Did they witness it?"

"I think so. They say there's proof."

"Proof of who did it?"

Madison's shoulders swayed. "Possibly."

"Why don't they give it to you? Are they credible?"

The question made Madison pause. Was her father's illness making him unreliable?

Teresa shook her head. "It's been years since we published any of Amelia's works. She just stopped sending us anything and quit all communication. Her poetry was good, and her back story was intriguing, which is why I remember her, but quite frankly, I haven't given her a second thought in years. I was surprised when Evan told me she was still in prison. I figured she had been paroled, moved away, and put all of that in the rearview mirror."

At that point, Madison wished she was the one putting it behind her. "I've been trying to get more information, and I saw the article that had the two of you together. The information I've been given is pretty vague, but I think it's worth looking into. I thought you might have contact or more insight into why she pled guilty."

Teresa lifted her eyebrows and sighed. "I wish I could help you. And if you do find there is credible evidence, this could be a huge story. I hope you'll stay in touch if something does pan out. We don't like playing catch-up, especially with stories that are part of our market. We'd make it worth your while to give us the exclusive."

Madison nodded. She wasn't about to commit to anything and was already regretting the information she had revealed.

As she drove out of the city and toward her hometown, she pondered the reason she had never aspired to be something more than a small-town reporter. Did she lack the hunger of reporters like Evan? Is that why she'd stayed so long at the tiny paper until her job simply dried up? Was she dried up? When she left home and made her way to the University of Las Vegas, her dreams of writing and investigating were as fresh and strong as her ambition to prove that her family was wrong. But the years passed quickly, and now she found herself doubting her choice of career. Was standing up to her parents about her path also wrong? She scoffed at the thought but felt the years of anger and fatigue.

The girl who was so lost as she drove away from that small town was now driving back, feeling just as unsure and adrift as when she left.

CHAPTER 17

I t had been a sleepless night. Madison braced herself as she stepped outside. The cold wind that whipped down the valley as she walked to the car awakened her and made her miss the heat of the desert.

When her mother answered the door, she looked surprised. Madison had told her she was leaving on Wednesday, and here it was Thursday. But she wrapped the sweater around herself and hurried Madison inside. Small flurries of snow tumbled with the biting breeze, making the orange glow of the fire roaring in the family room especially inviting.

"You're still here," Darlene said. "For some reason, I thought you said you'd only be here until Wednesday."

"I decided to stay a bit longer." Madison's heart dropped, realizing her mother hadn't even bothered to try and say good-bye when she thought she was leaving. *Stop expecting things*, she told herself.

Darlene raised an eyebrow. "I'd like to go out and run some errands. Do you mind staying with him for an hour or two? Once in a while, he tries to get up, and he wanders. I found him all the way out at the mailbox about a week ago."

"Of course, I'll stay with him," Madison said, although she was sure her father wasn't able to even walk to the bathroom, let alone anywhere else. She watched from the large front window as her mother pulled out of the driveway. Then she went to the back room.

"Dad, did you kill that girl? Did you push her off that cliff?" It's what she wanted to ask, but even idle conversations about the storm the night before, or how Darlene always burned toast, were a struggle for him. Along with the concern over aggravating his illness, the idea of getting clear or even intelligible answers about his involvement in the murder had Madison's head spinning with indecision.

"Just find the proof," he mumbled when she finally asked him to explain more. She gave up and let him rest.

She took deep breaths and tried to figure out her course of action as she struggled to stay awake. She pulled the album from her tote and flipped through it yet again, wishing something would miraculously jump from the pages. The low drone of the TV, her father's soft snoring, combined with her exhaustion from the stress, had her sinking deep into the plush recliner and in a battle with her eyelids.

Her Uncle Syd woke her up as he shuffled through the bedside drawer. He startled when he saw she was awake.

"Hey there," he whispered. "Your mom's not here, so I let myself in. I'm just looking for some papers that your mother can't seem to find."

Through blurry eyes, she saw him standing at the bedside, holding the album. She blinked and looked down at her lap where she'd put it. Confused and concerned, she sat up, trying to shake off the drowsy fog. She looked over to her father and saw that he was still sleeping. He was turned on his side, his face covered in the blankets, but his back showed the rise and fall of breathing.

Saul stirred, and Syd put his finger to his lips and motioned her to step out of the room. She followed, and once in the hallway, he closed the door softly. Madison looked at the album in his hands, and seeing this, he shrugged. "Not sure why he's still thinking about this."

She reached for the album, and he reluctantly handed it to her.

"I know why you didn't want to tell me who the boy was at that cliff when it happened. I found him in the court records," she whispered. "Why couldn't you just tell me?"

"The court records?" He flinched back. "Why are you looking into this? It's over. Don't dredge this up."

"I'm not dredging up anything. I'm trying to help him. It's what he wants," she said, standing firm.

He looked at her, confused. "Why would he want that?"

"Because that girl has been in prison for forty years."

He shook his head, frustrated. "She confessed to pushing Sara off the cliff." His voice rose with each word, and his neck and face began to turn red. He was getting more upset than she expected. Why did he care?

The sound of the front door opening gave Madison a welcomed reprieve.

"Syd?" Darlene called. "Are you here?"

"Yes," he called back.

She came around the corner and saw the two of them standing alone in the hallway, both agitated.

"Is he okay?" she asked, placing a brown bag on the hallway table and coming toward them.

"He's fine," Syd answered. He put a hand on his sister's arm.

Then another thud of the front door closing, then voices came from the foyer. Madison listened a moment and heard her brother Vince's voice. She groaned. Soon came the sound of others entering the house. Madison wondered if another family gathering was planned; she dreaded the thought.

"What's this about?" Darlene asked, approaching the kitchen. She, too, was obviously unaware they were coming over.

Soon, Madison saw her three brothers and their wives peering pensively down the hall.

"Is Dad okay?" asked Troy.

"He's fine," Syd said again. He walked Darlene toward the kitchen, leaving Madison alone in the hall. She felt the weight of her brothers' stares upon her.

She wanted to avoid what she knew would be conflict and stay sequestered with her father. There would be nothing constructive about this visit. Vince seemed to revel in confrontation, and with the high-stress situation, she was sure he would be ready to pounce. Before she could go back into the room, he called to her.

"We need to talk," he said gruffly.

She stiffened but turned toward him, refusing to be intimidated. Walking toward them, she held her chin up. "What about?" she asked.

Madison came into the foyer, where Ben and Natalie stood together by the door. Her mother looked pensive and wrung her hands as she swung her eyes from face to face, confused.

"You couldn't just stay away," Vince hissed at Madison. "You had to come here and try to cause us problems by bringing up a bunch of shit."

"Vince!" Darlene scolded from the kitchen. "Don't talk like that."

"What's this about?" asked Syd, standing between Madison and her brother.

"I'm not bringing up anything," Madison defended. Then she looked at Natalie, who lowered her head. "You told them?" she asked, deflated. She shook her head slowly. "You promised you wouldn't say anything."

Natalie raised her eyes apologetically.

"She's my wife. She doesn't keep secrets from me," said Ben.

Madison scoffed. "Really?" Then she turned to Natalie. "So, I suppose you also told him about the rest of our conversation? What my dad told you?"

"Please don't," Natalie begged, cutting her off.

Ben turned to his wife. "What did he tell you?"

"What's this about?" Syd tried to break in again.

"She did the right thing," said Vince, ignoring him. "At least some of us are loyal to this family."

"Loyal?" Madison asked with a sarcastic lilt. "Well, if keeping secrets means you're loyal, then what does that make you? You're the one who couldn't wait to run to mom and dad with your story."

Vince shrugged but looked uncomfortable. "They needed to know."

"That wasn't all they needed to know," she spat back.

The look on Vince's face made it clear that Madison held his shame in her hands.

"I should have told Mom and Dad the truth about you from day one," she said. Madison gave a sarcastic laugh.

"You don't know what family loyalty is."

Both Vince's wife and Darlene turned to him for an explanation.

"Told us what?" asked her mother.

Vince pushed them aside. "Nothing."

Madison heaved a sigh. "You're all a bunch of hypocrites. I came here because Dad asked me to come. Yes, he told me some things, but..."

Vince sneered. "You can threaten me with lies about the past, but if you pursue this ridiculous idea of Dad confessing to a murder, I'll..." he lunged toward Madison and snatched the album from her hands. He lifted it high when she tried to take it back. "Is this it? Is this the stupid bunch of pictures he told you about?"

"Give that back," Madison said as she tried to reach the album he held above his head.

"Murder?" Darlene cried out, trying to grasp what was being said.

Ben stepped forward and tried to stand between Madison and Vince. "Stop this, please."

"I'll stop this for good," Vince yelled, and he stomped toward the fireplace in the family room.

Madison pushed Ben aside and went to where Vince stood, blocking her as the fire crackled and burned.

"Don't you dare!" Madison yelled, grabbing for the book. Vince tried to deflect her, and as they struggled, both the book and Madison went down. She hit the floor with a slap that sounded much worse than it felt. The album splattered across the floor, plastic, cardboard, and photos scattering everywhere. She quickly gathered herself up and scrambled toward it. "Way to be all dramatic, asshole," she scowled back at him. "You can't stop me from doing what I need to do, even if you were to destroy these pictures."

Darlene began to cry, and Syd tried to comfort her.

There was a knock on the door, and the entire group turned to it. Darlene pushed her way toward it but then turned and looked at the whole group standing silent, eyes wide, waiting for their scolding.

She looked through the peephole. "It's just Morey," she said, wiping her eyes. She took a deep and annoyed breath and then opened the door, ignoring him as he walked in.

Immediately he could see that things were awry. Madison was kneeling on the floor.

"What happened?" he asked, going to her.

Vince scoffed as he watched her sweep up the photos that were strewn about. She hastily scooped them back together and then held the mangled book close. She turned toward Vince, ignoring Syd and her mother's desire to keep things sane. "You come near me again, and I'll call the police."

"Go ahead! I know you've already talked to Daniel West about this."

"What?" asked Morey.

Darlene shot a look at Madison. "Daniel West?"

Madison rolled her eyes, exasperated at her mother's continued pathetic yearning for the past. "Yes, he knows." she huffed, and gave Darlene a disappointed glare. Her mother, feeling her daughter's disgust, put her hands over her face and wept.

Vince stepped forward, pointing angrily at Madison. "It's that stupid bunch of photos and dad's off-the-wall talking. She thinks she's digging up some dirt on our family. She's still trying to prove something."

Syd, with his most sincere and solemn look, went to Madison. "Maybe I should be the keeper of the photos just until this is settled. They seem to be the source of a lot of conflicts."

Morey went and stood with Madison. "Photos of what?" he asked, confused.

Madison stood and faced him. "My father asked me to come here, and this is why," she said quietly, holding the tattered album. "He wants to make things right, and it's obvious none of you would have helped him." She turned to Vince to make her point, as he stood glaring at her. Then he looked away, as though he couldn't stand the sight of her any longer. When the others turned as well, she gathered her tote and started to leave.

"Oh, you're such a saint. You don't care about making anything right," Vince called after her.

Madison turned on her heel. "And you're not really worried about these photos or about what Dad did. All you care about is the fact that you're not going to get the money," Madison shot back. She turned to Natalie. "Sorry, I guess I should have kept our secret," she said with a sarcastic lilt.

Seeing this, Ben puffed out his chest. "Leave her out of this," he said. "She's not the problem."

"I'm the one who's the problem?" Madison asked. She was ready to flee.

"You've always been the problem," Vince barked at her. "And then you waltz back out here and cause even more problems."

Madison felt her face flush. The rage inside her was at the surface. "I could cause lots of problems. I could have told them about your own little secret problem."

"What problem?" Vince's wife asked him pointedly.

"Nothing. She has nothing, and she's just trying to turn things away from what she's doing. Unlike her, I have nothing to hide," he said, mocking her.

Madison and Jenny had huddled together in their hideout on the back porch, and with a flashlight, she revealed the items she had taken from her brother. With her heart pounding, she had searched his room and found a paper bag. Inside was a note, a medical bill, a white plastic wand, and the gun. It was all stuffed in the bottom of his underwear drawer. She knew he would blame her when he found it missing, but what could he do? Having her father find out he had the gun would be worse than what he had possibly planned to do with it. She would have to take her chances that he never caught her alone.

The medical bill was from a clinic in Colorado. It read "second-trimester abortion."

"Abortion," Madison said, stunned.

The wand was a pregnancy test. Vince's girlfriend was pregnant but had had an abortion. Then she read the small note at the bottom of the bag. It was her brother's handwriting. It was unfinished and rambling.

She scanned it quickly and then gasped. "I told you I'd kill myself if you went through with this." Madison read it aloud to Jenny, who put her hand to her mouth. Madison had wondered and worried about what role the gun played, and now she knew.

"Do you really think he was planning to do it?" Jenny asked, reaching for the letter to see the words for herself.

From the scene she had viewed from the crack in his door, Madison felt confident of what he was planning and knew taking the gun was the only option.

She put the pregnancy test and invoice back into the bag and then studied the gun. "I need to get rid of this. I want to take it and throw it into the canal. Will you come with me? We can go first thing in the morning before anyone wakes up."

"Don't you think you should tell your parents what he planned to do?" Jenny asked urgently.

Madison felt tears begin to well in her eyes, along with her desperation. "I don't know what to do. He'll kill me if I tell."

Jenny leaned forward and embraced her. She held her closely as Madison rocked and sobbed, repeating her fear.

"I don't know what to do. I don't know what to do."

The roar of his frantic search rose to new heights when he found them with his possessions.

The girls screamed when he ripped open the drapes they had pulled around the alcove, bringing Saul and Darlene scurrying to the scene.

"I'm going to kill you," he yelled, grabbing for the bag.

"What is going on out here?" Darlene frantically whispered. She looked around, obviously worried the neighbors would hear more than whether Vince really was going to kill Madison.

In the soft shimmer of the moon were guilty faces and an accusation that would change Madison's life forever.

Madison grabbed her purse and searched for her keys. Then she felt the paper bag that held the gun. Her breath was ragged. *So, Vince thinks he had nothing to hide? What about the night he altered my life forever?* Her rage boiled to the top and spilled over in an uncontrollable seethe.

"Nothing to hide? Really? Then, how about you tell everyone what this is?" She was frazzled and furious as she tried to open the bag, wanting to see his face when she revealed his weapon. Let him squirm and explain it now! But in her rush, the bag spilled open and the gun fell out, landing with a clatter and sliding on the hardwood floor.

All eyes were wide and mouths agape, watching it.

Darlene gasped. "A gun!"

Troy and Ben both rushed forward. "What are you doing?" they said in unison.

"I'm not doing anything," Madison shot back. She immediately regretted her hasty decision to expose the gun. "I didn't mean ..." She stopped.

Troy's face was full of doubt. Ben stood in front of Natalie as though blocking her from harm.

"I'm tired of him trying to act like he's so innocent and that I'm the cause of all these problems." Madison knew she was trying to justify what she'd done and felt worse, now that her vengeance was laying there, solid and exposed.

Vince picked up the gun, looked it over quickly, and then

turned to Madison. "Where did you get this?" he snapped.

Morey walked to Vince. Confused, the older man reached out.

"This was my father's," said Morey.

Vince relented and handed him the gun.

"Grandpa's?" Madison asked.

Morey nodded. "Yes. It was part of his collection. He noticed it was missing years ago but wasn't sure when it was taken or if he had just misplaced it. None of the other guns were missing, though the gun case had not been broken into." He looked at Madison. "Why do you have it?"

"It was with the stuff dad gave me. I thought it was the gun from..." she turned to Vince.

Vince glared at her.

His attitude stoked Madison's anger. "Ask *him* where the gun came from," she said, pointing to Vince.

Morey turned to him. "You took it?"

"I didn't take it. I found it in Dad's closet years ago. I was just looking at it. I was going to put it back, but then she stole it from me." He glared at Madison.

Darlene came forward. "Stop this. Why are you bringing this up again?"

Madison's heart dropped like a rock. She was still being blamed for her family's strife.

"She's right. This isn't helping anything," said Syd, by Darlene's side. "The only thing that matters now is letting Saul have some peace during his last days. He deserves that."

Her face wracked with sadness, Darlene quickly left the group and went to the bedroom. Troy waited until she had closed the door. "Enough, okay?" He directed it at Madison.

Ben stepped forward. "I agree. I've stayed quiet ever since you got here, but this has to end. If you can't leave all that stuff in the past, then just leave."

Madison was again the center of their anger. Even level-headed, quiet Ben was against her. Why did she agree to come back for this?

Refusing to let them see her pain, she stomped out the front door, letting the screen door slam against the frame. When she hit the sidewalk, she heard the screen slam again and Morey calling out to her.

"Madison, wait."

She turned, and seeing they were alone, her shield came down along with a flood of tears.

He put a hand on her shoulder. "I knew this was likely to happen when you told me you were coming. I should have warned you."

Shaking her head, she took a deep breath. "You knew about the murder and Dad's photos?"

Morey shook his head. "Murder? What murder? I thought this was supposed to be a meeting about the will."

"Is that why everyone was there?" she asked.

He nodded, looking perplexed. "What does this have to do with murder and Saul's photos?"

She groaned. "Dad told me about the murder of Sara Voorhees while he was at the youth camp. And he told me that the other girl was innocent."

Morey's jaw dropped. "How would he know that?"

The front door closed. Syd came toward them. "Don't you think *everyone* should talk about this?"

Morey bowed up to him. "Can't you see she doesn't want

197

to talk to any of you? She comes home after all these years, and this is how she's treated?"

Syd gave a condescending chortle and put a hand up. "Morey, it's more than fighting about past issues. Saul is telling Madison things about the Sara Voorhees murder. I don't know why he's bringing this up now, but it's not going to help anything. Plus, there are other issues that we need to take care of regarding the will." The breeze was strong, and Syd kept having to brush away the hair from his face. Even the large amount of gel he used couldn't keep it slicked back in place. He turned to Madison. "I've been asked by your mother to be the executor, and with this other stuff, there are concerns ..."

Madison let out a grunt. "Concerns? Don't get your garments in a bunch. I'm not here for the money. I didn't even know he had any."

Syd cocked his head, unconvinced. "Why did you say that Vince wasn't getting anything? What did your father tell you about the will?"

"Nothing. Natalie said he told *her* something. I'm sure he's not giving me anything. Besides, I came here to see him because he asked me to. That's all. And it wasn't until after I got here that he asked me to help with this stuff about the murder."

"Help how?" Morey asked.

Syd broke in. "It isn't just money that is concerning. It's your father's legacy. And this could affect your mother's standing in the community after he's gone. These rumors getting out would be terrible for her."

Madison laughed. "Why am I not surprised? Is that all you care about—what will people think?"

Morey turned and, ignoring Syd, spoke directly to her.

"Why didn't you tell me about this?"

Seeing his disappointment in her lack of trust, she sighed and tried to explain. "He told me the day I got here. I wasn't sure what it meant, and he told me not to say anything. I was going to tell you when I got him to explain it to me."

Syd turned on both of them. "This is a waste of time and energy. That girl confessed. It went to trial, and she never denied it," he said.

"Then why is my father so adamant she's innocent?"

"Your father is sick and delusional," Syd warned. "He's never said a word about this to anyone until now. This rumor getting out would be devastating. People will start making up things and blaming others. Consider your mother. Consider all of us." He turned to Morey as if looking for validation. "This will be a stain on this entire family." Then back at Madison, "Think of the good things your parents have done for the people in their ward and the students your father taught. Don't tarnish what they've built over a lifetime."

"According to them, I did that a long time ago. How much worse can I possibly make it?" She felt the heat rise in her face.

"This isn't about you, Madison," Syd scoffed.

"Let's talk about this later," said Morey, trying to usher her toward her car.

"Is this about revenge?" asked Syd. The question was lobbed over to her like a grenade.

Madison flung around and flashed him a glare. "Revenge!"

"Leave her alone, Syd," said Morey, trying to maneuver Madison away.

"This isn't my idea," she said, shaking off Morey. "I didn't even know about this until he told me three days ago.

He begged me to look for the proof and set things right."

Syd took a deep breath and then let it out slowly. "That girl was odd and had problems." He then turned to Morey. "How do you feel about her digging into this?"

Morey looked conflicted but shrugged.

Syd gave a frustrated huff. "Your father had nothing to do with this. Let him die in peace. Can't you just move on?"

Madison felt exhausted and defeated. But his last sentence grated on her. *Move on?* She had been estranged from her family for years, without any contact except Morey and a few Facebook messages from Natalie. How much further could she move?

When she refused to respond, Syd shook his head, disappointed. "Pursuing this will only cause grief for your family. I would hope that it still matters to you."

He went back into the house.

Morey began to talk, but Madison wanted to escape. She was done. She walked away from Morey, jumped in her car, and drove off.

When she was far enough away from the house, she pulled over to a curb and let the anger and pain pour out. She wondered if there would ever be a day that she wasn't a pariah in that house. More importantly, would she ever reach a point where she didn't care?

Her phone rang, but she ignored it. Regardless of who it was, she didn't want to speak to anyone. She wiped her eyes. It was ten years ago that she sat in a car in almost the same spot, wet-faced and red-eyed, vowing to never allow them to get to her again.

LOST

My love, my soul, lost.
Carried always in my heart.
Never forgotten.

CHAPTER 18

As she rolled into the condo's parking space, the sun was beginning to dip and spread across the horizon, a shimmering glow shooting across the valley. Madison watched, feeling incredibly small and weak. She might as well have been back in high school, just been given her family's ultimatum that had sent her away.

Her phone continued buzzing. She could no longer avoid it and pulled the phone from her tote.

"I'm so sorry, Madison. This is their problem, not yours. I've told you that for years, and it's still the case." It was a voice mail from Morey.

She wasn't ready to talk to anyone, even to him. Her heart ached when she listened to the message. She remembered those words from him, but the scab she had grown to protect her feelings had been ripped off in seconds. Madison knew from her family's scorn and rejection how they felt, yet deep in her soul, she had held on to some tiny glimmer of hope that they had changed. She wore a mask of indignation and indifference to protect her from the pain, but it was flimsy at best. Their cruelty hurt. This trip had only validated her fears that nothing had changed, that even Natalie was against her, and now Madison's mask was gone.

Without her Uncle Morey, she would have been lost. After her fall from grace, he was the first, the only one, to tell her she had done the right thing. The support he gave her wasn't just in the form of checks to help pay her bills, but also in messages of caring and acceptance that she needed more than anything else. He knew how her transgression was viewed, and yet he never made her feel like she was a miscreant. She believed he related to her due to his own feelings of ostracism. He didn't serve a mission, had been kicked out of BYU when he was caught drinking, and he was divorced. He maintained contact with his brother and the rest of the family but was never really part of the fold. He was the black sheep long before Madison one-upped him, and he empathized and came to her aid. After almost a decade, he was still her ally.

She debated calling him back but wasn't up to discussing it yet. She began to put the phone in her tote but noticed a missed call from Martha Johnson. Then she saw the long string of calls and texts from Daniel.

"Please call me ASAP," the last of the texts read.

Madison groaned and wondered what could be so urgent. Suppose he had discovered information about the murder. In that case, it couldn't possibly top the terrible new details she had already uncovered. With the backlash she had just witnessed from her family, she was already dreading what would happen if she continued to pursue her father's wishes.

"On my way to Jenny's condo. Huge fight with my family. I'll call you later." She sent the text, hoping it would suffice for the moment. She just wasn't up to it. He'd understand. She decided to call Martha once she had some time to settle in and rid herself of aggravation. She silenced her phone and threw it back into her tote.

As she walked up the stairs to the door, she felt eyes on her back and turned with a gasp. Her heart pounded as she scanned the area. There was nothing but the large junipers, softly swaying; however, the eerie tingle of someone watching her remained. Slowly, she turned back, and when she got to the top of the stairs, she froze. The window that ran the length of the door had been broken and the door was ajar. Her instinct was to flee, but instead, she took another sweeping glance around. Her breathing was hard and swift. Stepping back from the door, she thought about the gun and wished she still had it.

This is stupid, she thought, knowing it was statistically far more likely the gun would be turned against her rather than keeping her safe. But she felt naked without something to protect her from the unknown. She leaned back, and using her foot, she pushed the door open wider. She scanned the inside, hoping there was no one there.

Inside, it was chaos; furniture upended, drawers dumped, and papers strewn everywhere. A dreadful silence filled the room as she stepped forward and peered closer. "Oh, no," she moaned. Wondering if she'd left the place unlocked was her first fear, but then she looked and saw the busted window had allowed the culprits to reach in and open the door. Was it a targeted burglary or just a random crime of opportunity? The latter seemed unlikely since Jenny's place was so isolated.

Why would anyone drive that long winding road into the trees unless they were specifically coming to see her? Feeling vulnerable and exposed, Madison quickly went back to her car. She pulled out her phone and called the police, and then waited. As she sat, doors locked and looking around, she called Taylor, but it went straight to voice mail. She decided not to leave a message, then she made the difficult phone call to her friend.

"Are you okay?" was Jenny's first reaction after Madison told her what she'd found. No worry about her home or possessions, only of her friend.

"Any thoughts on who might have done this?" Madison asked.

"No idea. And there's really nothing that I keep at the house that would be worth anything. I guess except the one Jenny Elizabeth original I have in my bedroom, but I doubt anyone even knows it's there. I should get better locks or some type of security system."

"Not to mention blinds for the front windows. Even with a security system, it wouldn't take a high-tech burglar to break in, just someone with a rock."

"But the view is why I'm there. And besides, it's just one of the reasons I stay. You've always asked me why I still lived there. It's because I've never had to worry about this stuff. Even someone with a rock."

It was another stark difference from where Madison lived now. Even the smaller, safer community of Boulder City wasn't a place she would ever consider having her doors unlocked or be without the camera-equipped security system installed at their home.

"I think I'll be home the day after tomorrow. Will you be okay there until then?" Jenny asked.

Madison sighed. She wasn't sure. She told her she would have to call her later. The police had arrived. She looked at the time and marveled at how quickly they had responded, even in the tiny town of Lindon.

Madison got out of the car and greeted the police officer. He was young and tall, with a crew cut. He smiled as though he was almost excited to be there. She told him what she had found and then directed him to the condo.

"Did you go in?" he asked.

She shook her head and told him why she was there and why the owner wasn't.

He listened and then asked her to wait by her car, and with gun drawn, he entered the condo. After several minutes, he was back outside, letting her know the house was clear.

A detective arrived soon after, and Madison watched as the older man dressed in street clothes, took photos, and searched for evidence. The uniformed officer continued to ask Madison questions about why she was staying there and if she had seen anything odd or out of the ordinary. She couldn't think of anything except that everything she'd experienced since arriving was out of the ordinary, but she kept that to herself.

Both officers took her name and phone number, as well as Jenny's, and told her to document anything that was missing. When they left, Madison stood wondering what to do with the broken window and whether she was up to spending the night there.

She debated calling Taylor again but decided to wait until she could speak without sounding scared. Why cause more worry when nothing could be done from another state.

Madison wanted to go home, back to Taylor and the

comfort of their little house on Baker Street. Living in the bedroom community of Boulder City allowed them to afford a home and live in a town that had no resemblance to the glittery big city. If she left in the morning, she could be home and away from all this before dinner, she thought. And who would even notice or care?

After the argument at the house, she was sure her family members were reveling in what they would view as her retreat. The thought of Vince gloating made up her mind. She refused to let him or anyone else keep her from her quest.

Then she remembered the voice mail from Morey. She decided to call him and see if he could put her up for a couple of days.

There were more messages from Daniel. "Please call me ASAP." She sighed. He seemed pretty urgent. However, it was closing in on five o'clock, so she decided to call a glass shop first, to schedule the window's repair before everything closed for the night.

She put window repair in her search bar, and several businesses came up. She picked one that was the closest and called the number. A woman's bright, sunny voice answered. Madison explained what happened and what she needed.

"Oh, I'm so sorry," said the woman. "Here, let me see what I can do. Sorry, but I have to put you on hold a moment. Okay?"

"Sure," answered Madison.

"Sorry, Honey. I'll be right back."

Sorry. How many times did this woman feel she had to apologize? This grated on Madison, but it wasn't surprising.

It was something she found herself doing, and it drove her crazy. If someone bumped into her in a crowd, she would say, "Sorry." If someone held the door open for her, and she was a few feet away, but they waited, again, "Sorry." Even when she was working and called someone for an interview, she usually led with, "I'm sorry to bother you."

Madison knew that the word wasn't used as an apology, but she found herself saying it even when there was simply an awkward pause in the conversation. The word "sorry" was so easily used . . . and yet, when it came to her own father, the word eluded *him*.

She thought of her mother's offer to stay at their home. Asking to stay there now was out of the question. She pondered what her brothers must have told her mother about her father's confession and what she planned to do. She wondered if her mother would even allow her back into the house.

Madison waited on the line as the woman tried to find a time to schedule her in. She was surprised at how quickly they were able to come out and do the job. She was told the glazier could be there within the hour, and then the woman apologized again for making her wait even that long.

Madison thanked her and then decided to wait in the car. Even though she felt confident the condo was empty, she felt safer locked in the small confines of the vehicle. As Madison waited, she again thought about why she was still trying to do her father's bidding. It was a mystery, but rather than being intrigued by the complexities of what was being revealed, this puzzle was like a weight around her neck. Finding answers was work, and for what? Her father was barely lucid, and what she'd learned about Amelia seemed as though she had no interest, either.

She debated whether to call Daniel, but didn't want him thinking he should swoop in and save her, so instead, she decided to read her book—the odd book of poems written by the enigmatic person that monopolized her thoughts and energy. She pulled it from her tote and studied the cover. Hands awash in blood, the colors dark and ominous. She shrugged and then turned the book over and read the short description and the author's even shorter biography.

Millie Juarez lives in Utah. She holds a B.A. in creative writing. Her poetry has been published in numerous magazines and was awarded a Hispanic Heritage Poetry Prize. This is her debut collection.

Even though it wasn't her usual genre, Madison was intrigued by not only the author but also the tone of the poems. They were dark and brooding, but considering Amelia's place in life, they seemed fitting. The poems also gave her a venue to continue her talks with Martha. It seemed the mother was the only conduit in reaching Amelia.

She decided to call Martha back. Even the night's trauma couldn't dampen her curiosity as to what she might want. Again, she thought how odd the connection was to her former Sunday school teacher.

She dialed Martha's number.

"Madison, dear," Martha said before Madison could even say hello. "How are you?"

The question brought tears back to Madison's eyes, but she steadied her voice and lied. "I'm good."

"That's nice to hear," Martha said, tenderly. "I wanted to talk to you. I've been doing a lot of praying, and the night after we met, I believe the lord came to me in my sleep. I've changed my mind about having you speak to Amelia."

Thank God, Madison thought and then realized how literal that could be.

"I spoke to Millie yesterday on the phone. She's agreed to talk with you," Martha continued.

Madison's heart leaped. "Really?"

"I told her I had taught you in Sunday school. I gave her your married name, but I didn't tell her about what your father said."

"So, why did she agree to talk to me? What did you tell her I wanted to talk to her about?"

"I said you were a reporter and were reading her book and that you were interested in speaking with her about it. I know it wasn't completely true, but I feel strongly that she needs to hear what you have learned. I couldn't bring myself to tell her. She refuses to talk to me about any of it. I'm hoping she'll listen to you."

Madison took a deep breath, letting the information settle. "Okay. So, when do I call her?" she asked.

"It's a meeting at the prison. Wednesday morning is visitation. Will that work for you?"

"That's tomorrow," said Madison, surprised. "But what about the background check and credentialing? Won't that take a while?"

"Millie is putting you down on her list. You'll have to fill out some paperwork when you get there, but I believe it's all arranged."

When Madison hung up, she tried to sort the chaos in her mind. In less than a day, she would be face to face with the woman she had been trying to figure out from the moment her father told her the tragic tale.

As Madison settled back against the seat of the car, thinking through her imminent meeting with Amelia, a knock on her window made her jump.

There was Daniel.

She rolled down the window.

"Why didn't you return my call?" he asked. He was ruffled, and there was no patience in his voice.

"I told you. There was a big fight with my family. I had to leave, and well..." she pointed up toward the condo. "I got here, and I find that someone's broken into Jenny's place." She was overwhelmed and on the verge of tears again but refused to let Daniel see her weak.

He studied the door but didn't seem to relent in his urgency. "Did you call the police?"

She nodded. "They've already been here. Now I'm just waiting for the person to come and fix the broken window." Then an odd realization hit her. "How did you know where to find me?"

He paused. "I drove by your parents' but didn't see your car. I figured you'd be here."

"You know where Jenny lives?" she asked.

"I asked around." He took a sweeping view of the area, as if someone might be watching them.

"What's wrong?" she asked, seeing his angst. "Why are

you here?"

"I got a phone call this morning from a reporter at the *Chronicle*. He wanted to know if I was considering reopening the Amelia Johnson case."

Madison felt her stomach sink.

Daniel noticed the dread in her face. "Did you tell them you were trying to get the case reopened?"

"No, well yes, I went and met with them, but..."

Daniel leaned back and groaned.

"I didn't tell them I wanted the case reopened. I went there to try and get info from the editor. She did an article about Amelia years ago, and I thought that..."

Daniel cut her off. "What did you tell them? They think there's new evidence, and when I refused to discuss it with them, they started asking me questions as though I was hiding something."

"They're just fishing," said Madison. She was annoyed, knowing the reporter who called Daniel was that arrogant and aggressive reporter, Evan, who was in the meeting.

"If they do a story on this, it will blow up in our faces."

"Our faces? What does this have to do with you?"

"We'll have everyone convinced that she's somehow innocent and that I'm hiding something. He pointed back toward his car. "It's an election year. I don't need this crap."

Even as the sun was beginning to fade, Madison could see the "Re-elect West for Prosecutor" sign that covered almost the car's entire back door. "That's not going to happen. They can't do a story about nothing. All I told them was I may have new information about the case. They tried to press me into working with that reporter, but I refused. Don't talk to them."

Daniel shook his head. "Sometimes, that's worse."

"Not this time," she tried to reassure him.

"Have you talked to your uncle?" he asked.

She shook her head. "He was at the house when the fight broke out, but..." The question stumped her. "Why?"

Daniel let out a weary sigh. "He left a message on my phone saying he wanted to talk about some things regarding your father's past. I assumed that reporter called him as well."

Madison shook her head, confused. "Why would they call him?"

Daniel lifted his hands and looked to the sky, exasperated. "Why do you think?"

Her face showed him she was oblivious.

Daniel took in a long breath of frustration. "His career could certainly be affected by all this."

"As a contractor?" she asked, thinking of Morey.

Daniel shook his head, "No. Your other uncle." He then sighed. "The one running for Governor."

Syd was running for Governor. It didn't surprise Madison. He had used his looks and his cunning ability to charm people his entire life. The booming real estate business he owned had made him a wealthy man, and his high position in the church helped boost his stature in the minds and hearts of the faithful who voted. But why would the reporter call him? How would they even know that he was connected with any of this? He may be her uncle, but he was her *mother's* brother, a different last name, and a different side of the family. Daniel's warning that this could damage his run for office seemed like a grasp. Besides, having a brother-in-law with a checkered past hadn't hurt other, more prominent politicians. Why did Daniel assume this would be different for Syd?

After questioning Daniel further, she felt it was unlikely the reporter called Syd—it was Daniel's fears that were rampant.

"I don't know why Syd is calling you," she told Daniel. "He knows I've been asking about what happened, and he's probably just trying to figure out why. I really doubt it has anything to do with that reporter."

She placated him with reassurances that what she told them at the newspaper wouldn't result in a story. There was no evidence and no statements that could be used legitimately, unless Daniel were to give those to them. And she reminded him that he hadn't helped her find anything useful so far, so what could he give them? After a while, he seemed to soften, then he asked her a question that made her cringe.

"You aren't going to stay here tonight, are you?" he asked, motioning up to the condo. "Why don't you stay at my place?"

Madison's expression was all he needed to see for an answer. She couldn't imagine what he was thinking. Did this handsome, available, and successful man really have no prospects beyond an old flame who had rejected him years before and was now married? Nothing had changed. She wondered why he didn't see that. Did his wife's death ruin him to the point of pursuing something he knew would never happen?

"What?" he asked, annoyed. "Do you feel safe here? At least you know nothing would happen to you at my place.

We've proved that." He gave her a smile, but she wondered if it was just a lighthearted tease or a backhanded jab.

"There's nothing to prove."

He shrugged and again offered her his guest room. She thanked him and then told him she would be staying with Morey.

After Daniel left, she called Morey and told him what had happened. As she knew he would, he offered to put her up without hesitation.

Waiting for the glass repair person's arrival, her thoughts again returned to the fight with her family and the album at the center of it.

She reached into her purse and searched through the mess of the broken album and strewn photos, looking for one of Amelia. Fumbling through several, she finally found one of the girls. She studied their faces for hints, clues, anything that would bring what would happen to their lives into focus, but nothing in the photos revealed anything.

She bristled at the thought of Vince trying to throw the pictures in the fire, as well as Syd's condescending assumption that he should keep them as the neutral person in their conflict. Her grasp on the photos as she'd gathered them from the floor was as strong as her distaste for both of them. The idea of losing the pictures to either of them made her livid. She gazed at the tattered pieces of her father's album in her purse and decided to make it whole again.

When the man from the glass shop arrived, she left instead of hovering over him. Her desire was to go for a run to de-stress, but it was getting dark. Instead, she drove aimlessly toward town.

She found herself in a shop she'd never stepped foot in before. To enter a craft store the size of a small country was overwhelming. She had few domestic qualities. Taylor did the cooking, and while she kept the house clean, she had no talent when it came to decorating, so this type of store was outside her comfort zone. She started to look at the placards at the end of each aisle listing the various sundries but soon gave up and found a woman in a blue vest and name tag.

"Photo albums?" she asked.

The woman led her to the exact location. Madison thanked her and then stood back and marveled at the number of different colors, textures, and sizes. She sighed, wondering if people, other than Taylor, still used film and printed the photos. She hadn't had a photo processed since she was a teenager. She smiled, picturing Taylor in her mind, clicking away with the old Canon camera. It was a hobby that filled the walls of their home. The process was the appeal, or at least that's what Madison figured.

Using the archaic point-and-shoot camera instead of the slick and easy one everybody had on their phone seemed superfluous to her. And now, as she stared blankly at the mass of albums waiting to be filled, she thought about the stacks of scrapbooks and albums her parents had packed away in boxes. She dreaded the thought of possibly inheriting that pile of memories one day.

"Were you looking for something specific?" the woman asked.

Madison raised her shoulders. "Just something small," she said, seeing the large, thick binders. "I have some old photos."

The woman nodded. "Old photos from film?"

Madison nodded.

"Usually film rolls have twenty-four or thirty-six exposures...photos," she clarified. "You probably need a twenty-four-pocket. That's about the smallest we carry. We don't have many, but I think most of them are right over here," she said, directing Madison to the far end of the aisle.

Madison thanked her.

"Anything else I can help you with?"

Can you look at these photos and tell me who murdered Sara? Madison felt like blurting out. She was weary and frustrated. Instead, she thanked the woman again and began to search.

The rows of binders were beginning to blur into one when she found a small, dark blue version with only twenty-four pockets. She hadn't counted the exact number of photos her father had taken but knew she wouldn't need anything larger. She grabbed it and practically ran to the cashier.

When she arrived back at the condo, the man fixing the window had completed the job and was cleaning up. He handed her the invoice for the work.

"If you were my daughter," he said, shaking his head. "I'd make you get some type of security system or a big, mean dog."

Madison gave him the small laugh he expected, thanked him for his concern, and then went inside and locked the door. Then, the fright of the burglary and that she was now in the apartment alone flooded through her, jarring her nerves. She stood in the large living room and let the silence of the house fill her head like a roar. It wasn't even her house, and yet an awful sense of violation lingered in the air. Her heart began to race as she imagined where the burglar or burglars had stepped and what they had touched. What were they looking for? The numerous pieces of art on the walls were undisturbed. She walked to the office, where Jenny's files and other important documents were kept, and found it intact.

She wandered into the other room. The bathrooms were intact. If someone was looking for drugs, they would have surely rifled through the drawers and medicine cabinets, but they were just as she had left them. Jenny's master bedroom had obviously been searched. Drawers and closets were opened, but it wasn't until she entered the room where she was staying that she discovered the biggest mess. Her suitcase was opened and overturned. The bed she had made that morning was torn apart. The dresser and nightstand drawers were open and their contents spilled.

Madison's stomach clenched at the sight. She quickly went through the scene and inventoried what she could. Nothing jumped out as missing. However, the sudden realization that she was the target almost made her pass out. Whoever did this was explicitly looking for something Madison had. She shook her head, wondering what of value someone hoped to find from an unemployed journalist. Did they lie in wait until she was gone to make their move? Or did they know why she was there, as well as when she'd be away?

As she held the bag with the album she had just purchased, her thoughts turned to the photos. They were the only thing she could imagine someone going after. She had no money or anything of worth. The only thing she possessed that would rile someone to the point of desperation would be the possible exposure of the scandalous proof the photos supposedly held. Were they so damning that someone would risk doing this? And if so, who? Her father was the one facing scrutiny, and he wasn't even able to get out of bed, let alone commit burglary.

She quickly gathered her suitcase and left the condo. She made sure the door was locked but wondered what the point was. Whoever broke in could easily do it again, and that made her feel even better about staying at Morey's.

The drive was quick, and when she pulled down the lane to her uncle's farmhouse, her shell cracked. When he met her at her car, all it took was for him to ask if she was okay and the tears burst from her.

CHAPTER 19

The house was built in 1911 and was the family's original homestead. Madison's great-great-grandfather, Alford Woodruff, was the original owner. He and his wife Annie had eight children—seven girls and one boy. That boy was Madison's great-grandfather Thomas. He and his wife Ada added cherry trees to the already abundant apple orchard and had six children—three boys and three girls. The farm was then inherited by their oldest son Saul, for whom Madison's father was named. He took over the farm in 1961. He and his wife Leah had only been married two weeks when Thomas died, leaving them the orchards to tend. Ada lived with them until her death at the age of 82. Saul Sr. and Evelyn had six children—four girls and two boys, but only the two boys survived.

Madison knew the names and dates because of the regular discussions and importance placed on those who had come before. Their roots were as strong and deep as the rows of apple and cherry trees covering the one hundred and thirty-two acres of land.

Madison fondly remembered her time spent wandering the orchards and grazing on the season's ripe red fruits.

They came into the house from the back door. "It's never locked," Morey explained.

Of course it wasn't, Madison thought, shaking her head.

"How long have you lived here?" she asked, following Morey up the sturdy wooden stairs to the guest room.

It was the room where Morey and her father had slept as boys. Even in high school, they shared that room. Madison wondered where the other children would have slept if any of the other four had survived. The home only had two bedrooms. The kitchen and dining area were large, but the front room and the rest of the house were so small.

"Dad died in 2002. I moved in about a year before that to help him out." He stopped at the landing and looked over the front room.

The furniture was as she remembered—a small, floral sofa and a large blue chair, a china hutch filled with a collection of cups and matching saucers, and a long dining table with eight chairs made of oak that had darkened from time. The walls were still covered in barn wood, readily available and practical back then, and now it was considered rustic and artsy and was seen in the high-end salons and coffee shops all over Las Vegas.

Madison refrained from asking him if he planned to stay.

"I didn't have time to make up the bed," he apologized, showing her the folded sheets on the small dresser. "But at least they're clean."

Madison thanked him and took a seat on the bed. She pulled her long red hair back with a tie. "I feel like a stray."

He shook his head. "I'm glad you're here. The rare two percent need to stick together."

She smiled but still felt lost inside.

"This shouldn't have been your first time visiting since you got back," he continued. "But I understand."

And he was right. He was about the only one who ever did understand. He saw and accepted Madison for who she was, and she loved him for that.

He placed her suitcase on the floor next to her. The doorbell rang. "Pizza's here," he said, with a smile, and went downstairs to answer the door.

Madison glanced around the tiny room. It seemed so much bigger when she was there before. She stood up and went to the closet. Inside, was a box filled with painted wooden blocks and a few plastic green army men. In another container, she found stuffed animals and a doll. It was the toy closet, as her grandma used to say. This closet was the first place she went when her family came to visit the grandparents. "We're going to the farm," her father used to say, and Madison excitedly took her seat between her parents in the front of their wood-sided station wagon. It was a drive to the country. She smiled at how what she considered "the city" as a child was incredibly rural back then and still was today.

She went downstairs and joined Morey in the kitchen. He was grabbing plates and paper towels for napkins. She noticed the gun sitting on the counter near him. She sat as he put the dinner items on the table and then put the gun on the highest shelf in a tall cupboard.

"I'm not sure what I'll do with that," he said, wiping his hands on the front of his jeans.

"You said it was part of Grandpa's collection. Where are the others?" she asked.

He grimaced. "Sold. I needed the money when the housing market crashed. Besides, what do I need a cabinet full of old guns for?"

She smiled and agreed with him, but she also sensed his sadness with having to part with something that was obviously tied to his father.

"I would have bought beer or something if I had known, but the liquor store closes at five. And that's one thing they won't deliver."

Madison laughed. "You have to go to the liquor store to buy beer?"

"Good beer," he answered.

"Even though I could use a drink after today, it would probably just make me feel worse."

Morey looked down sadly. "I'm sorry about what happened. I left you a message on your phone."

"I got it," she said. "And I appreciate you. I don't know why I expected them to be different."

He nodded and tried to smile. "So, what is it that has them so upset? I know that Saul gave you some photos. What are they?"

Madison sat back and gave an exasperated sigh. "That's just it. They aren't anything. Just camping photos. Most are of trees and kids mugging for the camera."

"Can I see them?" he asked.

Madison shrugged. "Sure." She went upstairs and brought her tote back to the kitchen. She reached in and began placing them on the table.

"I went and bought a new album," she explained, as she shuffled around the pieces of the old one. She rummaged through the tote until she found the last of them.

Morey sorted through the photos, studying each one. Then he placed them together in a neat pile. "Is this all of them?" he asked.

Madison looked through her tote again and then nodded.

"There are only about a dozen shots. Not even a full roll of film. You sure?"

"Yes. That's all that was in the album. Why? What do you see?"

He gave a soft chuckle. "Nothing. I don't see what would have everyone so upset. What has them so worried?"

"I guess they're worried that Dad may be guilty of something, and it will make them look bad."

"Saul? Guilty. Of what?"

"Pushing that girl," said Madison, directly.

Morey's brow furrowed. "That can't be."

Madison nodded in agreement. "I know. It's hard to believe, but he said that Amelia is innocent and that he needs to confess and make things right."

"Did he confess?"

Madison rocked her head side to side in thought. "He said he needed to confess and that he needed to repent. He hasn't come right out and said he pushed her, but from what I've read in the court documents, he was the only one there who witnessed it. Or at least I think it was him." She then explained the redactions, initials, and his adamant stance that Amelia wasn't the one.

"Maybe he just imagines something. With his illness and the meds he's on, he could just think he remembers something." Morey flipped through the photos again. "I just don't see what the fuss is about. There's nothing here that would show what happened to Sara. What else have you found?"

"Not much. Just the court records and some newspaper articles." She thought about her upcoming visit with Amelia and wondered if she should tell him. "When Dad asked me to help him prove that Amelia didn't do it, I was intrigued. But along with the crap regarding my family, Jenny says even if my dad confesses to the murder, it will take a lot more for them to consider reopening the case."

Morey lifted his shoulders. "Has he told anyone else about this?"

Madison shook her head. "I don't think he's ever told anyone." Then she remembered her father telling her he had told his own father right after it happened, but she kept that to herself.

"What about Syd? Do you think he knows?"

Madison raised her eyebrows. "I don't think so. However, Syd has to act like he's in the middle of it. I think he's worried something will get out that will make him look bad or hurt his campaign. Why else would he be hanging around so much?"

"He wants to make sure the sale goes through." Morey hung his head. "When he gets his money, he'll be long gone."

Madison reeled back. "What sale?" Then she realized what he was referring to. "You mean the land, this land?"

Morey nodded. "He didn't get that rich by passing up an opportunity. Even if it means taking advantage of his own family."

"He's the one who arranged the sale?"

Morey nodded.

"What an ass." Madison sat and thought a moment. It was a difficult question, but she needed to know. "Is it true that grandpa gave everything to my dad?"

Morey scrunched his face as though it hurt to hear it. "Yes."

"Why would he do that?"

Morey gave her a knowing smile. "My punishment for not being the son that he wanted."

She shook her head. "What? You took care of him and this whole place. Didn't he see that? What did he want?"

He stopped her. "It's a bit more complicated, and there's nothing I can change now."

"You can fight it. It's not fair."

Morey gave a weary smile. "It's your fight now."

Madison then realized he knew what Natalie had told her. It was Madison who would be inheriting whatever proceeds came from the sale. Her breath halted. Could it really be true? Was her father giving her his fortune along with his confession?

"I don't believe he's giving it all to me. How could that possibly be? He disowned me years ago. I'll go to him and tell him to change it. I'll tell him to stop the sale."

"It's too late. It was done months ago. With your dad's state of mind, there is no changing it now. And besides, Syd seems to control everything."

Madison scoffed and rolled her eyes. "Augh. If I have to hear that name one more time. I know he's my uncle, but he drives me nuts. It's always been the amazing Syd Wallace." Then she paused. A chill hit her, and she repeated the name quietly. "Syd Wallace." Then she gasped. *S.W.* Had she really failed to associate the initials with it possibly being him? Syd was there at the camp. He admitted that to her the first day she saw him. And he was so reluctant to tell her who the boy was or even talk about what happened. And no wonder he wanted to keep the photos while trying to convince her to let the whole thing drop.

"What is it?" Morey asked.

She looked at him. She wondered frantically if she should tell him what she suspected. "Syd was at that camp, wasn't he?" she asked.

Morey looked down. "Yes. We should probably talk about that camp."

Her phone rang, and she jumped. Looking at the screen, she saw it was Jenny. Madison cringed, realizing she had forgotten to call her and give her an update on what the police had said regarding the break-in. She hadn't even told her she would be staying with Morey. "I need to take this," she said. He nodded, and she went to the upstairs room so she could unload what she'd found in private. She closed the door behind her and answered.

"I'll be home tomorrow," Jenny said.

Madison sighed. "I know you'd be welcome to stay here at Morey's until you get things secured at your place."

Jenny thanked her but declined. "I'll find a hotel until I can get some actual locks and a security system."

"It's about time," Madison scolded. "Do you need help?"

"No. Take care of what you need with your dad. But let's get together before you leave."

"Of course," said Madison. There was so much she wanted to tell Jenny, so rather than wait even a day, she poured out the new discoveries and what she suspected.

"I guess it makes sense," said Jenny. "You told me your

mom idolizes her brother. Maybe your dad was protecting him because of her."

Madison felt an angry burn start to rise in her face when she played back what Syd had said about her parents' loss of reputation if this got out. He had no concern for them. His own skin was all he cared about.

"Are you going to confront him about it?"

Madison sniffed. "He'd deny it. He's already trying to get me to quit digging."

"It's too bad you couldn't ask Amelia herself."

Then Madison realized she hadn't told Jenny about her impending visit with Amelia.

"What do you think she'll do when you tell her you know it was Syd?" asked Jenny. "Are you going to ask her why she pleaded guilty?"

"I don't know what will happen. She thinks I'm coming to talk about her poetry book. I hope I can at least tell her what I've found."

Jenny paused. "That's a big revelation. What then?"

It was a question that sat Madison back on her heels. What was her plan from that point? She had just assumed Amelia would be happy to hear that after decades seques- tered away, there was a glimmer of hope that she may be set free. The vision of Amelia hearing the evidence and a large smile spreading across her face in appreciation was the only thing Madison had expected. She hadn't considered that Amelia might not believe her or wouldn't want to hear what she had discovered. She was meeting her under false pre- tenses, and while her intentions were pure, what awaited her might be something completely different.

FORGOTTEN

Gray and beige. Clothes, walls, and food.
The muted life of one inside and forgotten.
Days fold into each other. No plans, no reasons.
Regret and shame. Like the person who holds them,
closed off, and kept safe.
Would I change the past? Would I reveal the lie?
Don't push. Don't pry. It's my truth to tell.

CHAPTER 20

adison barely slept. She played out scenarios of her early morning meeting with Amelia, over and over. In the morning, she told Morey she had to run some errands for Jenny regarding the break-in at the condo. She hated having to lie to him but wanted to keep the meeting with Amelia to herself until afterward.

When she was out the door and on the interstate that led to the prison, she felt her nerves begin to tighten. She would have to balance keeping up the half-truth Martha had told her daughter regarding the book, and stealthily revealing her real intention for the meeting.

Following Martha's directions on where to park and what door to enter, Madison was soon filling out paperwork, walking through metal detectors, and then waiting to be called back.

She imagined Sister Johnson each week, sitting in that same room waiting to see the daughter she loved regardless of what she had done. If Amelia was truly innocent, the revelation had the possibility of not only freeing Amelia from that prison but Martha, as well.

When the guard came in and called her name, Madison jumped, startled from her musing. She gathered her things and followed the indifferent woman to a room of small cubicles with seats separated by thick plastic shields and dropped into a hard chair.

When Amelia was led in, Madison felt her body tense as if she were starstruck. She had become so obsessed with this woman and her plight, it seemed unreal that she was actually seeing her in person. Amelia looked younger than her age, with shoulder-length dark brown, almost black hair, and large dark eyes. She was pretty and petite and looked nothing like a woman who could push someone to their death.

She took the seat across from her in the small cubicle, then gave Madison a nod.

Madison smiled and began to talk, forgetting there was a pane of thick plastic between them. Amelia motioned to the phone receiver hanging to her side, and Madison quickly grabbed hers.

"Sorry, I've never done this before," said Madison. It sounded awkward, and she apologized again. She groaned inside. *Always sorry.*

Amelia sat up straight. "My mother said you wanted to talk to me about my book?" she said. She seemed interested but also abrupt.

Madison cleared her throat, feeling the heat of her lie rising in her face. "Yes. I'm reading it now."

"She said you were a reporter? It's been a long time since it came out. Are you doing an article about it?"

Now that Madison was there with the woman at the center of her father's dilemma, she knew she had to get to the point, but she felt tentative and unsettled due to the ruse she and Sister Johnson used to get her there. "I'm originally from Orem. That's how I know your mother. I was interested in learning more." She took a breath. She hadn't completely lied and told her she was doing a story. "Tell me what made you decide on the subject matter of the poems."

Amelia shrugged. "I write what comes to me. I had written so many I decided to create a compilation. I feel the poems relate to what many people face."

The answer made Madison sit back. She hadn't really planned on discussing the book, only hoping to use it as a catalyst.

"Your mother said you used to write a lot. This book was published almost twenty years ago. Are you working on another book?"

Amelia thought a moment. "No."

"Why?"

"I have nothing more to say."

Madison cocked her head, surprised. And then she found herself with nothing more to ask, except for the real reason she was there. She cleared her throat, feeling the awkwardness forming. "I was also hoping I could talk to you about what happened that day at Echo Lake."

Amelia took a deep, long breath, and blew it out slowly, annoyed. "I don't talk about that day. My mother should have explained that."

"I know, but I have some information that might help you." She couldn't just say it. To come right out and exclaim that her father said he had proof she was innocent was too much. Madison felt the need to gauge her mindset first.

"Help me with what?" Amelia asked curtly.

What should be good news felt like a burden. Why did she feel so tentative about giving Amelia her father's revelation? She had the right to hear it. After spending years in prison, Amelia deserved that possible reprieve.

"There is someone who says they have proof that you weren't the one who pushed Sara off that cliff." It came out quickly and brusquely.

Before Madison could say anything more, Amelia's eyes shot wide, and she was standing. "You lied to me. You didn't come here about my book."

"Wait," Madison called to her. "Please, let me tell you what he said."

The guard walked over, seeing Amelia's distress. "Is everything okay?"

Madison nodded, and Amelia did as well, taking her seat. Her face was full of dread and fear. When the guard walked back to her post, Amelia put the phone back up to her face and whispered, "I don't want to hear it."

"Why? He wants to help you," Madison pleaded.

"Help me?" Amelia said, taking a seat and looking cautiously back toward the door and where the guard stood. "No one wants to help me. All they want is to get some notoriety from what happened. I've had dozens of you people trying to 'help' me." She used her fingers to emphasize the word. "I don't want your help. I want you to leave me alone."

Madison held up a hand in appeal. "But he says you're innocent. He says he has proof that you didn't kill that girl."

"Who's he? And proof?" she scoffed. "What proof could he possibly have?"

"There are photos and . . ."

Amelia shook her head, unconvinced. Her irritation was palpable.

Madison took a deep breath. "I think my uncle was the one who pushed Sara."

Amelia's face turned frustrated. "Your uncle?"

"Yes. My uncle is Syd Wallace." There it was. Madison sat, her skin buzzing as she waited for the reaction.

Amelia's brow pinched. "Who?" she asked.

Madison leaned forward as if Amelia would understand her more clearly. "Syd Wallace. He's my uncle." She waited for Amelia to gasp at hearing what Madison knew.

Instead, she shook her head. "I don't know who that is or what he's been telling you, but he doesn't know anything."

Madison sat back and bit her bottom lip, wondering where to go from here. "Syd Wallace wasn't the one who pushed her?"

Amelia had had enough. "No. Who are you? My mother said she knew you."

"Yes. We were her neighbors for years when I was young."

"What did you tell her about this?"

"I told her my father says you're innocent and has proof. She felt you should know."

Amelia leaned back unconvinced. "Your father? If he has proof, why isn't he here? Why go through you?"

"He's very sick. I think he's been afraid to tell who it was until now."

"Who's your father?" She then looked down at a small notebook in her hand. She tapped the top of the page with her pen. "It says your name is Madison Moore?" She raised her shoulders, confused.

Madison nodded. "Moore is my married name. My

maiden name is Woodruff and..."

Amelia's back straightened. "Woodruff," she said, low and with disdain. She looked at Madison and shook her head. "You're *his* daughter." She studied Madison with reproachful eyes. Her face went to stone as her glare circled Madison's face and head. "I should have known."

Seeing Amelia's reaction cemented her fears that her father really was the one. "Yes," muttered Madison. It came out as an apology.

Amelia twisted in her chair, agitated.

"He's dying. He has cancer. He asked me to try..." The words bubbled up and poured out.

Amelia scoffed. "So, he's dying and wants to make himself feel better. He has no right to talk about me." She stood up and began to place the phone back in the handset on the wall.

"He wants to confess. He wants to help you," Madison cried into the phone.

She shook her head, and a look of defiance spread over her. "Now he wants to help? He made me take the blame. You can tell him I hope he rots in hell." She slammed the phone into the handset and turned toward the guard.

Madison sat, stunned. She called out. "Wait!"

But Amelia couldn't hear her and was soon out of the room.

Still perplexed at what she'd heard, Madison slumped in the car in the prison parking lot and sat, unable to do anything but ponder what had happened. *He made me take the blame.* Amelia's statement looped in her mind. Amelia *was* innocent and what her father said was true. She pulled down the sun visor of the car and opened the mirror. Amelia's glare of comprehension confused Madison. What did she see that connected her to her father's terrible deed?

As she steered the car toward the exit of the prison parking lot, her phone rang. The number was her parents' landline. It was Madison's childhood phone number, one she still remembered. A terrible chill went over her, and she pulled the car to the side of the road. She answered the phone, and her mother's voice was garbled and broken.

It was two words, and their finality hit Madison like a punch. "He's gone."

When she arrived at the house, there were so many cars, Madison had to park up the street and walk. When she reached the front door, she knocked and a woman she didn't know answered.

"Can I help you?" the woman asked. Her face was somber but kind. She held a kitchen towel in her hands, as though she'd been cleaning.

"I'm Madison, his daughter."

At first, the woman looked suspicious, then her eyes popped. "Oh," she said. "Yes. Um, come in."

Inside, women scurried around in a sedate but resolved and coordinated dance of various chores. It was as though the house needed to be prepared for what came with death. They were the women from the ward, and they knew their assignments and were experts in doing their service.

Madison saw Natalie standing in the family room, speaking to yet another woman. Were there only women here? *Where are my brothers,* thought Madison, even though she was dreading the thought of seeing them. Natalie turned and saw Madison. She hesitated, but then came to her.

"I'm sorry, Madison," she said, with lowered eyes. She began to reach out but then held back.

Madison nodded and tried to accept her condolences.

Natalie's eyes began to well. "I'm sorry about everything. I didn't mean to cause you more problems with the family. I didn't know what to do."

Madison shrugged. What Natalie did was the least of her hurdles when it came to her family. It didn't help, but she was too tired to continue being angry with her.

"Where's my mom?" she asked.

Natalie motioned toward the hallway that led to the bedroom. "The family is in there." That's when she noticed Troy and Vince's wives huddled together at the fireplace.

"My mom and brothers are with him? Is he still in there?"

"Yes."

Madison's heart sank. She knew he was gone, but she didn't expect him to be lying there in that bed, in that room.

"I believe Syd is offering a blessing," Natalie continued. "You should be in there."

She took a deep breath and held it. She wanted to scream. Her family had gathered together, but of course, she was again on the outside. Even Syd was included. When she released the breath, it was a loud hiss.

Dismissing Natalie, Madison walked toward the room.

As she approached the door, it opened. Troy and Ben came out, and when they saw her, the hallway became cramped.

"The people from the mortuary will be here soon," Troy said. His words were awkward and halting. He stepped to the side, offering her a path into the room. Then Vince appeared at the door. When he saw her, his mouth curved into a sneer, and he backed up and away, but Madison stood tall and continued into the room, ignoring him.

Syd was at the bedside, and her mother was leaning over, straightening the sheets as if her husband was simply sleeping. When she looked up and saw Madison, her eyes showed both sorrow and relief.

"I'm so sorry, Mom," said Madison, walking toward her. Then she saw her father's sallow and frozen face. Her voice halted along with her heart. It wasn't him. It was a shell. The memory of the man she once thought was larger and stronger than life. Seeing his body, sunken and inert, actually gave her a sense of hope that his spirit truly did leave and would live on in a happier, better place.

For several minutes, she stood arm in arm with her mother, silently thinking and looking down on him. When the men from the mortuary arrived, the family removed themselves from the room, and met with the sympathetic faces of the women in the living room. They congregated around her mother, and instead of being left alone with her brothers and Syd, Madison stole away to her old room to find solace.

It wasn't long before the stretcher carrying her father's body covered in a purple velvet drape was wheeled by. She closed the door and watched through the window as they loaded it into the hearse and made their way slowly down the street. The house seemed to heave a sigh of release, and soon others made their way out the door and to their cars.

Small drizzles of rain crept down the glass as Madison peered out. A knock startled her, and she turned to find her mother peering into the room.

"I wasn't sure where you'd gone," she said softly. "Almost everyone has left."

Madison gave her a tired smile. "I just needed to be alone for a while."

Darlene nodded in understanding and then stepped into the room. She handed Madison a large manila envelope. "I found it in his desk when I was looking for some papers. It looks like he was planning to mail it to you a while ago. He didn't have your address and must have forgotten about it."

Madison took the envelope. It was sealed and stamped, and when she saw her name in his flowing script, she felt the burn in her nose and throat from stifled tears. She and Taylor had lived in the house in Boulder City for three years, yet her parents didn't know her address. She looked up at her mother and placed the package in her lap, letting her know she wanted to open it alone.

"I'm going to start cleaning up," said Darlene as she turned to the door.

"I'll be out to help you in a minute," Madison called to her.

Darlene gave her a muted smile and then pulled the door closed.

Madison sat on her childhood bed as she opened the envelope. Inside was a note, some newspaper clippings, and six strips of film negatives. She studied the negatives, trying to distinguish what they were by putting several of them up to the window's light. They were dark, and nothing was clear, but they looked similar to the photos from the album—trees, kids posing—nothing stood out. She set them aside and figured they were simply the negatives of the pictures she already had. Then she unfolded the letter.

> *Dear Maddie,*
> *I wanted so badly to be a good father to you, and I feel I've failed. Instead of following the still small voice within me, I allowed others' voices to determine my actions. I was wrong, and I wish I could take back all those years of neglect, when I should have been there for you. I know that an apology will never be enough, but I wanted you to know how sorry I am for abandoning you.*

There it was. The thing Madison had so desperately wanted to hear. So badly, she'd hoped for those words to come from his lips, but instead, they were on paper. Even though she knew from the time she'd spent with him that his regret was genuine, Madison wished she could have been able to look him in the eye and tell him he was forgiven. Tears welled in her eyes, and she took a moment to wipe them away so she could continue reading.

> *I also need your help. I'm sending you these newspaper clippings that I've kept all these years because I want you to help the girl they are written about. Her name is Amelia Johnson. She is in prison for murder, but I know she didn't do it. I should have spoken up years ago when I witnessed what*

happened, but I was afraid, and again, I allowed others to direct me instead of doing what was right.

These are photos that will show what happened that day. I hid them away, not wanting my cowardice to be exposed, but also to protect those I love. Please help me by doing what I couldn't do. Reveal the truth about Amelia Johnson and set her free.

Madison finished the letter and then just held it, touching the words of her father. She looked at the negatives again. Why couldn't he have just told her what happened? Why put her through the hassle of piecing together a puzzle if what he wanted was to confess what he'd done? And again, the question of why her? What made it so crucial that she ferret out the truth?

CHAPTER 21

enny sat reading the letter on the sofa of her condo, surrounded by the chaotic mess left by a stranger going
through her things.

Yet, Madison found it more peaceful than her family
home. She needed a few hours of calm before the funeral
the next day. She was also desperate to show her friend the
letter and tell her what took place at the prison, though she
held back her desire to inundate Jenny; it was the first time
either of them had been back to the condo or had a chance
to talk for any length since the break-in.

They'd gone from room to room, surveying the mess
and trying to determine what might have been taken. There
was nothing either of them could discern was missing. The
two of them then sat for hours talking, drinking wine, and
trying to make sense of what had finally come to a head
regarding Madison's father.

Now, Jenny turned the paper over as though she was
searching for more to help validate what Madison was facing. "I still don't understand how it could be your father. How
could he have pushed her and also be taking the photos?"

Madison considered this. "Maybe the photos were simply proof that he was there at that camp?"

Jenny shook her head. "But he isn't in any of the photos. He just took them and then kept them hidden all these

years. Maybe the person who killed Sara knows about the photos and wants to get them and destroy whatever they might show." She motioned to the room and the mess the burglar had left.

Madison's mind leaped to Syd. Maybe he was the one who broke in. It obviously wasn't her father. And Syd was at that camp and had the same initials as the boy in the court files.

"Amelia didn't recognize the name when I said 'Syd Wallace,' but maybe he went by a nickname. My dad said they all had them." Madison wanted it to be Syd and was grasping at anything that would point to him and away from her father.

Jenny appeared unconvinced. She sat up and chewed the side of her lip. "But if it was Syd, why wouldn't your dad have said something when it happened?"

"Because he wouldn't want to hurt my mom. Syd's her brother, and she idolizes him. My dad would want to protect her."

Jenny raised her brows in thought, but soon they lowered. "But your parents weren't married back then. Your dad would have had no reason to protect Syd if he had killed Sara. Besides, the people who seem to know what happened that day are your dad and Amelia, and the name she remembered wasn't Syd's, it was your father's."

"So, you think it was my dad?" Madison asked.

Jenny began to answer but then tilted her head and lifted a shoulder. "I'm not sure of anything when it comes to this case."

Madison slumped back into the sofa. "Me either. This whole thing's exhausting. Just thinking about it all. For years, he's pushed me away, and when he finally wants to confess that he killed someone, he welcomes me back." She took another sip of wine. "Now I'm here, and my brothers blame me for trying to ruin the family name. To make things worse, I find out my grandfather left everything to my father, and now my father has possibly left everything to me." She rubbed her temples. "And from the sale of farmland that I didn't even realize was valuable. I thought it was just a bunch of fields."

Yet, those acres of fields and trees were priceless to her. They held so many positive memories of her childhood. The rows of sturdy trunked trees with their branches opening up like bowls toward the sky, and the rich reds of both the cherries and apples tasted like nothing she found in the grocery stores or even the farmer's markets in Boulder City. Just the thought of them being bulldozed crushed her, left her feeling helpless knowing there was no stopping it. So many things she had come home to were disappointments, but what remained warm and whole in her heart—those elements of her childhood and family history that mattered— were being swept away like the dead leaves of autumn.

At the funeral the next morning, Madison found an isolated spot in the pew behind her mother. Her brothers and their families surrounded Darlene in a protective barrier of solemn rounded shoulders and lowered eyes. When Syd and Katie entered the chapel, they pushed in beside Madison, making her groan inwardly. Deep down, she had hoped that

Syd was to blame. It would have made her feel justified in all her years of disliking him. Now it brought her both guilt and angst. It wasn't Syd's name who Amelia remembered but her father's. *Woodruff* is what made Amelia's face flush with rage. Now Madison felt certain it was her father who had committed the crime. She had denied the fact and made up excuses to help her deal with what he was confessing, and now he was dead, and she was left shouldering his shame.

Morey came in late and sat on the other side, near the front. He leaned back and scanned the chapel; when he saw Madison, he gave her a comforting smile. Madison gave him a small smile in return and wished she was sitting next to him.

She was back in the familiar church. The wooden benches were shiny and simple, and the chapel's muted decor was bathed in the soft light that came through the large frosted windows. The coffin holding her father was at the front, draped in a large spray of orange and yellow carnations and sunflowers. Over a dozen other large arrangements were placed around the chapel, overwhelming Madison with the smell of the flowers. The sweet scent was so strong, she wondered if she would now associate the smell of flowers with death and no longer enjoy it.

I'm just a bundle of joy, she thought. But what better frame of mind to have at your father's funeral?

She held the program and stared at the smiling photo of her father, obviously taken before the illness had hit. His graying brown curls were cropped short, and he wore his traditional attire—dark suit, white shirt, and blue striped tie. It's what she always remembered him wearing. She wondered how many of the other men sitting in that church had closets filled with the same set of clothes.

She pressed her back against the hard bench and longed for Taylor. It had been over a week, and she was ready to be home.

Home. Sitting alone in that pew, she felt the significance of the word. For years, she had mourned her childhood home. The memories . . . the molding . . . this place and the people were bittersweet, deeply-entrenched components of her life, and now she knew what mattered wasn't determined by scenes from the past but rather the sense of belonging and going forward.

When the soft, melodic tune of the large pipe organ stopped, Syd stood and walked up the stairs to the pulpit. He gave a brief scan of the audience and then folded his arms and bowed his head to pray.

"Our dear Heavenly Father, we come here today to say good-bye to our cherished brother, father, grandfather, husband, and friend . . ."

The room was utterly silent as Syd spoke, except for a stray cough or stifled throat clearing. Madison listened to the prayer and realized she could have recited it herself. So many of the traditions and familiar sayings were etched in her memory. She looked around, and seeing her niece, Bethany, eyes open and scanning the church, had Madison choking down a laugh. When the two made eye contact, Bethany turned away quickly, squeezing her eyes shut.

When Syd finished, he looked up as though expecting applause, something that never happens in a Mormon chapel. Madison was surprised he didn't finish the prayer with "I'd like your vote" rather than "Amen." He gave the congregation another somber yet comforting gaze and then stepped down and took his seat in the pew. Katie patted his arm with approval, then an older man in the customary dark suit and tie stepped to the podium and introduced himself as the bishop of the ward. In the gentle and calm voice that many of the church leaders used, he spoke of the gift of eternal families and, that while Saul's passing was a sad time for those who would miss him on this earth, they would be reunited in the celestial kingdom.

"It will be a joyful time, when he will welcome you home to live with him for eternity." The man made sure to speak directly to Darlene, who nodded, teary-eyed but uplifted.

Traditional Mormon hymns were softly sung by those in attendance, as well as a rendition of "I Am a Child of God" by five of Saul and Darlene's grandchildren. And again, the message of being together in the afterlife was evident. The last line rang out: "Teach me all that I must do, to live with him someday." The words and melody were something Madison instinctively remembered. The songs she had sung as a small girl in Sunday school were still taught today. The familiar comforts of the words and music wafted around her like a blanket. It felt warm and good, and for the first time in years, she remembered why she had been so devoted to her religion and why it had been difficult to leave it behind. The feeling of belonging and being a part of what was preached as a grand plan toward salvation was comforting.

As she sat in that pew, the message of never losing a loved one and the promise of one day living again surrounded by those she cared about was intoxicating. The feelings of security it evoked made Madison realize why the pain of being cut off from all of that was so traumatic and why she had never wanted to come back.

The life sketch was given by Troy and was filled with Saul's constant devotion to teaching the gospel and the effect he had on those with whom he came into contact. He told stories about Saul's mishaps during camping trips, which brought laughter and sighs from the crowd, his love of ketchup, and the accolades and images he had taken with his photography.

The mention of cameras brought Madison back to the awful reality of what her father had taken besides photographs—a life. She imagined the difference in tone this service would have if the truth about what he had done was known.

Madison drifted off, overcome with anxious thoughts of how she would tell her mother about her father's terrible act. She wondered how Darlene would react when she learned the murderous secret of the man she had loved for almost forty years and now mourned. Would she blame Madison and accuse her of stomping on her father's grave? It was eventually going to come out. She was determined to follow through for Amelia's sake, but having her mother hear the details from someone other than Madison would simply be cruel. As she sat playing out the scenarios in her mind, she began to squirm, dreading the outcome and thinking how strange it was that during her only trip home, she would again reveal something that would upend her family and make her the target of their disdain.

She sat with Syd, Katie, and her mother in the long

white limousine that followed the hearse to the cemetery. Her brothers and their families had their own vehicles. The drive was silent; Madison's heart ached for Darlene as she thought about her spending her days in that house alone.

Walking to the gravesite, she put a hand on her mother's arm and was surprised when she leaned in and gave Madison a hug. They stood together as the others gathered around the draped grave and waited for the pallbearers to bring the casket from the hearse. Syd and Troy walked on opposite sides at the front, and Ben and Vince were positioned behind.

Morey was there but was the odd number and fell back to where he simply followed. Madison wondered why he didn't stand up and take his place as her father's only brother. Still, she also knew following behind was something he had become accustomed to over the years, and the funeral was not the opportune time to make a statement to the contrary. She would miss Morey and worried about what he would do when he was forced to leave the farmhouse and the land.

They had driven to the funeral separately. Madison planned to meet Jenny back at the condo when the day was over. The only positive about the break-in was the extra time at the farmhouse with her uncle.

The wind was cold, and her heels sunk in the moist grass as the family stood awkwardly together for photos beside the flower-adorned coffin.

Even with the funeral over and a large reception and lunch held afterward in the church, the procession followed back to the house, filling it with somber well-wishers. Madison was polite, but hearing the phrase "He's in a better place" was no longer comforting. It wasn't that she didn't believe in some type of afterlife, but after hearing the same thing being uttered by so many, it soon lost its sincerity and grated on her.

While trying to avoid her brothers, Madison meandered through the clusters of people, most giving her sympathetic smiles, but some looks of cynicism. "That's his daughter," she heard them whisper, and she knew what came next.

It had been over ten years since she'd left, first found guilty of her brother's accusations and then revealing that she no longer believed in her parents' church and its teachings. She'd been labeled a sinner and then an outcast. She tried to ignore what they said. Another reason she didn't visit. She'd been sparing her parents the awkward pain of trying to explain their wayward girl.

The crush of bodies was both stuffy and stifling; yet, even with the house being packed and humming with voices, she felt alone. She made her way through the kitchen and tugged open the sliding glass door to the outside patio. The air was cold, but it felt good to get out of the cramped and condescending mass.

The yard was almost unchanged from her time as a child. The trees were taller, and the wooden fence was sagging in spots, but she could envision herself as a child, running with her dog and doing cartwheels on the grass. And she also saw her father, standing at the grill, flipping burgers and humming hymns.

She stood looking up at the mountains and suddenly had an overwhelming urge for . . . something. A cigarette, maybe. She didn't smoke. She had never smoked, but at that moment, she needed a release and a rebellion. She took a deep breath of the cold air, then pretended it was a drag off a cigarette, slowly blowing it out and creating a smoke-like haze. It was childish and silly, and suddenly an enormous wash of guilt hit her as she recalled the disease that had just killed her father.

She put her hands into the pockets of her long sweater. Her fingers encountered the folded paper of her father's funeral program. She pulled it out and opened it. The list of participants was filled with her father's loved ones. Madison was listed with the family but wasn't asked to be part of the ceremony, and being the other black sheep in the family, neither was Morey. When she read the names of the pallbearers, he wasn't listed there, either. Instead, Syd, the brother-in-law, was listed first. Knowing her mother and Katie did the planning, it didn't surprise her. Next, her three brothers, the oldest grandson, Patrick, Troy's son, and then a Seymour Woodruff, were listed.

Madison squinted at the name. *Seymour Woodruff?* she thought, not remembering any of the grandsons or nephews with that name. There were many of the extended family that Madison didn't know, but if someone was listed prominently at her own father's funeral, she figured even with the years estranged, she should know who they were.

She heard the whoosh of the sliding glass door and turned to find Morey coming out to join her. "You okay?" he asked.

She shrugged.

Morey put his hands into the pockets of his jacket. "It's getting cold out here."

She gave him a halfhearted lift of her eyebrow and thought how fitting his remark was, considering how she felt inside the crowded but warm house.

He shuffled from one foot to the other. It was odd that he was that cold, she thought. After all, he was wearing a suit jacket, and Madison had only a light sweater.

"Have you given any more thought about what you're going to do?" he asked.

She knew what he meant. They hadn't spoken much about what she'd learned, about the photos or her father's confession. She hadn't told him about her meeting with Amelia or what she'd learned. The emotional chaos following her father's death and the plans for the funeral had kept them busy. She knew she would take the information to Daniel, but she wanted to speak to Jenny first. It was just one of the many uncertainties in her life, like going home in two days and having no idea what her plans were for finding employment.

And what about the other unanswered questions she'd had before she even stepped on any plane? What about a child? It was something she hadn't considered in so long, and yet now, as she was surrounded by reminders of why she had avoided being a parent, the idea kept creeping into her thoughts. She wondered if it was really what she wanted, or was a baby just a consolation prize?

She shook her head. "I wish I could forget about what my father told me," she said. "No one seems to care if Amelia is innocent. I don't even think she does. The only thing I know I'd be accomplishing is pissing my family off even more."

"I think you're right. I'm sorry that things got ugly with the others," he said, rubbing his hands together. "I had hoped it would be different."

Madison shrugged. There was nothing either of them could do to change things. For a moment, they both stood in silence. What more was there to say? Madison held up the program. "Who is Seymour Woodruff?" she asked.

Morey leaned his head back and groaned. "Why do they always have to use your given name with these things?"

Madison looked at him, confused.

He pointed at himself and smiled. Then, the realization hit her.

"You're Seymour," she asked. "Morey's a nickname?"

He gave an exasperated chuckle. "And it's not like they named me after anyone. Who names their kid Seymour?"

Another person with a nickname? she thought. Her father was right when he said they all had them.

Then, as they stood with the breeze swirling the dry leaves on the concrete patio, the initials from the court documents flashed into Madison's mind, and her heart sank. "S.W. Seymour Woodruff." She said it under her breath and then again in her head, hoping it wasn't true.

"What was that?" he asked.

She continued to look at the program to keep from having to make eye contact. *S.W.* Her mind began to race with the things her father had said. Was it Morey he had been protecting all these years? Amelia had reacted to the name Woodruff. But . . . was *Morey* the Woodruff she remembered? And what about the way she saw something in Madison—the studied look she gave her? Was it her distinct red hair, the same color as Morey's? *We're the rare two percent*, he always said.

"My God," Madison gasped, as the awareness settled it. She looked up at him. "It was you."

He cocked his head and gave a confused wince. "What was me?"

"You're the one they were fighting over at Echo Lake. It was you."

His face went from quizzical to fearful. He started to speak but instead glanced back toward the house. "I was going to talk to you . . ."

Madison saw his unmistakable guilt. "You made both those girls think you cared about them, and then, when you were found out, you not only pushed one of the poor girls to her death, you let the other one take the blame and rot in prison."

"Madison, I didn't kill that girl . . . That's not how it happened," he stuttered.

Beads of sweat formed on his face as she watched him squirm and reveal his culpability.

"I've been running around trying to get answers and all this time..." She could hardly get out what she wanted to say. She wanted to shake him, to release what he had kept bottled inside. But she also felt the need to flee, before finding out anything more. Her breathing was shallow, her chest was seizing. The bitter realization rose in her throat.

"Madison, I know this looks bad, but please listen to me." He reached out to her, and she recoiled, giving him a glare of disdain. All these years, she had trusted him. The last person she felt connected to in her family had shattered everything.

She tore through the house without acknowledging anyone or being aware they were even there. She could hear her name being called but didn't look back for fear it was him chasing after her.

She was in the car and driving toward Jenny's when she realized her things were at Morey's. *Seymour's.* Again, the wave of betrayal shook her, and she had to tell herself to breathe. She called Jenny as she drove, and without explaining what had taken place, begged her to come and pick her up at the farmhouse.

Madison decided to park behind the house. She quickly made her way to the back door that was never locked and, once inside, ran to the upstairs room. After shoving everything into her suitcase and tote, she went back to the front room and peered out the window, silently willing Jenny to drive faster. She feared Morey would try to get to her, knowing the secret she held and what he might do to keep it hidden. Madison didn't know what he was capable of. She didn't know him at all.

She was reaching high into the cupboard when he came through the back door.

He stopped, red-faced, gasping for breath, when he saw her holding the gun. "Madison, please listen ..."

"Stay back," she warned. She held the gun and raised it slowly toward him. Her broken heart was racing, and the gun trembled in her hands.

"I didn't do what you think. I didn't kill her," he pleaded. "You have to believe me."

"It was you who broke into Jenny's house. You wanted my dad's photos because you knew he was there at that cliff and saw what happened." She shook her head, and closed her eyes hard to stave back tears. "I trusted you. No more."

He spread his arms wide. He held out his chest to her. "If you aren't going to listen to me, just shoot me now. Don't think I haven't thought about it myself at least a million times."

A knock at the door made Madison jump. She glanced through the small window and saw it was Jenny. Holding the gun on her uncle, she moved quickly to unlock the door.

Jenny's eyes went wide when she saw Madison holding the gun.

"What are you doing?" she asked.

"Help me with this," Madison said, motioning for her to pick up her suitcase. Jenny leaned into the house and lifted it, but did a double-take when she made eye contact with Morey, leaning against the kitchen counter.

He was slumped and defeated, his eyes wet.

Jenny looked back to Madison. "What's going on?"

Madison didn't answer, only saying, "Let's go." She pushed out the door and quickly piled her things into the back seat of Jenny's car.

"What happened? What's with the gun?" Jenny asked when they were both in the car, and Morey was nowhere in sight.

"Please, just drive. I'll tell you later," said Madison urgently. "I need to get away from here quickly." She sank into the passenger seat and tossed the gun into her tote. As they turned onto the main road, she let her breath release and her guard down. She stared wildly out over the land that was once her favorite place to be. "It was him," she said.

Jenny looked over in shock. "Morey? No."

Madison put her hands to her head. "Yes. It was him. He was the one."

"How do you know? Did he admit it?" Jenny asked, having a hard time keeping her eyes on the road.

Barely able to speak or even think, Madison just sat and let what she had learned settle into her soul. It wasn't only the knowledge that her uncle had killed Sara but the betrayal of him knowing the truth while she agonized, thinking it was her father. And then there was Amelia. Truly innocent and spending years being vilified and locked away.

HIM

Flutter of the aspen leaves, yellow flashes white.
Scent of Baby Soft and pine, float in sun-burnt sky.
Hushed words tipped in sin that may reveal too much.
Stolen moments, shy and new. Lightly, fingers touch.
Does he notice, will he see, what burns so deep inside?
No looks should linger or reveal.
Smiling eyes are what we hide.
So much at stake because this love
comes with a heavy cost.
Risking all for what we know and surely will be lost.
Steal away to shelter from the harsh and glaring light.
Took a chance to be as one and hold each other tight.
Assumed to be hidden, far from them, up here high above.
Guards come down. Emotions rise. Careless show of love.
Smooth skin, hair of silk, dewy cheeks from tears.
Deep sighs, questions, lies, and culminating fears.
Whispered promise for secrets kept,
in dread of being caught.
Crunch of needles underfoot, but hear them we did not.
Followed at a creeper's pace until the light turned dim.
No escape and life now lost. All because of him.

CHAPTER 22

For hours, the two friends sat and mulled over the awful situation. There were few words, just quiet contemplation of what Madison had ultimately revealed.

They were back at the condo. Jenny hadn't had time to do anything new in the way of security or alarms, but Madison didn't care. With everything that had taken place, she knew the only place she would ever truly feel safe again was with Taylor.

During Madison's phone call home, Jenny sat and let the new information sink in. Madison had explained the events again, giving Jenny the chance to consider, as an attorney rather than a friend, what avenues she might have. There was still no concrete proof, just initials, Amelia's reaction to the name Woodruff, and Morey's lack of total denial. He hadn't admitted to pushing Sara. He hadn't admitted to anything.

Nothing Jenny could say would sway Madison's determination that her uncle was guilty, at least at that moment, and Jenny stayed silent as if processing what she'd learned. The avalanche of misfortune that had afflicted Madison was so overwhelming, and she needed time to digest not just what she thought Morey had done but also her father's recent death. Having just lost him, so much of Madison's sorrow was that he died, never knowing if she had given him his final wish.

Jenny helped Madison take her suitcase and tote back to the guest room.

"What's in this thing?" Jenny asked as she picked up the heavy bag. "It weighs a ton."

Madison rolled her eyes, not at Jenny, but at the amassed stash of dread the tote held. Along with her wallet, laptop, lip gloss, and other essentials were also the puzzle pieces she had secured away during her quest for the truth—the photos and broken album, the proofs, the new album, Amelia's book, the envelopes with her father's letter and negatives . . . and the gun.

While Jenny made tea, Madison removed the brown bag that held the gun from her tote. She placed it on the bed, but then remembered the note that was also in that bag. She brought it out and unfolded it. There was the large, rounded cursive signature with a simple but swooping *S*. But now she wondered if it was Seymour, not Sarah, who wrote that note.

The angst in the letter, as she read it over again, was raw. *Some days I want to die.* She lifted the gun out, and a chill shook her with what she imagined. Was it Morey who was filled with so much pain? Was the gun something he planned to turn on himself, and was that why her father had taken it and kept it hidden? Why else would her father keep the note and gun together? The chill of seeing her own brother contemplate that gun made her shiver. She wondered when the nickname Morey had come about and if he had decided to go with the nickname, knowing his real name might tie him to the crime.

Madison wondered if Morey was somewhere in the photos. She realized she had never considered looking for *him* as she'd studied the images. Had he been hiding in plain sight as she searched for clues?

She dug out the old tattered album, the new album, and the photos, and placed everything on the bed. Removing the craft store album's plastic packaging, she carefully began arranging and putting the pictures in their new home. Having a number of the slots unfilled, she remembered Morey's comment about how few there were and that it wasn't even a full roll of film. Again, she searched the purse for more but found nothing else.

She counted the photos—fourteen. There were ten empty slots. Considering the number of exposures on a roll of 35-millimeter film, it was odd that almost half were missing. She again rummaged through her tote, eventually dumping everything out to make sure she wasn't failing to find any missing photos.

With the scattered contents laid out and accounted for, she shrugged. That was all of it. There were no other photos, and none of the proof her father had so adamantly professed she would find.

Disappointed but accepting the fact, she gathered up the pieces of the old, empty album and folded them together so it would fit in the trash can. The old brittle cover snapped easily, showing decades of wear, and as she pushed it down into the mass of crumpled papers and other trash in the can, she noticed something protruding from the broken cardboard slip of the back cover. With just the corner visible, it appeared to be another photo.

She retrieved the piece from the trash can and carefully drew out what was peeking from behind the flap. It was a page of small, black-and-white images, six in total. There were pine trees, a far-off lake, and young people, one of whom she recognized immediately. She studied each frame carefully. When she got to number three, she felt her breathing become laborious, and her heart begin to race. At photo number six, putting a hand to her mouth to keep her horrified gasp contained, she shook her head in disbelief.

Her eyes began to sting as tears welled, and her throat tightened.

"Proof," she whispered. What she held was literally that. It was the proof her father had been searching for—a proof sheet of six photographs. The images were black-and-white and weren't crystal clear, but they revealed what happened that day with unmistakable clarity.

In a frame-by-frame sequence, the photos showed that Amelia was nowhere near Sara when she fell from that cliff, the horrifying last shot showing the moment Sara went over the edge. But that wasn't the only thing Madison found in those hidden pictures. And what it exposed was even more shocking.

Her phone had been going off for hours. Morey had left several messages. "Madison, please believe me. I didn't push that girl," he pleaded.

What he said was true.

It wasn't Morey who pushed Sara. It also wasn't Saul, and it wasn't Amelia. It wasn't anyone. The photos showed Sara was far away from them when she fell from the cliff.

Was she really seeing it correctly? The proof photos showed where Sara was standing, and almost out of the frame were both Morey and Amelia. Maybe the image was distorted or the distance skewed, but from the onset, it looked apparent that Sara had simply stepped off the edge and ended her life.

There was a fight. That part was true. But during the struggle between Morey and Amelia, neither of them was aware nor anywhere near Sara. She wasn't part of it. A letter was the source of their frenzy. Morey was the last to have it, and he held it high, victoriously, while Amelia reached for it. Was that *the* letter her father was also hiding? She picked up the letter again and read it over.

I don't know what to do. Some days I want to die. I'm scared, but the one thing I know is that I love you. That will never stop. But I'm so afraid about what will happen if they find out what we've done. No one can find out. If I act weird, please don't think I am mad or that I no longer love you. It's only because I don't want anyone to ever know. Someday, we will be together. Remember, I will always love you.
Love, S

Some days I want to die. That line continued to ring in Madison's mind. With the proofs showing Sara taking her own life, she was now even more convinced that the letter had been written by her. She and Morey had not only betrayed Amelia but had done something Sara was both ashamed of and terrified that others would find out.

Again, Madison assumed it was sex and the repercussions that would have in regards to her beliefs. Was Sara pregnant? Did she have an abortion? Madison sat back; a dizzying realization swirled through her head. Was that the reason her father wanted her to know the truth?

Madison imagined Amelia had come upon the two and tried to get the letter, proof of their infidelity. Amelia was angry with them both. She had discovered her best friend with her boyfriend. Sara, distraught and guilt-ridden, couldn't live with what she'd done, not to mention the shame when others learned of her sin.

As the scenes in the proofs progressed, it was as if Sara left the fray and surreptitiously slipped closer to the brink. And then, with Amelia and Morey distracted and fighting for the letter, Sara stepped off the edge and was gone. In the final frame, only a wisp of blonde hair appeared above the rim. The sight was both horrifying and oddly whimsical. Amelia and Morey were far from her, both physically and consciously.

But while the photos showed the sequence of events that day, and the complete lack of fault regarding Sara's death, Morey Woodruff was far from innocent. The proof sheet showed clearly that Morey didn't end Sara's life, but he did nothing to save Amelia's. That was also her father's shame. It was what he regretted and wanted to confess. They both allowed Amelia to shoulder the blame and spend her life in prison. Now Madison had the proof and knew the truth about Sara's death. What she didn't know was why. Amelia was behind bars. She confessed, and both Morey and her father let her take the blame for something that didn't happen, even though they all knew the truth.

"Now what?" That was the debilitating unknown. "What do I do?" Madison asked as she and Jenny sat on the bed, studying the proof sheet.

"You call Daniel," said Jenny quickly. "You show him what you've found. He's obligated to advise the court, as well as Amelia, of this new evidence. There is a professional conduct rule. I'm not a prosecutor, but I know that he has to show any evidence that might prove innocence in a case, and because it's his jurisdiction, he'll have to remedy the conviction."

It sounded like lawyer-speak, and even though Madison dreaded that call, she knew it was inevitable. "I'll call him," she assured her.

"What about Morey? Are you going to talk to him?" Jenny asked carefully.

Madison flinched at the thought.

"He obviously didn't kill Sara," Jenny continued. "And even though he didn't help Amelia, we don't know what really happened. I think you should tell him what you've found and at least hear him out."

All those years of Morey keeping it hidden were so calculated that Madison's lifelong adoration and trust in him had been ruined and replaced with a grim fear of what he might do to keep his shame a secret. It was the reason when she was frantically packing up her things that she went to the kitchen and took the gun she had watched him place in the cupboard.

"Do you think Morey will be charged with anything?" Madison asked. Madison could only imagine the shame and regret Morey had felt for decades. At least she hoped it was how he felt. He was young when it happened and obviously scared, and even though he could have explained it to the authorities, he was probably convinced he would somehow face the blame. After all, he was the one who had deceived both those girls into thinking they were the one. To think he had pulled off such a lie and then to see the horrifying consequence of that lie would surely be traumatic. What he did wasn't right, but Madison couldn't help but feel the angst and confusion of what he'd kept hidden for so long.

Madison sighed. There was a question that continued to dig at her: Why?

Why did Amelia take the blame?

CHAPTER 23

Holding the proof up, Madison said, "I still can't imagine a girl that age looking down a huge cliff and deciding to jump. I know young people end their lives, but with girls, it isn't usually guns or jumping off a cliff. It's usually pills or something..." she paused, trying to choose the right words. "... less violent." She scrunched her face at the oddity of what she'd said. It was suicide. It was violent regardless of what form it took. "I mean ..."

Jenny put up a hand. "I know what you mean. It does seem like a strange way to choose to die, but maybe the situation played a part. Maybe she was so upset that she acted on emotion and opportunity. She was probably so devastated knowing that her best friend now hated her. At that age, it would seem like the end of the world. Instead of facing what she had done, Sara just killed herself."

"But they were teenagers," countered Madison. "This wasn't a real relationship. It was at most a crush."

Jenny sat back and tilted her head at Madison. "No teenager has ever felt it's just a crush. You know that."

Madison raised her eyebrows. "Yes, but that was different."

"Was it?" She took the photo and looked at it. "I think Sara was so devastated that she acted on passion."

It made sense, and yet it didn't. Madison studied the

photo again. She couldn't imagine the young girl stepping off that cliff on her own accord.

Jenny then squinted closer, examining one of the photos. "What is it?" Madison asked.

"What's in Morey's hand? It looks like a piece of paper."

Madison reached for the letter. "I think it's this," she said, handing it to Jenny. "This letter was in the bag with the gun. It's signed with an *S*, so at first, I thought either my father or Sara wrote it. When I learned that Morey was actually Seymour, I thought it might be him. But now, seeing that Sara killed herself, I think it has to be her. It's been torn, and part of it is missing, but..." she pulled her reading glasses from atop her head and read, *"Some days I want to die."* She looked up sadly. "I think that's pretty telling."

Jenny read the note and then looked at the other photos. "That's got to be what they're fighting over. It makes sense since it was proof of the affair."

"Affair?" Madison rolled her eyes. "Morey and Sara were kids. And it still doesn't explain why Amelia would confess to pushing Sara. I don't understand that at all."

Jenny nodded in agreement and continued to study the proofs. "Look at where they are. Even in black-and-white, you can see how immense it was. I can't believe they were even allowed to go up somewhere that high and dangerous. Weren't there any adults watching these kids?"

Madison turned to Jenny. "Have you ever been up there?"

"I've been to Echo Lake, but not up along the cliffs where they were. Aspen Veil was a church camp. Remember, I wasn't part of the club."

So often, Madison forgot how much of an outsider her closest friend was because Jenny's family hadn't attended the "right" church.

"What about you?" Jenny asked.

Madison gave a sad, reflective smile. "I was never allowed to go. I went to girl's camp at Cherry Creek, but never to Aspen Veil. My dad never allowed any of us to attend. At the time, I was really mad at him about it. He said that there weren't enough chaperones. You know, boys and girls actually sleeping over at the same time."

"They weren't in the same barracks, were they?"

Madison scoffed. "Oh, hell no, but that was his excuse. And yet, he never volunteered to go and be a chaperone." She sighed. "I remember even my mom thought it was over the top."

Jenny's eyes went wide. "*Aretha* thought it was over the top? Wow, that's saying something."

Madison laughed. "Yes. But now it kind of makes sense why he didn't want any part of it. With the memories of all that happened there and what he witnessed."

They sat and pondered it—the frantic scene in the photos and Sara's last moments of life. Saul was there. He'd captured it on film while witnessing the tragedy.

"Do you want to go up and see it?" Jenny asked.

"Aspen Veil?"

"Yes. Aren't you curious?"

Madison's brows furrowed. Initially, she was put off at the thought, but then a sense of intrigue came over her. "You mean, go out to the overlook?"

"Yes," Jenny said, motioning to the photos. "Your flight

isn't for two days. It would be nice to get out. And don't you want to see where this all took place?"

Madison took a deep breath. It wasn't so much the idea of seeing where the horrible tragedy happened, but experiencing the place that had haunted her father for decades. She didn't expect to find new answers. It was merely to be there, to stand where they stood and wonder why.

The narrow road winding up Provo Canyon was bordered by the crimson and golden colors of autumn. Hues were rich and so vibrant it seemed an odd contrast knowing their arrival was nature's display of death. The drive was oddly silent, especially for two friends who had rarely seen each other in years. They had forged their own paths but had held onto their ties to each other. It was a solid bond that should have been unlikely, considering what had happened between them, but it remained strong.

Madison's parents never approved, and when her revelation took place, their distaste for Jenny grew. Madison refused to let them blame Jenny, but nothing would change their ideas of what caused her destructive downfall. And even years later, after years of success and triumph, they still saw only rebellion and worldly influences. Jenny knew her part in it, and yet never balked at their accusations or even held a grudge.

Madison looked over to her resilient friend, her tanned and toned arms glistening in the sunlight. Jenny lifted her eyebrows and gave her a big "we're going on an adventure" grin.

Pulling down the paved path leading into the camp, Jenny squinted and then groaned. "That gate is huge."

Madison sighed. "And it's chained. Oh, well ..." she said, relenting.

Jenny scoffed. "We're hiking. We'll park down away and hike in."

"We don't even know exactly where we're going. How are we going to find it if we don't take the path from the camp?"

Jenny rolled her eyes. "We are going to hike into the camp from around the back. They can't fence in the entire camp. If we get caught, we'll say we got lost."

Madison didn't argue but hoped Jenny's legal mind knew what she was doing.

Jenny parked. She produced a backpack and handed Madison a smaller fanny pack and a water bottle. "It can't be much of a hike, so this should be fine."

Finding a clearing in the trees, they started off toward the compound. The fence attached to the gate went partially around, but it was easy for them to find access from the woods. Once in, they cautiously walked through the empty camp and around the old barracks. It was early November, which meant the campers were in school.

"The court records say they used a trail that started just behind the main lodge," said Madison pointing at the large log structure that was obviously the focal point of the complex.

They walked to it and searched the back area for signs of a trail. In the thick brush, they found a sign informing campers of the rules to stay within the camp's boundaries unless escorted by a camp guide.

"I'm surprised they didn't put a picture of the weeping lover on the sign to scare them into staying away," Jenny giggled.

Madison shook her head. "It's the Leaping Lover, not Weeping," she corrected her. "And the ghost story may be intriguing enough to get them to break the rules."

Jenny then pointed to the area just beyond the sign. "Look. I think that's it, or at least the remnants of it."

Madison followed, and they stepped into the dry grasses and up a small path scratched into the dirt and brush. The trail was thin but visible and soon turned steep. They both found themselves sliding along with the loose rocks and sand as they climbed. They continued as the path turned to a narrow switchback through thick woods.

Madison's heart was thumping. She was anxious about where they were headed but also surprised at the steep and uneven terrain. *The view must be incredible for young kids to make this type of trek*, she thought.

"If this trail wasn't as obvious as it is, I would think we went the wrong way," said Jenny. The trail seemed challenging even to her, an experienced hiker.

And then, as they reached the top, through the shaded and dense forest, they saw the deep, clear blue of the sky. Madison felt her breath catch at the sight of it.

"Look!" Jenny exclaimed, hands on knees, panting.

They struggled forward, and soon, the path opened up, leading to the overlook. The large, thin pines buffered the view like the curtains of a stage.

"It's incredible," said Madison, looking out over the vista. The overlook was a small, flat mesa elevated high above the green-blue shimmer of Echo Lake.

Jenny walked to the edge, and Madison felt her heart leap. She was uncomfortable with heights and was fine standing back to experience the view.

Jenny turned back to her. "I see why they would want to be here. Young lovers, sneaking away from everyone else, to sit and look out over all this." Then she pointed to an area near the edge. It was a natural alcove chiseled into the rock of the cliff by centuries of wind. "I bet they were snuggled up in there when Amelia found them together."

Madison's reverie with the view came to a halt when the reality of why they were there and what happened next hit her. She felt a chill and looked at Jenny. For a moment, they shared a common thought of how this melded in with their own lives. It was like a gut punch. Jenny's face turned reflective and sad. She cocked her head in question but didn't speak. She didn't have to. Madison knew that Jenny had also been forced to remember when their past was the source of confrontation and sorrow.

Jenny walked toward the edge.

"Be careful," said Madison, nervously. She hated heights, and while the view was incredible, the awe was replaced by a growing angst in her gut.

Jenny turned to her with an unconcerned smile, and when she turned back, her toe caught a small indentation of the rock surface, and she stumbled forward, arms flailing out as her legs buckled.

Madison watched as if it were in slow motion. Her chest seized.

Jenny landed on all-fours just inches from the cliff edge,

and before she could take a breath of relief, Madison was crouched down and gasping in terror.

Jenny may have been the one who almost went over the edge, but it was she who went to Madison to comfort her.

"I'm sorry," said Jenny.

Madison looked at her perplexed and shaken.

"I'm sorry about everything."

Madison felt her shell shatter. The emotions came roiling up like a geyser. So much confusion and betrayal. She knew coming home would be hard, but she had no idea of the wound she would uncover and how quickly it would fester.

As the sun began to hide beneath the crest of the mountain, the two sat huddled, unable to speak. The tears on Madison's cheeks turned cold, and that was when it was time to make their way back down the trail.

"Are you okay?" Jenny asked her as they braced each other to standing.

Madison gave an unconvincing nod. She felt poised for the next terrible thing to happen. She wondered how she would ever be able to move forward, unsure what direction would ever be right, convinced any step she took would have her hurdling toward the edge.

THE FALL

Crisp orange and red remove the spring.
It calls of cold and snow to bring.
Steal away in a secret nest,
and forbidden boundaries there to test.
From that vantage high above,
there are two so much in love.
Comes a threat and much dismay.
Lost and defeated, one fades away.
As she ponders there on high,
she steps into the unforgiving sky.
Crushing sorrow, angst, and shame.
One left behind and one to blame.
As any who could watch and see,
the loss is hers, the guilt is he.
And that which perished forever gone,
will rise again and see the dawn.
For love persists past earthly strife
and becomes anew in the afterlife.
Be strong in sorrow and in grief,
and keep faith close, avoid hope's thief.
The hurt remains, and echoes call
to remind her of her lover's fall.

CHAPTER 24

Madison closed the book and sat back with a gasp. "Echoes call. Her lover's fall," she whispered to herself, contemplating the last line of the poem. She then flipped back through the pages. She paused on another poem and read, "As any who could watch and see, the loss is hers, the guilt is he." She sat, stunned. These weren't just verses Amelia had written; these poems were the cryptic and tragic tale of Amelia's own life.

She leaned back and released the breath she hadn't realized she was holding and then stared at the book, wondering how she could have read so far without it becoming obvious. The hands covered in blood was the guilt Amelia had been carrying since before the accident. The prose described what really happened that day. The fall from the cliff, who was really to blame, and how Amelia had shouldered the guilt. She hadn't pushed Sara, but in her heart, she felt she had.

Again, she studied the cover. "Millie Juarez—Amelia," she repeated the names, as her father's musing about nicknames flooded back to her. *It was as though they knew they'd have something to hide.* Madison pondered this a moment, wondering why that idea pricked at her so. She had the evidence to prove Amelia was innocent, and yet, she was tormented with the unanswered questions surrounding her confession. Why would she take the blame for something she didn't do? Or did she actually feel she was at fault simply because of social norms? It was an eerie parallel of her own mottled past. She, too, had taken the blame for someone else's transgression in an attempt to hide her own. So, why did she find it hard to believe Amelia would do the same? The idea bore a hole in her soul as she tried to answer that question.

Daniel recused himself from Amelia's case. The prosecutor who was assigned looked at the evidence, along with Amelia's time served, and then declined to retry her for the murder of Sara Voorhees. After months of post-conviction hearings and other legal loopholes, the photos, and Morey's testimony, along with Amelia's new statement to what happened that day, was eventually enough to exonerate her. Even Sara's family supported the court's decision.

Madison had turned over the evidence she had gathered to an attorney Jenny knew from the Utah Justice Alliance. She then stepped away. Except for a few phone calls with Martha and regular updates from Jenny, Madison felt it was best to remove herself from whatever notoriety may come from her family's involvement. She felt good knowing that Amelia would finally live outside the prison walls but unsure how "normal" her life would ever be.

Morey eventually admitted to what happened that day. However, even with the evidence showing Sara wasn't pushed off the cliff, some were demanding justice in the form of someone's head, and with Madison's father now dead, the fingers pointed to Morey. The proof showed he hadn't touched Sara, let alone pushed her, but his silence over the years was viewed as being complicit when it came to the other victim in the tragic story. With the loss of the farmhouse and the community's indignation, he left the place he had always called home and moved to another state to escape the scorn.

Madison was initially angry at him for what he didn't do and felt his compliance and regret were forced. Her father's decades of silence was also a source of disappointment. He had the proof to free Amelia but kept it hidden. Thinking about what he did started the anger to rise in her chest, but just as quickly, the reality of his death would set in. What good was being angry with him now? She at least knew he'd felt remorse.

Even with the unmistakable verification of the events of that day, her mission to seek out the full truth and bring justice to someone wrongly convicted had been a challenge. Not only did she have to convince the legal system to consider the new evidence, but also the very person who falsely confessed to the murder.

So sure of her place in that prison was Amelia that one time they spoke, Madison was surprised when she heard that Amelia was finally working with the attorney.

Strangely, it was Amelia who accepted Morey's apology and refused to see charges or any other form of punishment befall him. She wanted him to fade into the background as much as she hoped to.

Madison was surprised when Amelia cooperated in her exoneration. She'd initially refused to testify and wanted

Madison and everyone else to leave her alone. But without her testimony, the case would be hard to prove, with her confession being the crux of the state's evidence against her. She eventually told the court, through her attorney, that she was traumatized by what she saw that day, and along with being angry, felt no one would believe that Sara had taken her own life.

Some still felt she was guilty, even with a witness and photographic proof, but regardless, the court agreed to hear the case and eventually ruled in her favor. And yet, for Madison, the contentment of knowing Amelia would be free and seeing her father's dying wish come true was tarnished; a piece of her closure was missing.

A year and six months later, Madison was back at the prison visiting area. It was the morning of the day Amelia was scheduled to walk from the gates of the prison and begin her new life as one of the exonerated.

Madison now knew why Amelia refused to come forward. It made sense as to why her father felt she was the one who would diligently try to help.

Madison walked into the prison, holding the proof. Not the six black-and-white photos showing how Sara really died, but four more Madison had processed from the negatives in the envelope with the apology letter from her father. These four were the start of that sequence of events on that fateful day, the reason Amelia took the fall along with Sara. While Amelia may have felt she deserved her sentence,

Madison now held the vital evidence that her guilt was not only inaccurate but based on something that had nothing to do with Sara's death. It was instead an inner shame that Madison herself tragically understood.

Madison and Taylor had stood shoulder to shoulder in the darkroom as the four missing photos became clear. She'd already helped prove Amelia's innocence with the six images showing Sara taking that step off the cliff, alone and of her own volition, but for Madison, that wasn't enough.

When Madison returned home, she spent nights lying awake, going over the checklist of evidence and clues she had gathered. The letters, the initials, nicknames, and of course, the proof sheet. She thought about the photos in the album.

It was still dark the morning that Madison sat up in bed and realized what she was missing.

She'd placed her father's letter he had planned to send, with negatives, in the top drawer of her nightstand. She turned on the small lamp, and when Taylor stirred, she apologized for the early hour. In the dim light, she opened the envelope with the negatives and counted the number of exposures. There were twenty-four of those brown, reversed images—the typical number on a roll of 35-millimeter film.

Fourteen of those photos were in the album, and six were on the black-and-white proof sheet. Four were still a mystery. Could they hold the clue she was searching for?

It was Monday. Taylor wouldn't have to leave for the

restaurant until the afternoon. In the specially built dark-room in the basement of their house, they waited in silence for the images to emerge, and as the sheets were hung and dripping in the red light, Madison gasped when she saw what the photos exposed.

As Madison waited for Amelia to be brought into the visiting room, she felt the corners of the small stack of photos tucked away in her jacket. She would have to ease Amelia into what she'd found. It was decades ago, and obviously, something Amelia hoped would stay hidden. It was what had kept her silent for decades, and even now hesitant in pursuing her freedom.

Madison took a deep breath, hoping to calm herself, but when Amelia was led to the cubby, she had to put her hand on the counter to steady her nerves.

"Good morning," Amelia said, with the phone receiver to her ear. There was no smile. However, there was the sound of relief in her voice.

Madison nodded. "I'm glad you agreed to meet with me again."

Amelia's eyes widened, noticing Madison's enlarged waistline. Madison placed a hand on her swollen belly and smiled, "A lot has happened in the last year."

Amelia raised her chin. "I appreciate what you've done for me. I can't imagine it was easy for you."

Madison agreed. "I think my father would be happy. I'm glad that I was able to help."

The two sat for a moment in silence, both contemplating the events that took place.

"I finished your book," said Madison.

Amelia lifted one brow. "You read it?" she asked, skeptically.

"I did. And I'm sorry I wasn't truthful about that our first visit, but I did read it."

Amelia's face brightened. It wasn't a smile, but she seemed genuinely pleased.

"Can I ask you a question about it?"

"Yes," Amelia answered.

Madison sat straighter, but her conviction began to bend. She swallowed and looked down. "The poems are all related."

Amelia nodded. "The book is a compilation."

"But they tell a story."

"Yes, I suppose," Amelia answered, hesitantly.

"They tell your story."

Amelia shrugged. "I write about things in my life."

Madison raised her eyebrows and sighed. She pulled the book from her tote, opened to a page that was tagged, and read, "No escape, and life now lost. All because of him." She stopped and looked up at Amelia. Then she continued. "The hurt remains and echoes call, to remind her of her lover's fall." She paused and again looked up. "These are related to what happened that day."

Amelia's face turned dour.

Madison continued to read. "Regret and shame. Like the person who holds them, closed off, and kept safe."

Amelia then shook her head. "What are you getting at?"

"After all these years, you're still listening to that little voice in your head telling you to be ashamed."

Amelia sat back and contemplated the question. "No. I'm not ashamed. We proved that I didn't do what I was accused of."

Madison tipped her head to the side and raised her eyebrows unconvinced. "Yes. But there's more to what happened that day."

Amelia glared.

"It's a fact that you didn't kill Sara. The photos prove that, but you didn't see all of them. My father had the negatives hidden and gave them to me in a letter that explained what he saw that day. Now I know why you spent all this time in prison."

Amelia scrunched her mouth, and her eyes showed fear. "What do you mean?"

"You took the blame because you didn't want anyone to know the truth."

The late summer of 1981 was exceptionally hot, even in the elevated mountains of Provo Canyon. The camp was full of squeals and laughter and the chaos of hormones and youthful energy. The young men and women of the 4th ward of the Orem, Utah, stake were winding down their five-day outing at the Aspen Veil camp and preparing for the culmination of their trip. The final event at all the youth camps was a dance in the common area surrounded by large trees and hung with strings of lights that illuminated the make-shift dance floor. The smell of pine and juniper filled the sun-drenched air, and there was no shortage of red and blistered noses as tables were being moved out to give space for the event.

Their final group dinner in the lodge had just ended, and while most of the girls hurried back to their bunker to get ready, Sara and Amelia stole off to the one place they had found that allowed them solitude. Or at least they thought that was the case.

But some watched and wondered what it was that had the girls continually leaving the group.

It was this curiosity that had both Dubby Woodruff and, separately, his older brother Morey making their own journeys to that isolated clearing.

Morey had asked Sara to prom that fall, long before any-one else had a chance. The school year wouldn't even start for weeks, but he had no intention of losing that chance. She had accepted his offer. He made it almost impossible for her to say no, organizing an elaborate and public display. He had a large group of friends surprise her at the food court at the mall where she worked. They danced around her while a boom box played "Dance with Me" by Orleans, and then Morey made his way through the group with a handmade sign that read "Prom?"

Had she said no, it would have been an incredible embarrassment, so he made sure there was adequate peer presence and pressure to give merit to his creative invita-tion. She smiled and nodded when she saw the sign, but her attitude was lackluster. She didn't even appear happy until the others began to applaud her decision.

However, even with Sara's lack of enthusiasm, her

acceptance was just short of them being an actual couple in Morey's mind. It bothered and frustrated him that Sara seemed uninterested and found any excuse to avoid being near him.

For Dubby, he was simply intrigued. He barely knew either of the girls, but because Sara had been kind to him at church, he found himself continually staring at her and daydreaming impossible scenarios.

Morey had seen the girls make their way to the path the previous day, so he climbed to the clearing before them and hid in the trees and grass. However, not knowing his brother, Dubby also followed Sara and Amelia from a distance and had almost lost them. If it weren't for hearing their soft voices when he made it to the top of the trail, he'd never have found them. He stayed back, hidden in the trees, but used the large lens of his camera to watch them. After several minutes, he began to document what he refused to believe he was seeing.

Amelia had a note and was reading it quietly as Sara sat next to her and listened. Dubby wasn't close enough to hear all the words, but what was on that page made Amelia put her hand to Sara's cheek and cup it softly. When Amelia finished, she folded it tenderly and then leaned in and kissed her. When Amelia opened her eyes and smiled, Sara pulled her back and kissed her again. The kisses then continued, and soon the two were lying on the soft forest floor entangled together and unaware of the eyes upon them.

Dubby heard Morey before he saw him. The sound was like a loud accusatory roar.

"You love her?" his brother shouted at the girls. He then

let out a sarcastic laugh. "I heard you! I saw you!"

He stomped toward the girls in a blustery show.

Amelia and Sara were stunned and quickly slid away from each other. They tried to look unaffected, but their faces showed fear.

Morey lunged and made them flinch back. Sara was pulling her blouse closed, and Amelia was standing and reaching for the letter Morey had snatched and now waved above his head. Dubby wondered if he should go back and find help, but he hesitated, mesmerized by what he was witnessing.

"I knew there was something wrong with you," Morey snarled at Sara. "Both of you are disgusting. Lezbos."

The word made Dubby sit back. What did that mean? He again brought his camera up and peered through the telephoto viewfinder to get a better look. He continued to photograph the conflict that was turning frantic and violent.

Amelia kept trying to grab at the letter, and yelled at Morey to leave them alone. When she was able to snatch it back, he tripped her as she tried to get away. She landed hard, and he was soon on top of her, violently tearing at her as she held the letter beneath her. They were rolling on the smooth surface of the mesa, Morey ripping at her arms and Amelia fighting back. As he straddled her, he sat up triumphantly with the letter held high.

"Wait till they all see this. They'll all know." He seethed. "You make me sick," he yelled over to Sara, who stood, face ashen with fear. "You're disgusting."

Amelia reached up, trying to grab for the letter, but he held it higher. She grabbed at his face and scratched it. He screamed out in pain and, with eyes red with anger, hit her hard, making her cover her face. He put a hand to his own face and recoiled at the blood she had drawn. Rage roiled across his features.

Then Dubby heard a scream. It was guttural and choking.

It came from Amelia, who wriggled violently out from under Morey and toward the edge of the cliff. She fell on her knees. Her wails wafted out over the valley.

Morey came up behind Amelia, looking around the mesa, confused. "Where is she?" he asked.

When he peered over the edge, Dubby saw his brother's face turn to horror. Dubby closed his eyes as he imagined Sara's body sprawled and bloody on the ledge below.

"Sara," Morey shouted.

Dubby's breath released as a sickening rush washed over him.

He saw Morey rub at the bloody scratches on his arm. Then his brother crumpled the letter in his hand. "You did this! She was fine until you moved here," his brother yelled, shaking the fist that held the letter. "This is your fault! If you two hadn't been doing what I saw, this would have never happened."

Amelia was now sobbing on the ground, her face in her hands, but when she heard what he said, she shook her head. "Why couldn't you just leave us alone? This is your fault."

Morey growled back. "I'll tell them what I saw. And..." he held up the torn and battered letter. "I have proof of what you are," he sneered. "You did this, and if you say anything different, I'll tell them all what I saw and show them this.

God hates gays, and that's what you are. It should have been you that fell off. You should die for what you are."

Through the thick plastic pane of the prison cubicle, Madison watched and waited for Amelia to respond.

Amelia's knees were bouncing; she put her hands on her thighs to quiet them. "You don't know anything. You weren't there and have no idea what really happened."

Madison frowned at the immensity of what she knew. She reached into her jacket and pulled out the photos. She drew one from the back and looked at it. "You didn't fight with Sara. You fought with Morey."

"Why are you doing this? He didn't push her. I saw the photos. It shows that." Tears rose in her eyes, and she sat back in the chair, looking from side to side, worried someone might overhear.

Madison lifted her shoulders. "That may be, but he *did* threaten you."

"No."

"Yes. But it wasn't to push you. Morey threatened to expose you. You and Sara."

Madison placed the photo against the clear plastic between them.

Seeing the image, Amelia's eyes went wide. She quickly placed her hands over it and looked behind her, frantic about what the photo showed. "Where did you get that? Put that away," she demanded.

"Morey caught you and Sara together. And so did my

father...on film. You didn't see him hiding and taking pictures. My father's photos caught what happened when Morey found the two of you together." Madison lowered the photo and placed it back in the stack. "You confessed and went to prison rather than have anyone know that you loved her. You were more worried about that than being thought of as a murderer."

Amelia began to argue but then put her hand to her mouth. "Please don't," she whispered. "Please stop trying to bring this out in the open. It's over."

Madison brought out the note. The tragic and telling words written by Sara to Amelia.

I don't know what to do. Some days I want to die. I'm scared, but the one thing I know is that I love you. That will never stop. But I'm so afraid about what will happen if they find out what we've done. No one can find out. If I act weird, please don't think I am mad or that I no longer love you. It's only because I don't want anyone to ever know. Someday we will be together. Remember, I will always love you.
Love, S

Madison felt her own eyes begin to burn. "My father didn't say anything because he actually felt that your love was a sin, as terrible as murder. He felt you deserved it for what you did. It took him years—decades—to realize he was wrong."

"Sara is dead because of what we did," Amelia said softly.

Madison shook her head and leaned toward her. "You're wrong. Sara is dead because of shame and bullying. My uncle threatened to expose both of you, and the idea of that was so horrifying, Sara took her own life. And so did you. You did nothing wrong. What you heard and were told made you feel like you were dirty and sinful. You were young and thought you had no future because everyone around you would think you were immoral. The only mistake you've made is you believed them."

"You don't know what happened or what I'm thinking. Please just leave me alone." Amelia sat up straight and turned, like she planned to leave.

"Wait . . ." Madison pleaded.

"What do you think this does for me? I've spent my life with my mother and my church thinking I'm a murderer . . . I'm about to be free. Now you want to make them hate me all over again?"

Madison held up a hand. "Please wait. I promise I won't say a word about any of this. You can have the photos and the letter. I'll give them to you, including the negatives. Burn them if you want." She put them away in her purse. "You know what's right. If you don't trust that, you'll never really be free."

Amelia remained standing, agitated, ready to run away.

With only silence, Madison left Amelia and went to wait with the others just outside the prison walls, where the once-convicted murderer would walk out a free woman for the first time in over forty years.

"How did it go?" asked Taylor as they stood, leaning into each other, trying to stay in the small patch of shade coming from the building's overhang.

Madison tried to smile but couldn't. "She still thinks she's to blame."

They stood in silence as a dozen newspaper and television cameras followed Amelia walking through the large metal gates of the prison, stoic and shy, into her mother's embrace.

It had been almost two years since Madison sat in Jenny's living room with Daniel and explained what she'd learned, showing him the photos of what really happened that day. She had returned home and waited as the slow wheels of justice turned, eventually vacating Amelia's sentence and setting a date for her release.

Martha asked Madison to be there for the gathering she had planned for Amelia's homecoming. "I'm getting my daughter back because of you," Martha told her on the phone.

Madison discovered the new photos from the negatives her father had given her not long before Amelia's release. Along with the similarities in Amelia's poems, she was finally able to answer the one question that had continued to eat at her. Why? Why did Amelia take the blame for Sara's death? When she realized the answer, she decided to tell Amelia what she knew . . . but it was Amelia's decision to share her truth. Madison would not out Amelia.

With Taylor by her side, she entered the back room of the restaurant reserved for the celebration. The group consisted of mostly people from the Utah Justice Center, Martha's bishop, and a few others she assumed were Martha's friends.

When Amelia came in, arm in arm with Martha, she looked like someone who had just entered a foreign country. She would have to learn an entirely new way of life.

A small speech was given by her primary attorney, and then, with coaxing, Amelia quietly thanked those who were there and had helped her gain her freedom. Martha stood beaming. The bishop offered a prayer and blessed the food. When he finished, the group seemed to give a collective sigh. Then the spell was broken and everyone moved toward the long tables with platters layered with sandwiches and sliced fruit.

When Madison found a moment that Amelia was not completely surrounded, she approached her and motioned for her to walk toward an area where they could speak alone.

In a small hallway off the banquet room, where they were buffered from the noise and eyes of the gathering, Madison reached into her purse and handed Amelia the envelope containing the photos.

"This is everything, including the note," she said, quietly. Madison handed her the tattered letter.

Amelia grabbed the letter and envelope of negatives and quickly shoved them into a purse she held awkwardly. The crisp jeans and ill-fitted blouse were obviously new and unfamiliar. Everything about her at that point seemed foreign and uncomfortable.

Before Madison could say anything, Amelia thanked her curtly and then glanced around, as though afraid someone might have noticed the handoff.

Seeing Amelia's angst, Madison decided to leave. Then

she noticed Martha coming toward them. Amelia sucked in a fearful breath. She clutched the purse, as though that would help hide the evidence of her transgression.

When Martha reached them, Madison smiled. "I was just saying goodbye."

"Thank you for coming," said Martha, putting a hand on Madison's arm. "I know it's a long trip."

As though sensing it was time to leave, Taylor came to Madison's side.

Madison grinned. "Taylor, I want you to meet Amelia and her mother, Martha."

Martha smiled and put out a hand. "Are you one of the attorneys?" she asked.

Taylor laughed. "No. I'm here with Maddie."

Madison turned to Taylor and put her hand on Taylor's arm. She looked back at Amelia and Martha, who both wore confused expressions.

Their perplexed faces shifted to shock when they both realized what they were observing.

They saw what Madison's father had known, that Madison could empathize with Amelia's shame, even if she no longer shared it.

"Congratulations again. Enjoy your life," she said to Amelia. Madison could see that Martha's mind was still turning, so she simply said, "Goodbye, Sister Johnson."

Taylor put her hand on Madison's lower back as she guided her wife to the exit. She opened the door leading outside, and the late afternoon sun slipped through the narrow crack and fell across the room in a thin beam. Madison turned back and saw Amelia watching her leave. She was standing in the solace of the shadows, her face showing the conflict in her mind as she tried to reconcile what she had just come to know.

At that moment, as their eyes met, and the door slowly began to close, she watched Amelia step from the darkness and into a sliver of light.

Amelia's chin lifted, and her shoulders rolled back, and it was the first and only time Madison saw her smile.

As Taylor drove from the parking lot and onto the road leading away, Madison leaned back in the seat and let the possibility of what she saw warm her. She knew that Amelia's freedom would be a lifelong endeavor. Still, as she imagined what that might look like for Amelia, Madison hoped that tiny voice inside her would speak up and that she would find the strength to listen.

EPILOGUE

Vince had hidden the tokens of his guilt behind his back the night he exposed Madison's truth. No one saw the bag with the evidence of a pregnancy and an abortion. But Madison was left holding the gun. She tried to push it behind her, but the large, heavy weapon barely budged.

"Hand it over," Saul demanded, holding out his hand.

Madison swallowed hard while feeling Vince's icy stare bore into the back of her head.

"Now!" Her father rarely raised his voice. That was Darlene's job, which is why his tone startled her. She quickly put the heavy pistol into his hand. Together, he and Darlene gave a terrified gasp. He looked at her with astonishment. "I had this hidden. How did you . . . Why do you have this?"

And when Madison opened her mouth to refute what was happening, that's when Vince blurted out the words that would change Madison's life forever. To keep his secret hidden, he revealed hers, diverting his parents' wrath to his sister.

"What?" Darlene asked, horrified. "That's not true."

But it was.

Vince's eyes darted between Madison and his parents. He was desperate, knowing Madison had him in her grip, and could easily squeeze the truth into the open. But instead, she held his secret in and let hers out.

It was time. Madison had felt the weight of what she was hiding. In a strange way, she was empathetic to her brother's quandary. Taking the heat away from him wasn't her intention as much as eliminating her own thick sludge of burden. It was time, and while she hadn't planned to tell them at that moment, she did.

"Madison?" asked Saul, waiting for her to dispute her brother's accusation.

Madison shrugged and looked at Jenny, wishing she wasn't there and knowing she would end up shouldering the blame. She turned back to her parents and simply said, "Yes, it's true."

"That's ridiculous," said Darlene. Her face turned to stone, and Madison saw what was going through her mind. It fit how she felt about Jenny. It was as though Madison could hear what Darlene was thinking. This wouldn't surprise her. She felt all along that Jenny wasn't the kind of girl Madison should be spending time with. This was her fault.

"You need to go home," Darlene said, pointing to Jenny.

"Don't get mad at her," demanded Madison. "This isn't about her."

"We need to talk about this." Darlene was stern and unbending. "Alone."

Saul looked lost, dejected, still holding the gun. "You know this isn't what's right. Why did you have this gun?"

"I was just looking at it," Madison said as tears rose to the surface.

"I should have had this locked in my safe. What were you planning?" His lips now began to tremble.

At first, Madison didn't understand what he was

thinking. She was focused on her life being exposed.

And then the wave of realization came over her. What she thought was her brother's contemplation in that room, her father now believed was hers.

She looked at Vince, who gave her a vile sneer, and Madison knew then that anything she threw his way was for naught.

"Do your parents know about this?" Darlene snapped at Jenny.

Jenny began to answer, but Madison cut her off.

"I told you this isn't about her. Leave her out of it."

"Protecting her little girlfriend," Vince quipped, walking away. He knew he was now immune.

"Don't say that," Darlene hissed at Vince. She turned back to Madison. "You're being dramatic. I know this isn't true. What about Daniel?"

Madison rolled her eyes and scoffed. "You're the one who's in love with him."

Darlene raised her hand to slap Madison but looked at Jenny and lowered it. She was now seething.

Jenny stood up from the alcove and gathered her things. She had been Madison's best friend for so long that she knew the dynamic, and Madison could tell she was puzzled and scared. Jenny would wonder why Madison took the fall for someone who had never shown her anything but cruelty. She left quietly and quickly, avoiding Vince and giving Madison one last, sorrow-filled look before closing the backyard gate.

When Jenny was gone, Darlene turned on Madison in a rage. "Why are you doing this?"

"I'm not doing anything. It's not like I've hurt anyone."

Darlene turned to her husband, still holding the gun, looking lost and defeated. She shook her head, frustrated. "This will hurt a lot of people. It's the last thing I would ever want in my child. Do you realize how wrong this is? Think about what this means for you. If people find out ..."

"I don't care what they think."

"Maybe you should care!" Darlene bellowed at her. "You'll be excommunicated from the church for this."

Madison bowed up. She stood and, putting her hands to her mouth like a megaphone, yelled out over the moonlit backyard, "I'm gay! I'm gay!"

Darlene backhanded Madison so forcefully that she landed against the lawn chair with a clatter. Surprised and angered, she quickly righted herself in the chair. She stood up, facing her parents, tears pouring down her face, but in a calm and measured voice said, "I'm gay. If the church doesn't accept me, then I no longer want to be in the church."

"Then you'll no longer be in this family." It was Saul. His quiet but stern message was so unexpected, both Madison and Darlene turned toward him. His eyes went from the gun to Madison. He stood steadfast, his face was firm.

Madison's anger dissolved into sorrow. This wasn't a thoughtless emotional outburst. This was a strident declaration. And it was one the entire family adopted and embraced like a mantra. They considered her sin so incomprehensible, they refused to believe it. When Madison forced her family to face it, she learned her family was no longer really hers.

Less than two months later, Madison was sent to the Canyon Springs Center for conversion therapy, and then eventually, she had to decide. Not if what she felt was real, but whether she wanted to live her life hiding in the shadows. It would be a decision that would mean leaving her home, family, and place in their heaven.

It was made very clear. There was no discussion. Madison stepped off that cliff of doubt and shame by herself. The initial fall was drastic and deep, but eventually, she learned to spread her wings and rise. Yet, no matter how successful she became, to have the people she loved and trusted turn away because of who she was at her core was an unbearable pain.

But when the hurt came bubbling up to remind her of that loss, the truth spoke to her, giving her the assurance that she eventually learned to accept: Her life was her own. She was as valid and valuable as anyone else.

And her life was full, satisfying. Besides writing freelance articles she sold to the *Daily Chronicle*, she had written a novel. That, along with her wife Taylor and a baby due that summer, she had found happiness, being exactly who she was.

Her heart was whole, and the still small voice within her at peace.

#

Thank you for reading The Still Small Voice. I hope you enjoyed it. If so, please take a moment to post a review and tell a friend. Your feedback is important to me and will help other readers as well.

If you'd like to get notifications of new releases and special offers on my books, please visit my website at

www.brendastanleybooks.com